tell
me a
story

jennifer rebecca

Tell Me a Story

Copyright 2017 © Jennifer Rebecca

This book is a work of fiction. Names, characters, places, and incidents are the product of the author's imaginations and are used fictitiously. Any resemblance of actual events, locales, or persons, living or dead, is coincidental.

Unless you are the boys from 'Bama who mercilessly killed my baby girl's dragon in Minecraft. Regardless, of whether or not it was a "bad" dragon, E loved it. She cried for an hour when it didn't come when she called it and for that you had to pay. Thank you for being such good sports about it and willing to laugh when informed you would die. I am forever grateful. But not for killing Ellie's virtual pet.

Cover Design by:
Alyssa Garcia
www.uplifting-designs.com

Editing by:
Stephanie Atienza
www.uplifting-designs.com

ISBN: 978-1-7320747-0-5

For more information about Jennifer Rebecca or her books, visit:
www.JenniferRebeccaAuthor.com

dedication

For my mom who thought it was totally normal to read *My Last Duchess* and *Rebecca* to a little girl. She gave me her creativity and a little bit of her crazy.

And also for my dad. It takes a strong man to raise a daughter to believe she can be anything in the world she wants to be. And an even stronger one to keep watching and encouraging when it takes 33 years for her to figure it out.

tell
me a
story

prologue

i'm coming for you

A SHRILL RING WAKES me from a restless sleep—I had the dream again. My phone bounces around on the unfamiliar night stand that I must have left it on last night.

"Goodnite," I rasp, my voice heavy with sleep.

"Detective, this is dispatch," *the disembodied voice from my phone informs me.* "We were told to notify you that the body of a male child has been recovered at the rocks near the bottom of the falls. Possible match for your missing person."

"I'm on my way."

That's all I need to know, and I am throwing back the blankets that are tangled around my body—my *naked* body. I pull my jeans on—*without* panties—and then my boots. I quietly search for my bra, hopefully not waking . . . *not waking* . . . I look over at the bed where a man with warm brown hair and a stubbled jaw sleeps on the bed that I just vacated. *Nope, not ringing any bells*. At least he's good looking. I shrug.

I should be embarrassed about letting some random pick me up at a bar the next town over. But I'm not. This case has been . . . *rough* . . . and I needed to blow off some steam. Will I call him again? *Uhh, no.* Will he call me? *He'd have to find me first.* Did he have a good time? *You betcha.*

I see my bra hanging from a lamp shade and grab it, tucking it into my back pocket. I pull my tank top and t-shirt on, having found both rumpled on the floor. I reach into the front pocket of my jeans and find — *thank God*—a hair tie and toss my long, inky hair on top of my head in a messy bun. I pull on my coat that had been dropped by the front door.

I palm my phone and pull my keys out of the same pocket the hair tie came out of. I step out into the New Jersey cold without ever looking back at . . . *Mike?* No, that's not it. I shrug to myself, fuck it.

I beep the locks on my car and climb in. I unlock the glove box and feel the weight of my badge and sidearm in my hand as I pull them both out of their hiding spot, placing both on the dash. I fire up my nondescript Tahoe and head towards tragedy.

My name is Claire Goodnite and I'm the best damn detective in the state of New Jersey and you better believe I'm coming for you.

chapter 1

vote of confidence

36 hours earlier...

IT'S BEEN A LONG damn day. I have been on the go since five this morning. At this point, there is more coffee in my body than actual blood, and I am alarmingly okay with that. I have been working a domestic since last Thursday and I finally nailed his sorry ass to the wall.

We caught a break late last night. The husband got a little too drunk and decided to take his *issues* to the street, where a bunch of little old ladies who had raised decent sized Italian and Irish sons took to the notion to end his *issues* once and for all—*with their fists.* I'm sure we all feel sorry for him. Read my sarcasm here. I would have cheered them on and brought a folding lawn chair and popcorn, but they made me more paperwork. And I hate paperwork.

After the dust settled, the wife decided life as a

punching bag wasn't as great as her husband had originally promised. She finally decided to press charges
and file protection orders. Again, more paperwork, but
so, so worth it. And as of right now, I have just filed
my last report. The wife is in the hospital again, but
hopefully for the last time and the husband is in lockup
where he belongs.

I hit submit and logout of my computer. Those
crazy mothers that work in this station would post all
kinds of shit if I didn't. One time they set up a dating
profile for me and it was horrible. All foot lovers and
guys with some serious kinks. Oh and a few women.
The guys in the department had said they'd never seen
me date anyone—*man or woman*—so they weren't really sure.

I actually had to go on a date with one guy because
I lost a bet. He was a banker with a foot fetish and
cried when I told him I was a cop. Oh, and then he
asked me to call his mother for him to come and pick
him up. *Never. Fucking. Again.* I slip some side eyes
at Marshall who is the worst offender as I lock out my
computer.

I stretch my arms over my head and twist to pop the
tight spots in my back. I roll my neck around and drop
my arms. I see the looks I get from some of the guys
in the department. It's not cockiness or arrogance, just
. . . *observance*. Unreciprocated observance. I would
never date any of these guys, not because they are bad
guys, but because with my track record, it would end
in a fiery blaze of not glory and I would hate to have an

actual reason for my brother to fire me.

Speaking of Liam, as the Captain here, he is another big deterrent to anyone who would date me. He has never thought any guy that I dated was good enough. And within reason, they all turned out to be assholes.

Lastly, you don't shit where you eat. This station and my family, that's all I've got. I might be a little crazy, okay you got me, a *lot* crazy, but I wouldn't risk either this job or my family. For anything. Got it.

I push away from my dented metal desk and stand up. I make a move toward my BFF, also known as the coffee maker, and pour myself my 988,473,729 cup of the day. Well, not really, but it feels like it. Sometimes, I wish I could just get an IV tapped so that I can mainline caffeine the way that I need to in order to keep moving today.

Again, not really, because that would probably get me fired or thrown in jail and that place is gross. I'm tough and all, but I am not a fan of peeing in front of other people. No, thank you. I take that first hot sip and it burns all the way down. I sigh to myself just before I'm startled out of my daze.

"Goodnite," my brother shouts and I'm embarrassed to admit that I jump a little. "My office. *Now.*" I roll my eyes. It's definitely different having my big brother as my boss. My dad was the Captain of this station when I was a little kid. Liam has been working towards filling out old man's shoes ever since he got back from a stint in the Navy alongside his buddy who I'm avoiding for the rest of my natural life. It sure keeps things interesting.

We've always been pretty close even though he's eight years older than me. I used to follow him and his best friend, Wes, around all the time hoping they would let me play catch or hunt bugs with them, but they never did. I never lost hope though.

Then they had to go and get girlfriends and that was the most embarrassing show I have ever seen. So, when I finished college and Liam had just come back from his last tour overseas to join the local Police Department, I followed him there too. He was not real happy about that one, but I didn't let that deter me.

"Any day now, Goodnite!" he barks. Sheesh.

"Alright already!" I holler back as I chug half of my coffee and roll my eyes.

"And don't roll your eyes at me!" he shouts.

I pause and look around. There's no way he can see me. He's just guessing. I take a deep breath and start walking towards his office, but not before I shout back.

"Oh, are you going to run and tell mom?" To the tune of snickers all around the bullpen as I saunter into the Captain's office. I wink at the guys before I shut the door.

"Do you always have to be so ridiculous and insubordinate?" he asks me. I pause to look him in the eye.

"Is that seriously why you called me into your office?" I mean really, does he know me at all?

"No," he sighs and runs his palms down his face.

By his body language alone, I know the case is a bad one. But what he tells me next, explains everything. "If you weren't the only available detective I have, I wouldn't even be having this conversation with you," he says looking me dead in the eyes. It's creepy the way he does that, but I don't flinch.

"Thanks for the vote of confidence," I droll.

"I'm serious here, Claire. I don't want you on this case."

He doesn't actually want me anywhere near this department so I don't let his comments hurt my feelings. I have no room for that kind of negativity in my life.

"Thank you," I sigh. "So, give it to someone else," I taunt. I don't really want him to do that though and he knows it.

"Everyone else is working another stack of them. You just wrapped up the domestic, so technically, you caught this one," he tells me on another grunt.

"What exactly is it that I caught?" I ask Liam, but by his reticence, I already know.

"A little boy, six years old, was reported missing by his parents when they came home this evening from work," I hold my breath. "If there was anyone else available . . ." He squeezes his eyes tight.

This is hard for him, I get it, but this is me. This is my life and the past is in the past firmly where I buried it under six feet of dirt and two feet of concrete. Metaphorically speaking. It is not open for discussion. With

Liam or *anyone.*

"I get it, you'd choose them over me," I sigh, not even surprised anymore.

"It's not like that, Claire, and you know it," he says exasperated.

"I don't care anymore, Liam. Not even a little," I say. "Can I have the case notes? Who called it in?"

I reach for the file on his desk, eager to get this little meeting over with. He opens his eyes, the same violet ones fringed in thick, black lashes as mine. On me, they are unique, on Liam they stop you in your tracks. I can see he is firming his resolve to bully me off this case.

"It's not good for you to handle these types of cases, Claire," he says softly.

"Why don't you let me decide that for myself," I respond just a little too sharply. Making a statement and not asking a question.

"It's not good for me to have you on this case . . ." Liam starts, but I can't let him finish that thought. I hold up my hand to stop him.

"Don't . . ." I say, but it's too late, he's on a roll already.

"Damn it, Claire! I can't protect you out there." He slams his hand down on top of his desk so forcefully that his stacks of paper topple over and his coffee mug rattles.

"I don't need you to," I say softly.

"What about what I need, Claire?" he shouts as he jabs his thumb back into his own chest. I shake my head and close my eyes.

"It's my life, Liam," I say softly, opening my eyes but not quite meeting his. "You know I love you, right?" But he ignores me.

"What about Wes?" he presses on and my spine automatically stiffens.

"This has nothing to do with Wes," I snap.

"He was there that day too . . ."

I know what he's thinking. Wes can calm me down. Wes can reason with me. Wes knows my past and thinks that I can't handle this case or be in the department either. But Wes doesn't get a say and neither does Liam. I was going to catch a case like this some time. Better sooner than later, right?

"Enough, Liam." I slice my hand through the air to silence him. "This has nothing to do with you or Wes or even me. This has everything to do with a little boy who is missing from his family."

Liam looks at me just a little too closely, he sees too much and I have too much to hide still. I know if I looked at his eyes, I would see just a little too much sadness. I can't handle that. I can barely live with the consequences of that day. The day I made so many stupid, immature choices. Childish choices that robbed me of the rest of my childhood. Not only do I get to live with the consequences, so do Liam and Wes. So, do my parents. Everyone's lives changed that day and there is no one to blame but me. So, I reach across his desk and take the file that sits there before turning on my heels and running like hell.

chapter 2

what it's like

THE DRIVE TO 1312 Orange Drive is not a long one, but one fraught with a storm of thoughts twirling in my head. I hate fighting with Liam but this is unavoidable. He can't keep throwing my past in my face to keep me from living my life. Using it to hold me back.

It was hard enough being the weird girl in school. The kid everyone knew about but no one talked to. That was so much fun. Everyone has their opinions about what really happens when someone gets kidnapped. News flash, they're all wrong.

Girls pretended to be my friends to get the inside scoop. Boys wanted to date me because they thought being kidnapped meant I must be easy. Because if the monster had raped me, then I wouldn't have my virginity to worry about protecting anymore. Liam and Wes set those morons straight. And then there was everyone elses's parents who claimed they wanted to mother me and protect me. They didn't. They just wanted something else to brag about at their bridge socials and PTA meetings.

I shake my head side to side like an etch-a-sketch hoping to shake the dark memories from my mind. I'm going to have the dream again, I know it. Fuck, I hate those dreams. Dreams that are likely disjointed memories.

I pull up to the house where the missing child lives. Red and blue lights dangerously twinkle in the darkening sky of the late afternoon. The black and white units line the street in front of the house. I watch uniform officers canvas the upper middle-class neighborhood, knocking on doors and talking to neighbors. Hoping the little boy just wandered down the block. By the scowls on their faces and the tension in their shoulders, they know that is not the case.

I park my Tahoe a little down the way and head to the front door. My badge is clipped to the belt on my jeans, but it wouldn't matter, most of these officers know me and see me around regularly. But they also know my background and by the looks on their faces now, they think this is a mistake. Maybe it is, maybe it isn't, but one way or another it's happening.

"Hey Claire," Jones greets me. He's a nice guy about my age with a girlfriend and a baby at home. "You catch this one?" he asks.

"Sure did, Jonesy," I say softly.

"Sucks," he says, nodding towards the house.

"They all suck."

I walk into the house and take in a clean, modestly decorated living room. There are well kept sofas, nice, but not brand new, a large flat screen television, end tables, and a coffee table. Coordinating curtains hang over large windows.

On one of the sofas sits a well kept woman in her fifties. She has blonde hair streaked with gray and her tasteful makeup now runs down her face as she cries into a soft looking, linen hanky. She is wearing beige slacks and a white poplin blouse with a light blue cardigan over it. The whole thing is topped with a string of pearls and matching earrings and ends in low beige leather sling backs with a pointed toe.

"Mrs. Ascher, I presume," I say as I walk towards her. "I'm Detective Goodnite," I tell her. Hoping to ease her into telling me everything.

"Claire Goodnite?" she asks me. The well-dressed man in navy slacks, a blue striped shirt and tie tightens his arm around her as they sit together on the sofa. There's something there I can't put my finger on. Something is off.

"Yes?" I ask distracted.

"I remember when you were taken," she says softly. I feel the breath in my lungs seize but I force a benign smile onto my face.

"Honey, I don't know if this is appropriate," Mr. salt and pepper hair and wingtips tells me something I already know. It's not appropriate.

"She'll find him," she whispers, putting her hand on top of his on her arm. "You'll find him, won't you?" She says to me.

"I'm going to do my very best to find out what happened to your son Mrs. Ascher," I tell her hoping to defuse this bomb.

"But you're going to succeed because you know what it's like to be taken," she tells me. "You know what it's like," she chants, over and over.

"I do," I say firmly back. "Now, time is of the essence, what can you tell me about your son?" I ask.

"Anthony, his name is Anthony Donovan," she tells me. "His sister, Kasey, was watching him. She doesn't know where he is," she says with a sob.

"Kasey watches him after school until his mother and I get home from work. Then we have dinner and they do their homework," Mr. Ascher tells me.

"And you are, Sir?" I ask. I know who he is, but I need him to tell me everything.

"Jonathan Ascher," he states firmly. "Anthony's mother, Elizabeth, and I married six months ago. The children have lived here with us ever since." Honest and to the point. I like that.

"Thank you. I have to verify everything," I smile softly at him.

"Absolutely," his eyes soften but he does not smile. He may have real affection for the children. Time will tell. "We just want him found," he says. Interesting he didn't mention safe. Not home safe.

"Where would Anthony have gone other than here?"

"That's the thing, he wouldn't," Mrs. Ascher tells me. "He *knows* he is only to go with Kasey," she stresses.

"And where is Kasey?" I ask.

"Up in her room. She's just beside herself," she tells me. I would be too if I had just lost my baby brother.

"May I speak with her when we're done here?" I ask softly.

"I don't think today will be good," Mrs. Ascher says, flooring me. She just said she wanted her son found and now she won't let me interview the last person that saw to him safe. The shock must show on my face because she quickly recovers.

"I really do need to speak with her, Mrs. Ascher," I implore. "It's imperative."

"She's having such a hard time right now," she hedges. "Every time she lost a pet, Kasey took it so hard. This is her baby brother we're talking about . . . maybe tomorrow."

"Tomorrow then," I say softly, not wanting her to become defensive. "How often does she watch Anthony for you?" I ask.

"After school when we're at work and any other time we might need a sitter," Mrs. Ascher tells me.

"And how old is she?"

"She's sixteen."

"Does she drive?"

"Yes, her father bought her a car for her birthday," she shares on an eye roll.

"Do she and Anthony have the same father?" I ask.

"Of course." She narrows her eyes on me.

"Where is he now?" I ask in the same tone.

"Probably off with one of his floozies," she snaps. So, there is no love lost between the

former Mr. and Mrs. Donovan. Good to know.

"Can you tell me a little bit about Anthony?" I ask, changing directions. Her face immediately softens letting me know that Anthony is the beloved baby of the family.

"He is such a precious boy," she says softly, her eyes brightening. "Anthony is so sweet and so smart. He gets straight A's in school. He loves trains, cars, and trucks like all little boys do. He loves mud and climbing trees. He wants a puppy desperately," she says sobbing.

"We were talking about getting him one for his birthday," Mr. Ascher adds.

"That's nice," I say before changing directions. "And how about his friends. Who are they?" I ask.

"He plays with the Johnson boy down the way," Mr. Ascher informs me.

"Jason and Mark are his friends from school," Mrs. Ascher states.

"Can I have you write down their parents' names and phone numbers, please? Addresses will help too if you have them."

"Of course," she sniffles. "Anything to find my baby boy."

I am about to make motions to go talk with their daughter when there is an outburst at the front door.

Yes, today is going to be a *very* long day.

"Where the fuck is my son?" A large man bellows from the front door as the wood panel crashes open and slams against the wall. "What did you do to my little boy?" he cries. I look at Mr. and Mrs. Ascher, their faces have gone equally hard.

"Mr. Donovan," I say softly. "Can we talk privately outside?" I ask as I stand up from my seat in the living room, making my way to the front door.

I look around and see all the uniform officers are frozen solid, with their muscles forced loose, waiting to see what Mr. Donovan's next move is going to be.

"Who are you?" His eyes narrow on me.

"I'm Detective Claire Goodnite and I'm here to investigate your son's disappearance," I say softly. Hoping to not rile him up more because it's already been a shit day and this is not helping me find his son.

"I just want my boy back," he breaks down, nodding. I move to him and gently put my arms around him, guiding him out the door.

"Then help me find him," I say softly, with my head bent towards his. "Talk to me, give me the information I'm missing to find out what happened to him," I implore. I can tell my pleas got through to him when he lets out a soft sob and nods his head again.

I look up to find Marty, one of the uniforms I know and move to ask him on my way out to get the grief officer down here to the parents. But when I look up, it's right into eyes burning so bright they can only be described as true Irish whiskey. Unfortunately, those gorgeous eyes are on the face of my worst nightmare, also known as Special Agent Wes O'Connell with the FBI. And Liam's best friend to boot.

Fuck me, it really is going to be a long day.

chapter 3

dirty laundry

"I CAN'T IMAGINE WHAT would bring you into my jurisdiction, Agent," I snap looking into those God damned amber eyes.

"One would think with a missing child, you would do whatever it is to find him, exhaust all resources, and not sit on your high horse, Claire," he growls.

"This is not the time or place, Agent O'Connell." I respond baring my teeth.

"Let me take over," he says softly, but you could hear a pin drop. Everyone knows. Everyone is watching. And I absolutely fucking hate it. It's as infuriating as it is humiliating to have my big brother's friend here to take over the case that no one thinks little Claire Goodnite can handle. I'm not afraid to admit that it stings.

"Liam called you." I sigh. "So that's how it's going to be is it?"

I motion for a uniform to take the boy's father and put him in the back of a black and white to take him to the station. He needs to be questioned and not on the front porch of the home of his ex-wife and her new husband. I look up at the window of the second story and see the curtains flutter. *Interesting.*

"Hey Mickey, can you escort Mr. Donovan back to the station for me?" I smile sweetly at one of my favorite guys. "I'll be there as soon as I wrap up what I need to here."

"You got it, Goody." He smiles softly to me before he walks Mr. Donovan to his patrol vehicle.

"Don't you think it's just a *little* unprofessional to flirt with every officer?" Wes snaps and I lose my mind.

"Excuse me?" I bark back. My head snapping around to stare at the big bastard in disbelief.

"You heard me," he growls, leaning towards me. "It's unprofessional the way you flirt with everyone." My jaw opens and closes. Then opens again before snapping shut.

"I don't flirt with anyone!" I shout, "it's just your *little* ego and *tiny* dick that can't handle the fact that I don't flirt with you." I let those words hang in the air between us.

"You, of all people, should know that my dick is *anything* but tiny," he shouts back. I gasp. If I thought you could hear a pin drop before, now, the air was still. It was frozen, charged with the coming storm between Wes and me.

"You asshole!" I scream before launching myself at him. I don't get the chance to make contact because strong arms wrap around my waist and pluck me out of the air.

"Both of you, back to your corners," one of the older officers in the department growls. "I know the Captain thinks your shit is golden, *Sir*, but I'm not so sure he'll be thrilled when he gets the report on what just went down here with not only one of his Detectives, but also his sister. Think on that," he says. Still not releasing his hold on me.

I stand there glaring at Wes. I can't believe he went there. I feel the tears sting the back of my eyes but I beat them back. I won't let him see me cry. Wes doesn't deserve that. I knew he would want me off this case as much as Liam, but to air our sordid history stung. I have worked hard here to be treated as an equal. I busted my ass to make it as far as I have. Plus, the way he said it makes it sound like we're having an affair, not one stupid night twelve years ago. Fuck my life.

"Yes, Sir, I understand," Jones, the officer behind me, says into his cell phone. "Yes, Captain, affirmative," he says before disconnecting. Fuck. My spine goes straight at hearing he's talking to my brother.

"Would you do me a favor, *Officer*, and kindly take your hands off the Detective before I remove them from your body," Wes growls.

"Are you fucking kidding me right now?" I yell back.

"Both of you shut the fuck up," Jones snaps. "You are both to haul your asses into the Captain's office. He is not happy. Thanks for the ass chewing, by the way."

"I'm sorry, Jonesy," I say softly. Unable to meet his eyes through my own shame.

"No worries, Detective, a good ass chewing is good for the soul," he winks at me.

My jaw hangs open as I stare at him. I don't think I have ever seen him wink. Let alone at me. He's serious and never jokes around. I mean never *ever.* I close my mouth and nod once, then head for my department truck.

I beep the locks and step in, closing the door firmly behind me. I look over my shoulder out the window where Wes and the officer are leaning into each other, obviously having heated words. As if he senses me watching, Wes looks up and his bright gold gaze locks with mine.

I'm not proud to admit that I jump a little bit and quickly avert my eyes when I see that stupid ass knowing grin spread across his stupid handsome face. Fumbling with my key, I finally fit it into the ignition. I refuse to look back at him but know he's watching. *Me,* he's watching me. I put my truck in drive and peel out heading towards the station.

The drive is not nearly as long as I wish it was. Before I know it, I am pulling into the parking lot and isn't it just my luck, there is a space opening up right in front of the building. I wait for the other vehicle to pull out with my turn indicator on. Once they take off, I pull into the spot and put my truck in park, turning off the ignition. I sit there for a moment with both of my hands on the steering wheel, just staring ahead at the brown brick building that I really don't want to enter.

I watch a pair of detectives I know walk out of the building, clap eyes on me sitting in my Tahoe and then turn around to walk back in. I know what those assholes are doing. A bunch of *Benedict Arnolds,* they are. I sigh and bang my head against the steering wheel between my hands once, twice, three times for good measure. I pick my head up and open my eyes. And there is Liam, my brother, my boss, holding the door open and staring daggers at me.

Unless I am mistaken, that is not a happy look on his face, and I am definitely not mistaken. He raises his hand and extends his index finger, pointing directly to me and then jerks his thumb angrily over his shoulder towards the doorway he is standing in before walking inside, the door slamming behind him.

I sigh one more time to myself wondering why I couldn't have been a stripper or a carhop instead of a cop, it probably would have made our relationship more copacetic. Then pull my keys from the ignition and open the door to my truck. I step down and shut the door behind me. I stuff the keys in my jeans pocket and walk towards the door with my head hanging and my shoulder slumped. *Defeated.*

I will never let those two assholes know that they got to me, so just before I open the door to the station,

I roll my shoulders back and lift my chin high looking everyone in the eye that thinks they can get to me with the knowledge that Wes aired some old news at a crime scene. They don't scare me and they know it. Until my dumb brother breaks the silence with his shouts, making me jump.

"Get your ass in here now, Goodnite!" He bellows.

"You've done it now, Goody," the guys jest.

"Nah, it isn't the first time I took a swing at a fed, it probably won't be the last time," I wink.

"But I bet it's the first time you boned his buddy," someone says softly.

"Yeah, there is *that*," I admit.

"Better luck next time."

"Yeah, thanks assholes."

I can't deny it so I just shrug my shoulders and head towards the Captain's office. I raise my hand to knock but Liam's shouts beat me to it. Again. Jesus, how does he do it? I think before crossing myself in the hopes that our very Catholic mother didn't just hear me say the Lord's name in vain. In her mind. She's crazy like that.

"Jesus! Just get in here," he shouts. So, I walk in the door and shut it firmly behind me.

"So . . ." I hedge. "You wanted to see me?" I ask.

He just glares.

"So, I need to follow up with the officers at the scene and interview the dad . . ." I trail off. "So, if you don't need me . . ."

"Sit down," he says, softly menacing.

"Liam," I whisper, his purple eyes cold and menacing.

"I said, *SIT DOWN!*" he roars and I do just that. Without putting any thought into it, I sit down in one of the chairs in front of his desk. Folding my hands in my lap I lock my eyes on them, not willing to meet his eyes.

Liam runs a meaty hand down his face before slapping the top of his desk. Hard. He hits it again and I jump a little at the bang. *"God damn it!"* he shouts.

I sit there silently, saying nothing. Nothing good can or will come from confessing all my sins to my older brother. I was a naive little girl but I have left her firmly in the past. That girl is gone and she's not coming back.

"When?" he asks softly when he opens his eyes and looks at me.

"A boy, Anthony Donovan, age six, went missing sometime between the hours of three and six this evening . . ." I start to report on the case he assigned me.

"No." he silences me. "When did you fuck my best friend?"

"Twelve years ago. You were both home on leave . . ." I start but stop when Liam hurls his coffee mug that was resting on his desk across the room and into the wall, smashing it for good. He drops his face into his hands, his elbows resting on his desk.

"Did you love him?" he asks when he sits up again, looking at me.

"Liam, this doesn't have anything to do with what's happening right now."

"It fucking does if he's bringing it up at an active crime scene in front of all of my officers twelve years later!" I just nod. He straightens himself. I can see him physically forcing himself to calm down. "Did you love him?" he asks me again.

"I was young," I say softly, not wanting to admit that Wes was the only man to ever really hold and break my heart.

"How young again?" *Uh-oh.* He tilts his head to the side and narrows his eyes on me.

"Eighteen. Barely," I add because it's the truth. My brother growls under his breath. Shit. Wes just might be a dead man. I hate that. I never told him because I didn't want to poison their friendship even if I could never look at Wes the same again.

"You didn't answer my question," he states. And no I didn't.

"I don't want to."

"Claire," he sighs, rubbing his palms down his face.

"Liam." He stares at me, his eerily purple eyes burning into mine, and I feel myself waffling. "Fine! *Yes,* I thought I did. *But I don't.* It was twelve years ago so cut me some slack!" I throw my hands up dropping them harshly to my sides.

"You loved me?" A voice I can't bare to hear asks from behind me and my spine goes straight. I look up at Liam, that betraying bastard, who is looking over my shoulder at what is no doubt the one person who will unravel my whole carefully constructed life. With a God damned smile on his face. My brother is the biggest asshole! No, he's the second biggest. Wes still holds the number one spot in my book.

"I gotta go," I say standing and Liam's smile grows wider.

"This is going to be fun," he says as he claps his hands like a dancing circus bear.

"No, it's not. It's going to be nothing," I snap at him, flipping him off.

"God damn it, answer me!" Wes thunders, making me turn to face him. "You love me?" he asks again.

"No," I lie, wondering how I'm going to escape this office with Liam at his desk and Wes blocking the door. I know the windows don't open and I need to get back to Mr. Donovan.

"Bullshit!" he clips out. "I want her off this case right now," he says to Liam. I don't hear anything else due to the blood roaring in my ears.

"Don't you fucking dare!" I shout. "This is my case." I'm breathing heavily, my chest rising and falling as I turn to take down Wes. His eyes dart to my chest for a bit too long before he looks in my eyes.

"I mean it. She's gone as in yesterday," he says to Liam while looking at me.

"Don't even think about it, Liam," I growl, not turning around.

"You and I both know she should not be on the Donovan case. Let me take it over and put the full resources of the FBI behind it," Wes implores.

"You can't be serious."

"She's too close to this," Wes pleads.

"I am not."

"She was in this kid's shoes," he says.

"Not likely," I harrumph.

"You don't know that." Wes looks back at me.

"Actually, I do. The longer we sit here arguing the more likely it is that he's dead."

"She's not rational."

"That's it. I'm gonna shoot him," I declare.

"See?" Wes says.

"Oh, stuff it, you old blowhard," I growl.

"I see you've really matured," he says as he shoots me the side eye.

"Can I please shoot him?"

"NO!" they both shout at me.

"Alright, alright. I get it. No shooting the Fed. Cool. I'm cool. I swear," I placate with my hands held out in front of me in mock surrender.

"See?" Wes rallies. "She cannot be on this case. She's too close with her past. She can't see this rationally."

"And what about you two?" I ask. "Do you really think you both can see it rationally? Our shared past, my past didn't affect you at all?"

"No," he growls.

"No, it didn't?" I ask.

"No, it didn't." Wes folds his arms over his chest.

"Not even a little bit?" I shrug my shoulder.

"No," he scowls.

"So, there was no reason to bring up our shared past in front of my colleagues for any reason than to humiliate me?" His eyes widen when he realizes where I'm going with this. "I knew it!" I shout.

"I did no such thing!" he growls. "You are insane if you think that time in my life, those days, those hours, those minutes you were missing did not affect me. But it didn't happen *to me.*"

"That's right it happened to me," I snap back.

"And I am trying to protect you. Your brother is trying to protect you!"

"I don't need anyone to protect me from anyone except you two overgrown gorillas. And you are not going to take this case from me!" I shout. I toss my long, black hair over my shoulder for effect as I make my way to the door. "Don't worry, boys. I don't take candy from strange men anymore. At least not the kind that comes in wrappers!" I shout as I slam the door behind me.

Shit! They make me mad. I cannot believe that those two idiots think that they are going to protect me. Like I need to be swaddled like a baby. I am not a baby!

I start to storm my way down the hall, away from stupid Liam and his stupid office. I hear the door open and slam shut. Shit! I need to get out of here. Where am I going to go? I start to pick up the pace when a strong hand clamps around my upper arm.

"Oh no, you don't," Wes growls as he backs me into the wall. "No men. No strangers. No one but me," he snarls just before his mouth crushes down on mine.

I gasp and the back of my head hits the wall behind me. Wes needs no flags, no ticker tape, nor neon signs to proceed. His tongue licks into mine. There's an aggression. A need.

Wes's hand on my arm moves up and into my hair. Gripping it tight. Pulling. His other hand pushes me back at my belly until my back hits the wall and I'm trapped, pinned, by a big hunk of angry man. As he deepens the kiss further, his hand at my belly slides around my waist and down. Down. Down. Where he palms my ass cheek and squeezes it in his strong hand, Pulling my hips towards him. Wes groans into my mouth as the hardness of his cock connects with my body.

"You're mine," he kisses me again. "You've always been mine."

"Wes . . ." I whimper on a gasp as he squeezes my ass again, pulling me against his hardness. I moan into his mouth as he kisses me again and again.

"You were always mine," Wes says as he kisses me again. "I'm just surprised you capitulated so easily." He smiles against my mouth.

"Wait, what?" I ask again as the fog begins to clear. Wes kisses me again, but this time I'm not into it. Wes doesn't seem to notice.

"I'm glad we see eye to eye here, babe," he says softly. I'm babe now? What is happening here. "I promise, I'll take good care of this case. You don't have to worry."

"*My* case?" I ask even though I know. I just freaking know.

"Yeah, I'm taking it over. I can't believe you're being so agreeable about it, Claire."

"That's because I'm not!" I shout as I shove him back. "This is my case."

"Yeah, but now that we're together, I want to protect you. I need to protect you," he tells me.

"No, you need to back the fuck up. This is my case, Wes. And if you really cared about me, you wouldn't try and shit all over my job, a job which I happen to love. This just goes to show that we can't be together," I say as I duck under his arm.

"We'll see about that, Claire. We'll see about that,"

he growls. "You are mine, babe. Your body knows it and so do you."

"I can't hear you . . . la la la la," I shout with my fingers in my ears as I walk away. I always walk away.

chapter 4

ghosts

I'M SO FREAKING MAD. I'm sure there is steam shooting out of my ears as I stomp down the hallway to my desk. I grab the notes on top that let me know that Mr. Donovan is in *Interview Room #4*.

I roll my shoulders back and meet the eyes of every detective and officer in the bullpen that dares to look at me and pass judgement. They do not have the right to because I have not given it to them. I atoned for my sins a long time ago, vowing to live my life only moving forward.

I am not a small child who needs to be swaddled in cotton and tucked away in a safe place. Nor am I the little girl who took a candy bar from a stranger who said he needed help finding his dog because she was so mad at her brother and his friend for not letting her hang around them. I do not need to be *protected.* The word causes a bitter taste to take up root in my mouth.

I want to spit it out but I can't because it's not real. Just like I tell myself every day that my old ghosts aren't real. *But they are.*

I scoop up my case file and notes. Then make my way down the hall to the interview room. I knock twice before pulling open the steel door and stepping inside. I shoot Mr. Donovan a sweet smile hoping to both placate him and catch him off guard—*I'm the nice police lady, tell me all of your secrets and lies*—before sitting down in the metal chair across from him, nodding at the uniformed officer standing in the corner.

I flip the switch under the table that starts recording the conversation by both video and audio. It's not always admissible in court, but I want to have it so I can run it by a body language expert I know. Something is just *off* with this case. I am also aware that Wes would have those people at his fingertips with all of his fancy pants FBI resources but I'm still too steamed to talk to him. The sad part is, he's right. I'm going to have to pull him in on this case for Anthony's sake.

"Mr. Donovan." I dim my smile to a sad one directed at him. "I am so sorry about your son. I promise that we will do everything that we can to find him."

"I don't know what to do," he sobs. His face buried in his hands.

"Can you think of anything that you think might be important?" I ask him. "Anything at all?" He just shakes his head. Tears streaming down his face.

"No," he cries. "Anthony is such a good little boy."

"Can you tell me about the people in Anthony's life?"

"Me. He lives with my ex and her perfect husband. His sister. He's got some friends. He goes to school. Plays ball. I guess he knows a lot of people," he whispers. My guess, he's realizing we're now trying to find a needle in a haystack, before it's too late.

"Was there anyone that just seemed off to you?" I ask.

"No—" he starts. "Well, Liz's new guy is weird, but I figured that's just because he's married to my wife and that burns," he says honestly.

"Can you tell me why you and Mrs. Ascher divorced?"

"What does that have to do with anything?" he barks.

"I'm just trying to put all the pieces together so that we can find Anthony," I tell him calmly.

"I slept with my secretary. One time! One freaking time and Liz found out. She couldn't pack her bags fast enough. She was living with that douche by the end of the month," he snarls.

"I'm sorry, that must have been very hard for you."

"It was. But not bad enough to hurt my son!" he shouts. "Those kids . . . those kids are all that is right in the world. Those kids are my entire world," he sobs.

"Can you tell me if there was ever anything that gave you a weird vibe?" I ask. He starts to shake his head no, but I need to see if I can shake something loose in his brain. "Did you see the same car over and over? Bump into the same person again and again? Feel like someone was watching you? Watching the kids?"

"No," he cries. "I should have been there!"

"Did your kids ever seem like something was off or bothering them when you saw them or talked to them on the phone?" I ask. My questions coming faster and faster to try and make him give me *something*. Really anything that might help us catch a break in this case.

"No!" he shouts. "I didn't know. I didn't notice anything because I wasn't there. I didn't protect him!" he screams before dissolving into a broken puddle of snot and tears. He drops his face down on the metal table, and pounds his hands away on the metal slab as if it will offer up some answers about his son. Unfortunately, I can see that the answers aren't here.

I put my hand over his on the table and lean in, whispering in his ear that I will do everything that I can to bring his son home to him.

"One way or another, Detective?" he asks. His watery blue eyes meeting mine. He grabs my hand tight, to the point of bruising. "Bring him home. Even if he's gone. Don't leave him out there in the cold."

"I will," I say. Knowing that we should never make promises like that. But unable not to. One way or another, I will bring Mr. Donovan's son, Anthony, home.

I walk out of the interview room and head to the kitchenette in the office. I grab a bottle of water from the fridge and pound it back. But it can't wash away the weight of this case on my shoulder.

I pour myself another cup of coffee but I can't make myself choke it back. I look out the window and see that it's dark. It's later than I realized. I am so tired. So exhausted. So weary that I don't hear Liam sneak up behind me.

"Go home, sis," he says from behind me placing his hand on my shoulder. "There's nothing more you can do here today. Get some rest and tomorrow you can hit it again."

I nod because he's right. I'm useless right now. My stomach growls and I can't remember the last time I ate. Maybe a burrito on my way into work this morning. I dump my coffee down the sink and turn to head out for the night.

"You know I love you, right?" he asks softly when I reach the door. I just nod.

"Yeah, Liam, I know," I tell him. "I love you too."

I walk in the front door of my apartment and lock it behind me. I could probably buy a house if I wanted to, but I don't think I'd like being alone in a big space. The solitary lifestyle of my one-bedroom apartment is just right.

I drop my keys on the kitchen counter and toss my

coat over the back of my couch. I'm not the neatest person, but the only person who has to live with it is me so I don't care. I open the fridge and grab the carton of fried rice and the leftover egg rolls from last night. Or was it the night before? I shrug and grab a fork from the drawer, happily eating my cold leftovers as I kick off my boots.

I set my carton down on the counter and take a bite of my egg roll. I chew it as I unbutton my jeans and drop them to the floor. I put the egg roll back in my mouth like a cigar and reach under my shirt to unhook my bra and pull it out through the arm holes of my tee.

I grab my carton and continue to eat as I sit down on the old corduroy sofa and grab the remote. I flip through several channels, but the late-night news is covering the disappearance. My service picture—my face so fresh and bright straight out of the academy, no one would see the secrets that hide behind my eyes, but they're there—flashes across the scene with my name announcing my lead role in the investigation.

I'm glad when my fork scrapes the bottom of the carton, because the news has spoiled my appetite. I toss the cardboard in the trash and the fork in the sink. I pull a water bottle from the fridge and down the whole thing, tossing the bottle in the trash.

I pull my long hair up into a messy bun as I make my way down the short hallway to my bedroom. I pull the covers back and flop in face first. I'm asleep before I stop bouncing on the mattress, not even bothering to pull the blankets up over my body.

Wes and Liam are so mean! I can't believe they won't let me hangout with them. I bet they're just afraid that I'll tell mom and Mrs. O'Connell about the magazines they're hiding with the girls in bikinis in them.

I'm stomping through the woods behind our house. I don't need those gross boys to have some fun. And those boys are gross! They smell weird and put on too much stinky spray stuff when they think I'm not looking.

I just make it to the street on the other side of the trees from our house when a white van pulls up next to me. I hear my mom in my head telling me not to talk to strangers. I feel my eyes going wide as he steps out of the van.

"Claire!" he says and I wonder how he knows my name. "There you are. I need your help!"

"What do you need help with?" I ask.

"I'm so glad you asked, Claire," he says my name again like he says it all the time. It's weird but I don't think too much about it. "My puppy, Millie, got out. She's missing. Can you help me find her?"

"I don't know. I should probably go back home . . ." I say.

"No!" he shouts and it startles me and I jump a little. His eyes widen when he notices my reaction. "I

need you to look for her while I drive around. I'll give you this candy bar if you help me . . ." he offers, holding up my most favorite kind. I instantly grab for it, but he pulls it back.

"Okay, what does she look like?" I ask.

He smiles a creepy smile showing all of his teeth, but I open the front door and get in the van. He hands me the candy bar and I realize that I don't even know what his name is . . .

"She's little and fluffy and white . . ." he trails off as I dig into the sweets my mom never lets me eat before dinner. Ever!

All of a sudden, my head feels funny and my ears feel full of cotton like last summer when I got an infection from swimming too much. I open my mouth to tell him something is wrong, but my words don't work. They won't come out! I turn my head to look at him, a scream stuck in my broken mouth. He just smiles his big, creepy smile and everything goes black . . .

When I wake up I'm on an old, yucky blanket on the floor of a dark, smelly house. It's not my house. I know that. I rub the side of my head, it hurts so much. When I look up, the strange man is leaning back in an old torn chair, his feet spread wide and there's a strange bump in the front of his pants that he keeps rubbing his hands on. He smiles when he notices that I'm awake and for the first time ever, I'm scared.

"Hello, Claire, I'm glad that you're awake," he says to me in a scary voice. I just sit there staring with

my eyes big. "You may call me daddy."

I sit up screaming, pulling the gun that I tuck under my pillow each night and pointing it at nothing. The ghosts have won again. But then, I knew that they would. I have to focus to slow my breathing. Sweat rolls down my spine in waves.

I'd like to say that the old Chinese food brought on the nightmares, but that would be a lie. It was the Donovan case, I know it. That and the haunted look in Mr. Donovan's eyes when he realized that his son might not come back.

The ghosts old and new have me in their grip. I know what I have to do even if I don't want to. I grab my phone with the hand not currently holding a gun. I look down at the cold, black steel in my hand and wonder, not for the first time, just when those ghosts will finally claim me for good. When will they come for me with such a frequency that I crave the bite of my own bullet to silence them. It happens to more good cops than anyone realizes.

Will I be the next?

I stalk to the bathroom and place my gun and my phone on the counter. I fill up the glass that sits on the counter from the tap and chug it back. I stand there and sweat and shake, over and over again, waiting for the effects of the dream to loosen its grasp on me until

I turn and drop to my knees in front of the toilet and empty the contents of my stomach. No, the ghosts that I can't quite beat back won this round.

I wipe my mouth on the back of my hand before standing up on shaky legs. I run my hands under the faucet again and cup water to my mouth to rinse it out. I splash a little on my face hoping to cool down my overheated skin.

I stand there for who knows how long, looking at my reflection in the mirror. Always hoping that the image changes. One day, I want to see a beautiful, care-free woman who has smile lines in the corners of her eyes instead of red rims and bloodshot pupils. Maybe she'll be fat and happy with a baby in her belly and a gold ring on her finger. Or a little silver streaked in her jet hair and the knowledge of forty years with the same good man by her side.

But the woman in the mirror and I both know that will never be possible. The glint of the steel and the black glass of my gun and cellphone catch my eye. No, I won't be falling in love or having babies. I won't grow old with Wes or any man. Those dreams were all stolen from me twenty-four years ago. My only role now is to find the bad men and to make them pay, no matter how unhealthy those goals may be.

But before that, there's one thing I need to do. I pick up my phone, the metal and glass cool to the touch in my overheated palm. My thumb presses the circular button and unlock the screen. I open my call log and dial a number I know by heart now.

"Claire?" A voice husky with sleep asks when they pick up the phone.

"You were sleeping," I say realizing how late it must be. "I shouldn't have called. I'm sorry."

"Claire," she says before I have a chance to hang up. "Claire, you called for a reason."

"Yes," I whisper.

"You had a dream again, didn't you?" I hear sheets rustle and know that she must be getting up to take my call and turn it into a middle of the night session.

"I did."

"Which one?" She asks in her soft melodic tone. I clench my eyes tight and my hands into fists before I can answer.

"The one—" I have to clear my throat and start over. The rock in my throat is so thick I can't get my words around it. "The one where he takes me."

"And how does that make you feel, Claire?"

"Stupid," I say for lack of a better word because I was. How stupid do you have to be to willingly get into a car with a stranger. "Weak."

"Claire," she sighs. We're getting into dangerous territory. My regular sessions with Dr. Anna Chandler were one of Liam's many demands before I could sit for the Detective's Exam. Somewhere along the way, Anna became more than my shrink, she's a friend and confidant. "You were six years old. At some point you have to realize that you can't sit as your thirty-year-old self and judge the mentality of child you from the past."

"I know," I sigh. "I know it. I do. I just . . ."

"You can't let go," she says softly.

"Yeah."

"It's been a couple of weeks since you last had one of the dreams," she states. I know where this is going and brace for it, physically and mentally. "Has anything changed since we last spoke?"

"Yes."

"Are you going to tell me what it was?"

"I don't want to," I say petulantly.

Anna laughs. I sigh.

"Come on, Claire. Tell me. You know you want to . . ."

"Fine," I huff. "I caught a new case."

"What kind of case?"

"A missing person," I say honestly, feeling a little lighter.

"Hmm," she muses.

"It's a child," I confide. "A boy, a six-year-old boy."

"That's an interesting age," she muses.

"It's definitely a pretty big coincidence."

"I have to admit, I'm surprised Captain Goodnite gave you the case."

"He didn't have a choice," I sigh. "It's been a busy

week. I had just wrapped up a domestic. He could give me someone else's case and bump me from the new one, but he'd have a lot of explaining to do."

"Interesting . . ."

"He did spend a great deal of time trying to convince me to hand the case over to Wes willingly if it makes you feel any better."

"And how is the cold and calculated SAIC?"

"Not so cold and calculated," I mumble.

"What was that?" Anna perks up.

I sigh.

"I said he's more . . . warm . . . passionate maybe than cold or calculated these days."

"And why would you say that?"

"He kissed me outside of Liam's office."

"Shut up!" She squeals like a sorority girl just asked to the spring social by a big idiot named Biff.

"Yep." I pop the p from my mouth.

"Tell me all about it," she shouts. "Shit. I need a cigarette."

"I'm not sure you're the consummate professional Liam thinks you are," I tell her.

"Sometimes, I think what Liam doesn't know after hours won't hurt him."

I hear her click her lighter and take in a deep drag from the cancer sticks that will surely kill her one day. But I guess when you hear all the shit she does, you need a vice.

"I couldn't agree more."

"I take it he still wants you to quit the department?"

"Yeah, the fucker."

"It's because he cares," she tells me.

"Something like that."

"You know it's true. He just doesn't have a healthy way of showing it," she sighs.

"Yeah."

"Wes does too."

I snort.

"Oh yeah, he really cares." I roll my eyes but she can't see them. "He has a funny way of showing it if he does."

"He does," she argues.

"Yep, and he showed it when he announced to all of the officers and the victim's family at an active crime scene that I handed him my virginity on a silver platter like a moron."

"He didn't," she gasps excited for a juicy tidbit.

"He totally did."

"How did Liam take it?" I can see her rubbing her hands together with glee in my head.

"He was pissed for about a nanosecond and then he decided that this would be fun. Now their group goal is to get me to quit because he can't legally fire me."

I sigh.

"That bastard!" This is why I adopted her as my friend. Really, she's one of the best. Anna and the ME, Emma, are my only two female friends. We're an odd group, but it works.

"Yeah."

"You think you can get back to sleep now?" She asks.

"Yeah, I do. Thanks, Anna."

"Anytime, babe."

And then she hangs up.

chapter 5

non-negotiable

BEEP... *BEEP*... *BEEP*...

My alarm is blaring on the bedside table next to my head as I lay on my back, staring at the ceiling. I groan out loud but there's no one here except the ghosts of my past to hear me. Mornings like this are hard. I hate being alone after a night of the dreams, after a visit from the past.

My skin is cool, the sweat from my panic during my nightmares has chilled on my skin making my t-shirt stick to my breasts and my back. My legs are tangled in the sheets where I finally stopped tossing and turning, but my foray with sleep didn't last.

Without turning my head to look I silence my alarm, but I can't silence the ghosts in my head. Maybe Liam and Wes are right about me being on this case. But I'll be damned if I let them know it.

I roll out of my bed and head for my bathroom, not

even pretending like I'm going to make my bed. Because I'm not. I turn on the water as hot as I can stand it before stripping off my panties and tee, tossing them into the pile in the corner.

I hiss when I step into the scalding stream before forcing all my muscles to relax one by one. I make quick work of washing my hair and my body. Every time my thoughts stray to Wes and his kiss in the hall my skin heats and that makes me angry.

I don't *want* to want Wes. I fell for his charming song and dance years ago and learned really quickly that is not something I want to do again. It goes like this: get sucked in-sleep with Wes-get burned badly when he bolts. And he *will*. No, I already got the thanks for playing t-shirt and I don't need another one.

I shut off the water and step out, toweling off. I do manage to put the towel back on the rack before combing out my long black waves and then heading back to my room to dress. I pull on a lacy bra and panty set, which are definitely *not* for anyone specific. Then my usual work uniform of skinny jeans and tall boots. I like my boots a little loose so I can slide my drop gun and its holster underneath. Then a white, long sleeved thermal t-shirt with little buttons down the front exposing a light blue tank top underneath.

I head back to the bathroom. My building is old, really old, so I have to wait for the steam to clear from the mirror. I twist my hair up into a bun at the crown of my head, not because someone always loved my hair long and free. Then I slap a little makeup on my face like I do every day with a little blush, mascara, and a berry lip gloss.

I head down to the kitchen and pour myself a cup of coffee and make myself some toast. I give the bread a sniff as I pop it into the toaster because I can't remember when I bought it. I lift my mug to my lips, but freeze as I stare into the toaster and remember the morning Wes woke me from a nightmare…

"Jesus, what is that?" I hear Wes shout over a scream. It's then that I realize the screaming is me.

I back up against the headboard of his bed, as far away as I can get when he's looking at me like that. I pull the sheet up to my neck. I'm naked underneath. Bare. Vulnerable. I squeeze my eyes tight as I remember last night. What we did, Wes and me.

"Answer me," he thunders and I snap my eyes open. I open my mouth but the words won't come out. I clear my throat again before I can speak.

"Nightmare," I tell him.

"Do you have them all the time?" When I press my lips into a thin line instead of answering, Wes narrows his eyes at me. "I see."

"It's not a big deal, Wes," I whisper.

"I think it is," he says softly.

"Wes . . ."

"No," he closes his eyes. When Wes opens them again, I know that I've lost him. "This was a mistake. I'm going to head out for a bit. While I'm gone, you need to get home," he says quiet but firmly.

I bite my lip to keep it from trembling and nod my acceptance. Wes thinks it was a mistake to be with me. I have loved him my whole life and until recently, he thought of me as a burden. The annoying little sister of his best friend. Last night, I was something else. Something special. Someone that he wanted. But now, now I'm just a mistake. Well, that makes two of us. I won't be making mine again.

"I'm s—" Wes starts, but I steel my spine and don't let him finish.

"Don't," I say sharply. "I'll just be going." I say as I stand up, for once unashamed of my nudity and start pulling on my clothes. I open the door and I'm almost to freedom when Wes speaks again.

"Claire," he starts, the pain evident but I don't care. I won't ever care again.

"I thought I said, 'don't,'" I say and then slam the door behind me, never looking back.

My toast pops out of the toaster shaking me free of one more trip down bad memory lane. I grab a plate from the cabinet and place my now butter and jam covered toast on it. I take a bite, but it might as well be sawdust.

I take another bite knowing it may be the last thing I eat today.

I sip my coffee and hear in my head the sad way Wes said my name all those years ago, but I can't. He doesn't get to break me and then show up twelve years later asking for a do over.

I think about the way he kissed me yesterday and how I caved. *Again.* I'm secretly not sure I will ever be able to stay away from him for long. And I hate it. I had very little left of me that I liked after I was taken, Wes stripped me of the last of it twelve years ago. I see red and hurtle my mug at the wall across from me in the kitchen. I dump my toast in the trash can. I am no longer hungry.

Yep, the ghosts are out in force today. *All of them.* All set to ruin the life that I have carefully constructed for myself out of the rubble. This is why I can't have nice things. So, I clip my badge and my sidearm to my belt and head out into the day, locking the door behind me.

I park my Tahoe and walk into the station feeling the weight of an already shitty day on my shoulders. I head to the kitchenette and pour myself another cup of coffee, psyching myself up to go to my desk and get to work.

"Goodnite, my office. Now!" Liam bellows from

the doorway to his domain.

"Fuck," I say as I let my head hang down from my shoulders. My hands braced on the old laminate countertop. "What now?"

I push away from the counter and set my coffee mug on my desk. I briefly consider locking my guns in my desk in case my brother does something monumentally stupid and makes me want to shoot him.

"What's up, Captain?" I ask as I walk into his office.

"Wes and I have come to an agreement," he states. I raise my eyebrow in question.

"Oh, you have, have you?" I sneer.

"Yes," he says calmly. Too calm. "Wes is going to observe the case as it progresses. Any time we feel like it's too much, we're pulling you out."

"The hell you are," I grumble.

"Yes, we are. And be warned. This is non-negotiable. And the best offer you're going to get from me," he says, his purple eyes burning into mine.

"Fine." I pout, folding my arms over my chest.

"Good, now get out and find that kid." He smiles at me as I stand and start to walk out of his office. "I love you, Claire."

"I love you too, Liam." I smile at him over my shoulder. And I do.

"Just . . . hold onto that feeling over the next twenty-four hours," he says cryptically.

I just shrug and head out into the bullpen and sit at my desk. I flip open the file and am looking at the reports of businesses near the house that might have video surveillance, when I hear a chair shuffle and a throat clear. It's then that I notice there is no other sound in the building. You could hear a pin drop. I look up to see what has caused a stir and right into the whiskey colored eyes of none other than my FBI arch nemesis . . . and fall right the fuck out of my chair.

"God damnit," I shout when my ass hits the floor. That's going to leave a bruise for sure. "You have got to be kidding me."

"Nope, no kidding here," he rumbles in his deep, sexy voice. "Let me help you up." Wes offers me a hand to pull me up.

I reach up and grab his outstretched hand and I am electrocuted. Not really, but it feels like it. Like being struck by lightning. Or when you have to get tasered before you can carry one on patrol. It feels like that. By the widening of his dark eyes, Wes feels it too. I want to slap that stupid, sexy smile right off of his handsome fucking face.

I stand up and wrench my hand free from his. I sit at my desk and the bastard casually walks around to the other side of the partners desk I'm sitting at and sits right the fuck down.

"Umm . . . what are you doing?"

"Getting ready to observe." He smiles sweetly.

"Why are you sitting there?"

"Because this is my desk."

"No, it's not," I counter.

"Okay, it's my borrowed desk . . . *For now*." His eyes twinkle.

"No, that's Harriet's desk," I inform him.

"I know that, but Harriet is on maternity leave for the next six weeks, so the Captain said I could sit here while I help out with the case . . . and *observe*." I don't say anything. Okay, I might have growled. And yes, I definitely should have shot Liam.

"Don't do that. I'd miss you if you went to prison," he says still smiling, this time indulgently.

"What?" I ask.

"Don't shoot your brother. I'd miss you if you went to prison," he says, quieting his voice. "I can't kiss you if you're in prison . . . Or do other things to you . . . *With you . . .*" he trails off. I think I might be having a stroke because all I can do is groan and maybe drool a little bit. I shake my head to snap out of it.

"I don't know what you're talking about." I huff.

"You do, but I take it that you didn't mean to say it out loud." He chuckles. I just glare at him before returning my gaze to the file in front of me on my desk.

I start making a list of all the places that I need to check out before calling some of the responding officers to follow up. Then, I'll head out and start looking for creepy vans or bad people who might be looking to snatch a little boy.

"Don't you think we should interview the neighbors or the parents of Anthony's friends before we go looking for a creepy guy in a van?" Wes asks. I just look into his eyes and glare.

"No," I growl. "And what makes you think I'm looking for a 'creepy guy in a van'?" I ask.

"One, you wrote on your notepad, find creepy guy in a van," He ticks off on his fingers. "And two, I think we should do more interviews and find out if there even is a creepy guy in a van," he logics. Fucking logic. But I'm already too far gone with my irritation and angry that Wes and Liam ambushed me first thing this morning.

"Look, I don't show up at your work to slap the dick out of your mouth and tell you how to get shit done, do I?" Before I sigh. "Fine, asshole, we'll do it your way. Get in the car. Let's go interview some people," I say. Hoping to God that I don't feel the need to shoot him.

"I heard that!" he says and when I look up he's walking at a pretty fast clip towards the door. "And I'm driving!" he shouts as he breaks out into a run. The hell he is. Game-set-*mother effing match!*

chapter 6

determination

"**G**ET BACK HERE YOU asshole!" I shout as I sprint through the front door of the station, only to see him grinning like a lunatic from the driver's seat of my department vehicle! "Oh no you don't. Get the fuck out," I say as he turns the key and starts the ignition.

"Are you going to get in or what?" He laughs as he buckles his seatbelt.

"I'll kill you," I seethe.

"No, you won't," he laughs. "You can't fuck me if I'm dead. Now get in." I hear a feral scream and I'm pretty sure it's mine.

"I do not want to fuck you, you stupid shit. Conceited much?" I ask as I climb in the passenger seat of my car. And the big idiot just turns his head and winks at me before backing out of my spot and heading towards the Ascher's home.

"You do too, but that's okay. I'm ready when you are," that fucker winks at me. I feel the growl rumble up from deep in my chest and he just laughs. "Come on, let's go find some bad guys and interview some witnesses." I just glare at the side of his head as he peels out of the parking lot and heads towards the neighborhood of our missing boy.

The trip to Orange Drive is not long but it feels that way. It feels like years have passed as I sit in silence with Wes. Wes, who has always been magnetic. His energy doesn't pour off of him it radiates out and pulls you back into him. I'm feeling it vibrate off him now.

Wes doesn't try to make small talk with me. He doesn't hum to pass the time. And he isn't overall annoying. And I wish he was. This new Wes has me reeling and I don't know what to do about it. I should be focusing on what I'm going to say to the Johnson's and here I am trying to force myself not to think of Wes, to lean into Wes, to give in to all the temptation that is Wes. He's leaving me alone on purpose. Intentionally leaving me to my thoughts knowing that they would stray to him. Knowing that I love him. That I loved him when I was more girl than woman. That fucker.

Before I know it, he pulls up to the curb a few houses down from the Ascher's home. Wes kills the engine and then turns to me, his face open and honest. I don't like this Wes either. This Wes scares me. This

Wes makes me want to believe that I can trust him and I know, I know that I can't.

"I thought we could we could start with the Johnsons," he says, mirroring my thoughts. I just nod, still not looking at his face. "Hey, look at me."

"No," I whisper. I hear the click as he unbuckles his seatbelt and the sounds goes off in the quiet truck like a bullet from a gun. Before I know it, his hand is gentle on my cheek as he turns my face to look at him. "I agree. Let's go talk to the Johnsons." I say softly, my eyes downcast towards his shoulder.

"I said look at me, Claire," he says softly. He waits for my eyes to meet his. "It's going to be okay, Claire. I'm not going to hurt you. In any way." I close my eyes against his words. His face.

"No," I whisper.

"I'm not going to hurt you. I'm going to help you. I'm going to protect you. From bad guys, from yourself, but I am going to keep you from protecting yourself from me. I'm not the same man, Claire, and you have to recognize that." I just nod and wipe my nose on the back of my hand before unbuckling my seatbelt and leaping from the truck.

"Claire," he calls after me, but I just shake my head.

"Not now, now I'm working," I say as I march up the front steps of the Johnsons place and stab at the doorbell button.

I look over my shoulder to spy on Wes, but see the upstairs curtains of the Ascher place flutter as I scan past. I turn back forward as the dead bolt in the door turns. Mrs. Johnson, I assume, opens the door.

"Can I help you?" she asks, her full lips smiling wide and seductive over my shoulder. Fantastic.

"Yes, ma'am." I barely refrain from rolling my eyes and kicking him in the shins. "I'm Detective Claire Goodnite with the George Washington Township Police Department. We're here to ask you a few questions."

"Sure sure." She winks again over my shoulder. "And who are you, handsome?" I grind my teeth and press my hands into fists, my nails biting into the skin of my palms.

"I'm Special Agent Wesley O'Connell with the FBI." And I hear the mother effing smile in his voice.

So, now I see what the game is, he doesn't want me, he never freaking did. He was trying to woo me over so that he could get me off the damned case! Ugh. And now, he's trying to see if he can make me jealous. Angry even. So that I'll storm off and leave him to prove he can handle my case better than I can. Emotional maturity and all that bullshit.

"Oh, a *Special Agent*, well come on in. I hope you have to use your cuffs." She winks and I hear him start to choke. I smile. She's not just a cougar, she's a freaking man eater. This. Is. Awesome. He overplayed his hand. And I couldn't be happier. I want to clap with glee.

"Yes, let's go inside," I say. Mrs. Johnson looks

over at me like she'd like to tell me to take a hike, but knows that she can't. This is awesome. "I promise, we'll be real quick and then I'll leave you in the good hands of Special Agent O'Connell." I smile sweetly.

"What are you doing, Claire?" he growls in my ear.

"Getting you out of my hair so that I can get some real police work done while you do what you're good at." I wink at him.

"And what exactly is that?" He glares.

"That should be fairly obvious," I grin. "You are a manwhore. You just can't help yourself." I whisper back. His eyes are gold and glittering, probably a sign I should apologize and back off, but I don't. I pat him on the chest twice and the turn and follow Mrs. Johnson to the living room.

"Thank you for speaking with us, Mrs. Johnson,"

"Of course," she says sweetly. "Anything I can do to find that little boy."

"And what do you know of Anthony Donovan?"

"I know that he is a darling little boy," she answers. Pausing to gather her thoughts. "He's the same age as my son, Scott. They have played together in the neighborhood since the Aschers moved to town a few months ago."

"And what do you know of the Aschers?"

"I know that Jonathan is the vice president of the local bank. His family has owned it for years. And I know that Elizabeth works there, but I'm not sure in what capacity," she says. I find that interesting. Her knowledge of Mr. Ascher is lengthy, but what she knows of Mrs. Ascher is sorely lacking.

"And what about their daughter?" I ask.

"She's alright. She's always hanging around with her boyfriend when she's supposed to be watching her little brother. I've been meaning to say something to Jonathan."

"And what's her boyfriend like?" I ask.

"Do you know his name?" Wes chimes in.

"I don't know his name. But he looks decent enough." Fantastic. Not helpful lady, stop making moon eyes at my brother's annoying ass friend.

"Can you describe him?" Wes asks.

"He's pretty tall for a boy, muscles." She winks at Wes and I think I throw up a little bit in my mouth. "Blond hair. Always in polo shirts and jeans. Tennis shoes." Well, that was decent enough.

"That helps, thank you." Wes smiles his damn charming smile. The fact that it is directed at someone other than me is a nice reminder that he can't be trusted with my heart or my lady bits.

"I'll do anything to help you," she breathes as we stand to leave. "I know you'll catch who ever took him. I know all about you. I read you saved her when she was taken," she says as she wraps her hands firmly around his bicep. Wes tries to disengage when I ask for a private moment.

"Why don't you go on and bang some information out of her," I say quietly as I smile and nod towards Mrs. Johnson.

"What the hell does that mean?" he growls.

"Nothing, nothing," I placate him with my hands up. "I just think you'll get more information out of her without me here." He seems to mull it over for a bit before nodding. I look to Mrs. Johnson.

"Thank you so much, Mrs. Johnson." I smile. "I'm leaving you in the capable hands of the FBI." I wink at her before making my way out the door, clicking it closed behind me.

I walk down the steps and head to the truck to compile my notes. Glad I picked Wes's pocket when the nice neighborhood hoochie was pawing all over him. I'm not jealous or anything.

I climb into the driver's seat of my truck and start going over my notes, making more in the margins and lining up my questions. I look up at the Ascher house through the windshield and see the curtains flutter again. Someone is watching.

I tap my pen against my bottom lip and think who would be secretly watching. The Ascher's want their son found. Mr. Donovan had to be sedated last night because he was so distressed by his son's disappearance. *Kasey*.

It has to be the sister, Kasey. The sister much older than the little brother. Much like Liam and Wes are much older than me. Liam and Wes who are still so torn up about my own disappearance that they would do anything to pull me from this case. But Liam wouldn't have hid when the cops came. That take the bull by the horns attitude is what made him a great operator in the Navy and a great Captain with the police department. Liam is about as opposite of a shy, sixteen-year-old girl as you can get.

I'm lost in my thoughts of Anthony and Kasey, of Liam and me, and even Wes. The parallels are uncanny. My eyes stare forward at the Ascher house, unseeing, my mind trying to puzzle together the facts. But the past and the present are getting to jumbled together.

I jump when there is a knock on my window. I shake my head to loosen the facts bouncing around and shake free the memories that have nothing to do with now. I look up into those whiskey eyes that suck me in every time.

"What do you want?" I ask through the window. He looks . . . *sad*.

"We need to talk, Claire," he says softly. I shake my head again.

"No, I need to find a little boy," I say firmly with more bite than I meant but I brush that off. I'm still shaken from the dream, the memories, all of it just bubbling at the surface. "What you do in your spare time and with whom isn't my problem." For a second, if that, I see defeat flash across his golden eyes before resolution and determination harden there.

"Shall we go interview the sister?"

"That was my plan," I say sweetly.

"Then let's go," he says as he pulls open my door. I step down and tuck my notebook into my coat pocket. Together, we walk up the steps of the Ascher house and I can't help but feel like everything is about to change.

chapter 7

loved and cherished

THE WALK UP THE curb is slowly maddening. I can feel Wes behind me and my anger climbs to new heights with each step. My palms are sweaty and my hand shakes as I reach out to jab the doorbell, all while hoping that Wes doesn't notice.

"Hello," Mrs. Ascher says as she opens the door. "What can I do for you, detective?"

"I'm here to speak to Kasey," I tell her gently, not asking permission, but also not demanding aggressively.

"I'm not sure that now is a good time . . ." she trails off before she notices Wes over my shoulder.

"Ma'am, I'm Special Agent Wessely O'Connell with the FBI," he says over my shoulder. "I'm sorry to say, but there is no good time when there is a missing child. We need to speak to her," he finishes softly.

Mrs. Ascher just nods sadly and opens the door for

us to enter. We follow her into the living room where we will question the young girl.

"Please, have a seat. I'll go find Kasey," she says. We both nod and sit down. Wes on the smaller sofa, me on one of the arm chairs across the coffee table.

The sounds of soft footsteps padding down the carpeted tread of the stairs draw our attention. And I have to say, I could not be more surprised by what I see. Kasey Donovan is the polar opposite of her sweater twinset and pearl wearing mother. She stands tall in light wash skinny jeans and a snug white, vee neck t-shirt that showcase Jessica Rabbit curves on a fairly young girl. She has a black and red plaid flannel shirt tied around her hips.

Her hair is dyed black by the show of light roots at her scalp. And it's flat with no shine, I think uncharitably. I have always wondered why someone would choose this color, but who knows. Kasey has a matte, red lipstick smeared across her full lips. Silver piercings twinkle from both her right nostril and her tongue which she flicks as she winks at Wes. *Uh-oh. Danger, danger, Will Robinson! Jailbait dead ahead!*

By the furrowed brow on his face, I see that Wes notices it too. It's weird. Mrs. Ascher is sitting there with a blank look on her face like she doesn't see it. I still the shudder that's creeping up my spine.

"So, I hear you wanted to see me, Agent . . ." she breathes. BREATHES!!! All Marilyn Monroe like. Wes looks . . . concerned . . . Frightened. I decide to toss him a bone, though I'm not sure why.

"Actually, I did," I say, redirecting their attention to me. "I am the lead detective in this case."

"But he's FBI . . ." she pouts.

"I don't give two craps if he's the Pope, this is still my case," I say firmly. "Now, please have a seat. I have a few questions for you."

"Fine," she snaps as she lifts her chin and folds her arms over her chest.

I see the wicked sparkle in her eye but Wes does not. *Uh-oh.* She then moves and sits right next to him on the tiny little sofa. I almost want to laugh at how uncomfortable he looks, but he deserves this awkwardness for his behavior at the neighbor's house. A maniacal glee takes over me.

"I'm Detective Claire Goodnite, as I said before, I'm the lead investigator on your brother's disappearance," I tell her. "What can you tell me about the day he went missing?"

"We came home from school like always . . . and then you know . . . he wasn't there," she says and I sit there for a minute thinking, that's it? That's all she has to say about her baby brother's disappearance?

"It's really awful!" she screams suddenly and hurls herself at Wes, sobbing into his chest.

He pats her on the back once, twice, before dislodging the hormonal teen back to her side of the sofa. Mrs. Ascher just sits there like this is all totally normal, dabbing a hanky under her eyes. I, on the other hand, think that this is really fucking weird.

"Did anyone come over that day?" I ask.

"No," she sniffles as she rubs herself all over Wes. He's blatantly trying to remove her, but all of a sudden she's like an octopus of teenage girl proportions.

"So, no one rang the bell?"

"No."

"Did you see any suspicious vehicles in the neighborhood?" I ask.

She sighs, "I mean I guess. There was a weird white van for a while, but it left."

"Did it leave before or after you noticed your brother missing?"

"I don't know, maybe after," she barks. "Wait a minute, are you trying to pin this on me?"

"We're not doing anything," I say. "I'm just trying to piece together what happened that day so that I can find your brother."

"Maybe he just doesn't want to be found," she says cryptically.

"He's six years old," Mrs. Ascher says. "Don't be silly, he loves it here, why would he leave?" Kasey doesn't answer. I continue to question her.

"And you didn't have any friends come over?" I ask watching both Mrs. Ascher and Kasey for their reactions.

"No," she bites out as her spine stiffens. "Why are you being so mean to me?" she wails as she throws her arms around Wes's neck and throws her face into the crook between his neck and shoulder and nuzzles.

"We're not being mean," Wes wades in while peeling her off of his person.

For a minute I was thinking she was going to straddle his lap in front of her mother and me. And speaking of Mrs. Ascher, she just sits there looking extremely bored. Wes stands up and walks around behind the club chair that I'm sitting in. He places his hand on my shoulder in an effort to make it look like we're *together* together, and that he's not in the market for committing a misdemeanor. Now I understand his use of the royal we. I look up at him and smile sweetly, his eyes narrow, knowing that what I really mean is retribution.

"We're trying to explain to you both really, how important the first forty-eight hours of a disappearance are, and they've already come and gone," he admonishes.

"What we're trying to say," I wade in, "is the time to stop playing games is now. So, sit back and answer the questions."

"Fine." This kid is a brat. I hate to think badly of people, but I want out of this house.

"Alright then," I say as I uncross and recross my legs. It does not go unnoticed that Wes follows the movement. Kasey does not look impressed by my actions. Apparently, I've inadvertently issued a challenge. "Did you have a boyfriend over?"

"Which one?" she smiles coyly, looking up at Wes through her lashes. "I have many." This appears to have finally pushed her mother to some kind of action. Anger flashes through her eyes.

"Do you really have to be so crude, Kasey?"

"Don't be jealous," she coos to her mother. Mrs. Ascher clenches and unclenches her fists at her sides.

"I would never be jealous of a child."

"I wouldn't be so sure about that," Kasey says as she buffs her black painted fingernails on her torn t-shirt, a malicious smile twisting her lips.

"Did you see any suspicious people in the area that day?" Wes asks.

"Yes," she purrs. "I saw a very sketchy looking man."

"What did he look like?" I get excited.

"Well," she smiles seductively as she taps the tip of her index finger against her painted red lips. "He was very tall, with big, sexy muscles, and dark eyes. He had lush dark hair I just wanted to pull when he kissed me. He looked like a very, very bad man . . . I bet you're a very bad man, aren't you Agent?"

Well, that's the ballgame, folks. I stand up and pull Wes along with me. "Call me when you're ready to help us find your son, Mrs. Ascher."

They both follow us to the door. Mrs. Ascher pulls it open for us, but says nothing. Kasey on the other hand has sided up to Wes who is looking particularly uncomfortable. She runs a fingernail down his chest before speaking.

"Call me when you're ready to ditch the old chick," she purrs. "I promise you, I'm better." And then she kisses him square on the mouth.

"I seriously doubt that," I say to myself.

Wes and I walk down the block before climbing back into my waiting SUV. He climbs into the passenger seat, not even arguing with me about who's driving. Which is good because I'd hate to have to fill out the paperwork because I shot him.

"So, I take it you're mad . . ." he hedges.

"Do not talk," I growl before putting the car in drive and peeling out.

I drive around the neighborhood for awhile, taking turns down side streets here and there, but staying close to the street that the Ascher's live on. I take another turn and then back. I feel the hairs on the back of my neck tingle.

"Are you going to talk to me?" He sighs.

"No."

"Are you going to at least tell me where we're going?" he asks.

"No," I say taking another turn. "Actually yes. Could you at least try to be less appealing?" I snap.

"What?" The bastard laughs.

"You know as well as I do, flirting with the neighbor in front of me was fucked up and unprofessional," I growl. "But the daughter, that was messed up."

"Did you not see me pleading for help the whole

time we were in that Goddamned house?" he shouts. "I couldn't get away from Lolita fast enough. I have never been more uncomfortable and you just sat there."

"You're being ridiculous!"

"Really?" he questions. "Did you ever think I flirted with the neighbor because I want something from you? Anything really. Just give me something!" he thunders, but I've found what I'm looking for. A strip mall with a Subway, an electronics repair shop, a Starbucks, and other businesses comes into view.

"Bingo," I thump the steering wheel as I turn into the parking lot.

I pull my keys from the ignition and jump down from my truck. I head into the Starbucks first because coffee. Enough said. Wes is storming in behind me. I walk up to the counter and order the sweetest most disgusting coffee on their menu and a cookie.

"Add a large coffee," Wes says from behind me.

"Did you just crawl out from under a rock? They don't do larges here," I snap. The jerk just shrugs.

"I just want a coffee. Are you sharing your cookie?" he asks.

"No," I snap but he just laughs as he peels a couple of bills out of his wallet and hands them over to the barista that is sufficiently stunned by his smile. Stupid gorgeous life ruining bastard. He scoops up the bag with my cookie in it and his coffee then heads over to a table while I wait for my coffee and make small talk.

"Is your manager here?" I ask, snapping the star stuck barista out of her fog.

"Umm, yeah," she hedges. "Am I in trouble?"

"No, I need to ask her some questions about another matter altogether. You're fine," I add for good measure.

"I'm good," she sighs, eyeing my badge and gun on my hip. "I was worried. I swear, I didn't know there was pot in those brownies."

I sigh.

She keeps rambling on and on to me about her drug use.

"Look, you seem like a nice kid, but I'm going to have to ask you to stop talking right now before you accidentally confess to a serious crime. I'm searching for a missing person, so I'm a little busy to be busting you for recreational marijuana use, okay?"

"Okay," she takes a huge breath. "That's my boss over there." She points to the man walking from the back hallway.

"Great!" I smile brightly and make my over to the slightly chubby, middle-aged man with the florid face and pants situation happening.

"Oh shit," I hear Wes mumble as he jumps up and follows me towards the manager.

"Hello," I say as I approach him, smiling fully. He has beady little eyes and I don't trust him. "I'm Detective Claire Goodnite with GWTPD and I'm investigating the possible kidnapping of a child," I say as I show him my badge.

"I didn't do it," he flusters.

"I didn't say that you did," I say sweetly. "But I was wondering if you had security cameras pointing away from the shop?"

"Yes," he whispers.

"Can I see them?"

He just nods before leading us back down the little hallway where he just came from. I take note of bathrooms, a break room, a storage closet, and lastly, the doorway to a tiny office just before the emergency exit out back.

He pushes open the door allowing Wes and I to follow him inside. He rounds an awful aluminum desk much like my own at the station and logs into an ancient computer before pulling up the security feed.

"You wouldn't have a flash drive, would you?" he asks, but I just smile and pull a purple flash drive from my pocket, handing it to him.

"Of course," he sighs. I swear I hear Wes snicker, but he keeps it tamped down.

"Thank you," I say as we take my flash drive and our coffees and head out the door.

"Where to now?" Wes asks as we pile into my SUV. "More of the same?"

"Of course," I look over at him as I sip my coffee.

I drive us over to the bridal shop and pull into the

parking lot. I shudder as I step down from my truck and look at the offending building. It's like an invisible wall is built up between me and the building, not letting me pass. It's like I'm froze or I'm stepping in gum, or super glue. I can do this. I can do this.

I force myself to take a small step forward, and then another and another. I stop to take a deep breath, totally forgetting that Wes is there until he speaks his deep, sexy voice in my ear making me shiver.

"Not a big fan of weddings?"

"No," I choke out, shaking my head.

Wes runs his fingertips down the slope of the side of my neck and over my shoulder. "That's sad, I bet you'll make a beautiful bride."

"I'm not ever going to be a bride," I whisper.

"What would your mother say about that?" he asks. It's like he's got me hypnotized and I can't help but answer him. I'm stuck in his vortex until he releases me.

"She'd say I should find a nice man and settle down."

"Maybe you have found a nice man . . ." I snort because the idea of one of the guys I have hooked up within the last year being a nice man is funny. They might have been nice, just not when they were doing decidedly not nice things to my body.

"Probably not. Although, I don't usually stick around to find out." I sigh.

"That's over now," Wes growls, my spine goes

straight.

"What?"

"I'm not talking about the little pricks you play around with, I'm talking about me, Claire."

"What?"

"You're done toying with them and you know it," his voice rumbles in my ear.

"I know no such thing," I snap coming unglued from the parking lot floor. "Let's go get their tapes."

"Sure, we can walk into that bridal shop, and we can go get those tapes, but you do it with the knowledge that I'm done fucking around. So, pick a date, a dress and some fucking flowers, I'll be there."

"Fuck off, Wes!" I shout as I pull out of his grip and stomp into the bridal shop to retrieve their security footage, if they'll give it to me. Something tells me that Wes is going to be the one to walk away from this one as the winner of the footage. And I don't know how to feel about it.

The bell over the door tinkles as we pass through. I'm still scowling, but Wes has a big ass fucking grin on his face looking at all the tulle, lace, bullshit and lies filling up this den of horrors.

"How can I help you?" A pretty young thing in an awful sweater twinset and loafers asks.

"My fiancé is not finding the dress of her dreams," he purrs. "And there is nothing too good for my pu-dykins."

"Awe, that is so sweet," she coos. I try to control my gagging. "Well, what are you looking for?"

"Big!" the bastard booms. "The poufier the better, and lots and lots of lace . . . and buttons!"

"I know just the thing!" she cries with excitement for all things bridal. I'm pretty sure she has an apartment full of cats, bridal magazines, and toe nail clippings.

She pulls me to a dressing room, pulling the curtain back and shoves me. I'm ordered to strip down to my panties and she tosses me a fancy corset type bra. With one look I see she guessed my size exactly. I give her a questioning look and she just winks at me. Cat lady is good.

By the time I've wiggled into the crazy contraption that I must admit, makes my ass and boobs look amazing, she's back, breezing in with what has to be over two hundred pounds of tulle and lace and glitter.

She pulls back the curtain and says, "I think we'll try this one first. It's exactly what your fiancé described."

She quickly helps me into a white strapless ball gown that laces up the back and has a huge skirt of layers upon layers of rhinestone adorned tulle. I learned two things: No one in the bridal industry uses or appreciates the word rhinestone, and second, Cat Lady can lace up a dress to rival Scarlett O'Hara's hand maid.

"Let's just step outside and onto the block and take a look," she says. Since I'm basically here to do nothing while Wes does who knows what in the back with the manager, I decided to go along with it.

She pulls back the curtain and I step up onto the carpet covered block. As soon as I look into the mirror, I laugh. I look like the Abominable Snowman. Cat Lady makes a face and then busts up laughing too.

"Okay, maybe not this one."

She leads me back into the dressing room and has me out of the poufy monstrosity in seconds. She slides a plain white, no frills dress with a sweetheart neckline over my head. She does up the hidden zipper and the ties a wide pink ribbon belt with fake flowers around my waist.

Again, we step outside of the dressing room and when I look in the mirror, I don't laugh. I don't look silly, I look sweet and demure. Like a lady. Like a girly lady. I think that if things had gone differently, I could have been the girl who would wear this dress and walk down the aisle to guy like Wes, but I'm not. That girl is dead. And Wes had a hand in erasing her from the universe.

"I'm sorry, I didn't mean to make you sad," she says softly. "Let's try one more."

"Okay," I say.

She leads me back and pulls off the beautiful pink and cream dress and pulls an ivory satin dress with cap sleeves and a V-neck. This dress is different. It has a delicate lace overlay with bits of gold beads woven in. The skirt is not full at all, in fact it skims my waist and hips and thighs like it was made for me. The back has soft satin covered buttons that go from the back of my shoulders to the underside of my ass where the skirt is gathered and opens up into a tasteful train.

She walks me outside, and for the first time, I wish it were real. This is a dress I could wear and feel beautiful, but still feel like . . . *me*. She holds my hands as I step up onto the box again.

"Forgive me," she says and I don't know what she means until she laughs, "Okay, just don't shoot me," she says as she pulls the rubber band from my messy bun letting my jet-black curls fall almost artfully around my shoulders and breasts. Then she sticks a comb in my hair at the crown of my head hold a long, sweeping train of the same ivory color.

We both stand there, for however long, looking at me. I'm stunned to see a beautiful woman. Someone who could be loved and cherished, not thrown away and so casually discarded. It's only until I hear a masculine throat clearing, that I realize, I could be loved and cherished, if I let him.

At least, if the look in Wes's eyes is anything to go by. He's stopped at the mouth of the manager's office. Whether he got the tapes or not, you couldn't tell by his expression. The only thing there is reverence, a sparking sexual tension, and maybe . . . love.

I shake away those thoughts. This man whom I once loved deeply, discarded me like old toilet paper without a backwards glance for me or my feelings. He flirted his way through witnesses this morning to get to me and kissed me silly outside my brother's office. There is nothing professional or even safe about the way Wesley O'Connell is handling me and the only thing I know for sure is it's time to put a stop to it.

I step down from the pedestal and am about to tell Cat Lady, whom I've grown rather fond of until this moment that the dress isn't what I'm looking for. Playtime is over, there is no room for make believe or could haves and would haves, but Wes beats me to it, "We'll take it."

chapter 8

just peachy

THE DRIVE BACK TO the station is relatively un-
eventful. I think we're both too busy mulling over
what happened in the bridal shop. Wes wants things to
change, and me, I just want him out of my life, right?

As I pull into the station I firm up my resolve to
keep Wes at arm's length until he moves on to his next
conquest. Which he will. He always does. But this
time, I'm determined to keep the pieces of my heart
intact long after he's gone. Wishful thinking? Maybe.

"Tell me you have something," Liam hollers from
his office.

"It's uncanny, really," Wes says. "How does he do
it?"

"I think he has surveillance cameras set up all over
the station, my car, my apartment, and our parents'
house. It's the only explanation that I'm willing to accept. Otherwise, he isn't human," I nod.

"Well," Liam says as he rounds the corner.

"We have hours and hours of storefront surveillance to go over looking for a white panel van that may or may not be there," I sigh.

"What else? Wes?"

"Wes is still recovering from man whoring his way through witness testimony," I say petulantly.

"I don't need to recover."

"Okay, I do."

"What's going to with you two?" Liam narrows his eyes on us speculatively.

"Nothing," we both say at the same time, maybe just a little too quickly.

I sigh when he won't let up on his death stare, "Something is off with the Ascher's."

"Like what?" he asks.

"Like the mom is in a fog and doesn't seem to care that her son is missing," Wes explains to Liam. I nod.

"And?"

"And the sixteen-year-old sister was seriously hot to trot for your old buddy, Wes, here," I laugh. "Seriously, it was uncomfortable."

"It was," he shudders. "I think I'm scarred for life." I just laugh.

"She's a cold-hearted woman," Liam commiserates.

"Don't I know it," he nods.

"Alright, Casanova, let's start watching security feeds. You take your boon, I'll take mine," I tell him before I head out of Liam's office and make tracks for the galley to grab a cup of coffee.

I settle down at my desk and set my coffee mug on top after taking a long hit of my favorite jet fuel. I insert the flash drive into the side of my geriatric computer and hope for the best.

The little black window pops up and I groan, it's nothing but static. Fuck. My. Life. Wes can't do better than me. That would suck big time.

"Yippee!" I clap when the screen flickers and then images start to tick by on the screen.

"You alright, over there?" Wes smirks.

"Just peachy. You look for the van on your side, I'll look for it on mine."

"And we meet in the middle?" Wes asks.

"Not ever."

I go back to watching the tape tick by and see not one panel van. I sip my coffee and peel my eyes open. I scan the scenes as they play out in black and white and hope for the stupid van to make an appearance.

At three hours I have to get up and stretch my legs. I hit pause on the tape and stand up. My brain was getting fuzzy and I still haven't seen a panel van. Wes did his walk about an hour ago.

"Want more coffee?" I ask. "I'm headed for a refill."

"Yes, please."

I pace the back-hall way for awhile and then make my way to the galley for more coffee. I fill up our cups and head back to my desk. Wes isn't anywhere to be found so I set his mug on his desk and walk around to my side.

I twist side to side until my back cracks, then I sit down at my desk and fire the video back up. I see mothers with babies in strollers, businessmen grabbing another cup of coffee, minivans, SUVs, sedans, no white panel van. I sigh to myself.

I look at the clock in the corner of my computer screen and realize that I haven't seen Wes in over an hour. I look around. His desk is empty. His computer is shut down and his keys aren't in the top drawer. That fucker left me.

I head down the hall to Liam's office because if Wes is still in the building, he's with Liam. There's a nervous pit in my stomach and I don't like it. I have a great gut. It's kept me from getting shot, only ever got me stabbed the once, and it's currently telling me that there is something about Wes and Liam together, that can't be trusted.

The walk down the hall to the Captain's office is blaringly quiet. There's no one milling about in the hall which is weird on its own. When I get to Liam's office I see that the door is slightly ajar and I can hear voices inside. Voices of the two men in my life who keep telling me at every turn that they love me and want what's best for me. Those same men, it appears, also enjoy stabbing me in the back at every turn.

"Pull her off the case, Liam. Now," Wes barks.

"I'm not sure I have enough reasoning to."

"I found the van myself, she was off getting coffee, that's plenty of reason to pull her and you know it."

"You know that it's not. I'm also legally required to offer all of my officers a bathroom break and the option to eat."

"Ok, how about that I got this security tape all by myself while she was dicking around trying on fucking wedding dresses," he says as he throws me under the bus. Beep, *mother fucking beep*, here comes Wes the dirty dealer.

My gasp draws their attention to me standing in the doorway to Liam's office, obviously eavesdropping. Liam bites out a *"Goddamn it,"* but otherwise they glare at me like it's my fault that their conspiring to ruin my career.

"This is a private meeting," Wes growls.

"Oh, I got that," I say to Wes, feeling the tears burn in my eyes. I won't give them the satisfaction of seeing them fall. They don't get that from me. Plus, it would probably be the final nail in my law enforcement career coffin. Obviously, the girls are too emotional to be cops bullshit.

"You don't belong here, Claire," he says softly, reaching out to me, but I jerk away.

"You don't get to decide that. I know where you

stand now. I'll do my end, you do yours. Stay the fuck away from me."

"Claire," Liam pleads. "I don't want you doing this."

"Oh, I got that," I snap. "But listen to me, that is not what happened today. You and Wes both know it. Apparently tanking my career is more important to you than finding a little boy. This is your final warning. If I find you two colluding to sabotage my career and reputation again, I'm going to IA."

"You wouldn't!" Liam yells. "You know how hard I've worked for this."

"And you know how hard I worked for this, but apparently it doesn't matter. I know that Wes is a cheating, double crossing prick, but you, you're my brother, or at least I thought you were. Right now? I'm not so sure. Have fun looking for your van, I'm off the clock."

I walk straight out of Liam's office and don't look back. I don't care. This time, no one follows me. I guess I know how they both really feel. I don't care about that either. I walk right through the station and can feel the stares of fellow officers but I don't make eye contact, not out of shame, but pride. They all heard, they had to but I won't let any of them see how much Wes and Liam hurt me. So, I keep my head held high. I am not the one in the wrong here.

I beep the locks on my Tahoe and jump in. I lock my badge and sidearm into the special safe in my glove box. I sniffle, I feel it coming. I cover my eyes with my

hands as a sob tears free from my chest. I feel so be-
trayed. I lean forward, with my eyes still covered and
lean my forehead on the steering wheel.

I sit there and cry. For how long I don't know, but
until I feel eyes on me. I look up and lock eyes on Wes.
The smug, angry look on his face is replaced with one
of anguish. Liam is with him. I let them see. Let them
look at what they did to me. This is on them, not me.

Wes makes a move to step forward and I quickly
dash away the tears from my cheeks and start the engine. I buckle my belt and look over my shoulder as I
back out of my space.

The drive home is boring as usual, except for all
of the thoughts pinging around in my brain like rogue
bullets. My phone has been ringing constantly with
calls from both Wes and Liam, but I don't answer. I'm
off the clock, if something changes, dispatch will call
me, not those two assholes.

I climb the steps to my apartment and unlock the
door. It's the same disarray that I left it in this morning.
I lock up my sidearm and badge over the fridge and the
strip off my clothes on the way into my little bathroom
where I take as hot a shower as I can stand.

By the time I get out I feel moderately better, but
also restless. I need to take the edge off. I decide to do
what I'd usually do. Wes doesn't spare my feelings so
why should I spare his.

I toss my long hair up into a messy bun and pin it
in place. I throw on a silky gray tank top with lace trim,

jeans and my tall boots. The look does great things for my boobs. Nice. Then I pad back into my bathroom and slap a little man-eating makeup on my face. Mascara, a rosy blush, and a deep raspberry lipstick. It's the kind that's meant to stay on forever and doesn't come off on a cheek or a wine glass. It's the very color a man can't stop thinking about wrapped around his dick. And it doesn't smear. Double win.

I toss a dark peacoat over my shoulders and pocket my money and cellphone. I see that I've missed a bunch more calls from the guilty group but shrug it off. I unlock my sidearm and badge. Then check the magazine before pocketing them both.

I lock the door behind me and head down the stairs to my truck. I beep the locks and hop in, locking up my badge and gun. I don't need them on me at all times when I'm off duty, but I do need them near just in case. But I have found that it's a bit of a dick wilter to have a man stripping me down, only to stop in his tracks when he sees that my gun is bigger than his.

I fire up my truck and head towards my favorite bar. It's two towns over and a bit of a drive, but it keeps me from shitting in my own front yard. It's a bummer when your hookup turns out to be a detective from a neighboring station. That's totally not awkward when your paths cross professionally or anything. But I wouldn't know, as that's totally never happened to me.

When I pull into the parking lot, the dim lights are spilling out into the lot, as is the loud music. This is just what I need tonight. I feel my shoulders physically lower as I slowly relax and gain back some of my control. What I do not feel, is the presence behind me that's followed me here all the way from my apartment in George Washington Township. No, I don't notice it at all, I just lock my doors and pocket my keys, walking into my favorite bar and heading straight for disaster.

chapter 9

major mistake

"THE USUAL?" JOE, MY favorite bartender asks as I walk in.

"Yeah," I smile and take a seat at the end of the bar where I can watch the people who move around the establishment and pick my next victim.

Joe slides the seven and seven on a cocktail napkin in front of me. I smile my thanks as I pick up my drink to take a sip. I swivel around on my barstool and watch the crowd absentmindedly. There's a couple of cute guys, but nobody peaks my interest.

I feel someone sit down next to me and I look up. He's about five eleven or six foot with a mop a sandy blonde hair and brown eyes. He has an easy smile and he immediately turns it my way. I look back at Joe who winks and shakes his head. He knows my drill.

He looks at me and smiles, "I'll have what she's having," he says to Joe and I think he might do. But

I'm just not that into it. I'll see how it goes.

Joe slides the drink in front of him and he happily sips it while waiting for me to say something. I finally decide to help him out.

"Well, what do you think?" I ask.

"I think it's not bad. Is it your signature drink?"

"I don't have a signature . . ." But I'm stopped by Joe.

"She does and it is."

"I'm Mark," he smiles at me and holds out his hand for me to shake. As I take his hand in mine and notice a firm grip on a smooth hand with no calluses and clean trimmed fingernails. The callous on my index finger grazes his knuckles and he bites his lip.

"I'm Claire," I say smiling.

"So, Claire, do you live around here?" he asks. "Wow, was that as bad as it sounded?" I laugh.

I feel eyes on me and I start to scan the room. I come up short when I see Wes scowling from a table in the corner. A waitress with a trim waist and balloons for boobs grazes his elbow with her rock-hard nipples as she delivers his drink, a cold beer in the bottle, but his gaze stays locked on me. I roll my eyes and turn back to Mark.

"No, it wasn't that bad," I lie.

"So, what do you do Claire?" Mark asks.

Joe groans.

I bite my lip and shake my head no. I'm not going to tell him. It will end all the fun. There's no way Mr. Businessman or Mr. Lawyer wants to go home with a police detective. I look over at his polo shirt and jeans and think he's cute in a very country club sort of way.

"Oh, you want me to guess do you?"

I smile wider because he'll never guess while nodding my head. I sip my drink and wait for him to guess. This could be fun. And I need fun. The missing boy, Anthony, and Wes and our fucked up past have my emotions too close to the surface.

"A dental hygienist."

"Ew, gross. I would never stick my hands in people's mouths." I laugh. Although I have stuck them in a dead body. I'm not sure what that says about me.

"A librarian."

"Do I look like a librarian to you?" I laugh.

"Only in my dreams," he laughs. "That was cheesy too, right?"

"Yeah, kind of. What about you? What do you do?" I ask. I feel eyes on me again and I look over my shoulder. The waitress with the flotation devices and huge hair is sitting in his lap, with his ear caught between her teeth. Her crooked teeth, I notice uncharitably. I'll drop an extra twenty in the offerings tray on Sunday and ask for forgiveness. It was worth it.

"You know that guy?" Mark asks.

I look back at him and see him looking at Wes and

the hooker. "No," I say as I look at him. He's handsome and nice. I should choose a guy like him. I toss the remainder of my drink back and ask, "You want to get out of here?"

"Hell, yes."

"Your place, I'll follow you out," I tell him as I stand. Mark throws some money on the bar top for Joe and I see him tip his imaginary hat at me behind Mark's back as thanks for the huge tip. Or maybe it's my ability to leave with a guy in less than an hour. I mentally shrug, who knows.

As I found out following his nondescript sedan home, Mark lives around the corner from my local bar. That's going to be awkward later. I pull into the visitor spot closest to where he parked his car. He waits for me by the door like a gentleman and then leads me up the stairs to his second-floor apartment.

Mark holds the door open for me but as soon as it closes behind me I grab him by the shirt and pull him against my body, breast to chest, and kiss him deeply. Not bad. Not great, but not bad. Mr. Country Club is not an aggressive lover.

He breaks away from my body to push my jacket over my shoulders. I pull his polo over his head and toss it to the ground. Mark sees to it that my t-shirt and bra go the same way. He smiles his coy smile at me again before taking my hand and leading me to his bedroom where I make my second major mistake of the night.

chapter 10

rough

"COME SIT IN DADDY'S lap," the man coos.

I don't want to, I know that I don't want to. He holds out his hand for me and I shake my head no. I don't want to sit in his lap. He's not my daddy. His face turns mean and I'm scared.

"If I have to come get you it'll hurt worse. I promise."

"I don't want to hurt at all," I whisper.

"That's not a choice for you to make, pet," he says through gritted teeth.

I turn on my heels and run, but I'm so small that I don't get far. He snatches me back by my arm and I scream out it hurts so bad. He drags me back to the dirty sofa where he sits back down and stands me in front of him. I don't look at him. I'm scared.

He pulls my pants and panties down my legs. I

shake, I'm so scared but I can't stop. I know he'll be mad that I'm not holding still, but I can't stop. He tips me over his lap and I cry out.

"This hurts me more than it hurts you," he sighs.

I never get the chance to believe him as his hand hits me on my bottom again and again. He spanks me over and over. I'm sobbing. The words coming out of my mouth don't even make sense but he keeps hitting me harder and harder. The mean man who is not my daddy hits me twelve times, two for every year that I lived. Part of me hopes I don't live much longer. I don't like spankings.

Hot tears roll down my cheeks and I can't stop them even if I want to.

Then it's over. Except it's not. I go to stand back up, but his hand pushes my shoulders down and he touches me. Mama always told me not to let anyone touch me there, but I don't have a choice. He won't give me a choice.

He won't stop no matter how much I cry or yell or try to get away. He just won't stop.

"See? Daddy knows what his kitten likes," he says before he finally stops hurting me.

He places me on my feet right in front of him. My clothing is long gone and I'm embarrassed to be standing there in nothing but my t-shirt. I try to pull the bottom of it down so the he can't see my private place but he slaps my hands away.

"Now you give to daddy," he says as he opens his

pants.

He touches himself and he slides his hands up and down, up and down. He squeezes it tight and I don't want to watch. I try and look away but he yells at me, tells me to watch.

"Look at me, Claire! Look at what you do to me, what you make me do."

I just stand there and stare, hoping for it to be over. I hurt in a bunch of places and I just want to go lie down. No, I want to go home, but he hurt me when I tried to run away. So, I have to just stand here.

I stand here and watch as his hand that does mean things holds himself tightly. I watch as he looks at me as he slides in and out of his fist. He's making funny noises now. I want to cover my ears because I hear my name in there every so often and I don't like it. I know that he would be mad if I blocked out his sounds so in my head I'm practicing my math facts.

I'm doing everything that I can to not make this last any longer than it has to. He's getting faster now. Up and Down, up and down. His sounds are louder and louder. Will someone hear him? Will they come to rescue me? Somehow, I don't think so and that thought makes me sad. He moves his hand faster and faster. Then he shouts my name as he sprays my favorite t-shirt with something yucky.

He smiles at me, happy with himself. But soon that smile turns mean again. He zips up his pants and grabs me by the arm, shoving me back towards the closet he keeps me in. He shoves me inside and I fall to the floor.

I look up at him, but his face changes from the mean man to Wes's beautiful face when he says, "You were a very bad girl today, Claire. I'm so disappointed in you."

I wake with a start. Well, that's a new twist to the dream. That's the worst part, that I dream. Lately, it's every fucking night. It would have been a mercy if God took all of my memory, but no, I got to keep just enough snippets to slowly drive me crazy. The psychologists all said that it was a sign of my strong mental strength. That it was a sign that my mind was protecting itself. It was a sign of something. But that's not what woke me up either.

A shrill ring woke me up from a restless sleep. And I had had the dream again. My phone bounces around on the unfamiliar night stand that I must have left it on last night. I wipe the errant tears leftover from my dream from my face with the palm of my hand and answer my phone.

"Goodnite," I rasp, my voice heavy with sleep.

"Detective, this is dispatch," the disembodied voice from my phone informs me. *"We were told to notify you that the body of a male child has been recovered at the rocks near the bottom of the falls. Possible match for your missing person."*

"I'm on my way."

That's all I need to know, and I am throwing the blankets back that are tangled around my body—my naked body. I pull my jeans on without panties and then my boots. I quietly search for my bra, hopefully not waking . . . NOT waking . . . I look over at the bed where a man with warm blond hair and a stubbled jaw sleeps on the bed that I just vacated. Nope, not ringing any bells. At least he's good looking.

I should be embarrassed. Letting some random pick me up at a bar in the next town over. But I'm not. This case has been . . . *rough* . . . and I needed to blow off some steam. *Will I call him again?* Uhh, no. *Will he call me?* He'd have to find me first. *Did he have a good time?* You betcha.

I see my bra hanging from a lamp shade and grab it, tucking it into my back pocket. I pull my tank top on and then my t-shirt, having found both rumpled on the floor. I reach into the front pocket of my jeans and find a—*thank God*—a hair tie and toss my long hair on top of my head in a messy bun. I pull on my coat that was dropped by the front door.

I palm my phone and pull my keys out of the same pocket the hair tie came out of. I step out into the New Jersey cold without ever looking back at . . . *Mike?* No, that's not it. I shrug to myself, oh, well.

I unlock my car and climb in. I unlock the glove box and I pull out my badge and sidearm, placing both on the dash. I fire up my nondescript Tahoe and head towards tragedy.

chapter 11

it burns

THE GRAVEL CRUNCHES UNDER my boots as I hike down to the bottom of the falls. The crisp breeze cuts through my coat and clothes making me wish I had a warm hat and gloves on. But this isn't about me.

As I approach the cluster of officers I can already tell that it's bad; whatever it is that dragged me out of bed this early in the morning. Jones looks up and drops his chin to his chest once, silently telling me what I already knew.

I pull the picture the Ascher's gave me of Anthony Donovan out of the inside breast pocket of my coat and look down at the tiny bundle under the yellow tarp. One of the other uniformed officers pulls back the sheet so I can see the boy's face. It's bloated from being in the river for so long, but even through all the distortion from the elements, I can tell that this is our boy.

My heart sinks. I know in my head, that not all kidnapping victims end up back at home, warm and safe. I know that the chances of survival are slim. But I always hope. Later tonight, I'll feel the guilt associated with being one of the rare survivors. A kid who managed to escape. And I moved on to the best of my ability. But tonight, when I'm home by myself, with bad take out and whiskey to keep me company, I'll wish it was Anthony who was able to escape and not me.

"What do you have for me?" I ask as I roll back my shoulders.

"The body of a juvenile male was seen by teenagers partying on the footpath to the falls. They called their parents who showed up and then called it in at 0114 hours," Jones reads from his notes. "The teens were released into the care of their parents, but I have a list of names of those who were present and contact info for their parents."

"What else?"

"Juvenile male, appears to be between the ages of four and eight years old, and approximately forty to forty-two inches tall. Will know more following positive identification."

"Characteristics appear to match description provided by the victim's mother and stepfather. They also appear to match the picture provided by the mother. Will know more pending positive fingerprint and dental identification," I respond tucking the photo back into my coat pocket.

I pull out a pair of latex gloves and snap them on my hands. All around me officers are combing the area looking for clues as to what happened to this little boy. I crouch down next to him. His clothes are water logged. I pull his pockets out, there's nothing in them.

I don't see any obvious signs of cause of death and trust me, I'm looking. I look up at the footbridge, it is possible that he fell, but what was he doing here. If this is Anthony, and I'm pretty damn sure that it is, how the hell did he get to the falls. This part of town is nowhere near where he lives—where either of his parents live.

I look back down at the little boy, "What happened to you, Anthony? Tell me your secrets," I say hoping to find some clue as to what happened. Anything really.

Out of my peripheral, I notice movement, but there's always a lot of movement at an active crime scene so I quickly dismiss it. It's not until a pair of wingtips step into my view that I groan. Damn it.

"Get out of my crime scene, suit," I snap barely offering him a glance. Damn he looks good. Fucking the slutty cocktail waitress clearly agrees with him.

"If I was a lesser man, I'd have my feelings hurt that you didn't invite me to the party," he chuckles. I'm not laughing. He cuts his humor short when he sees the look on my face.

"I didn't want to bother you and the big boobed waitress."

"Tut tut tut, jealousy doesn't become you." He smiles.

"I am not jealous, I'm working," I growl.

"This site is out of your jurisdiction," he says softly. "It's time to hand it over, Claire."

"The hell it is," I snap, standing up and ripping off my gloves.

I stomp all the way over to Wes and shove him hard. He backs up a step and then I shove him again. I'm angry—not just angry—livid. Red colors everything I see. How dare he come here in the eleventh hour and try to steal my case. Again.

"This case started in my jurisdiction so it is mine," I growl as I push him again.

"Stop," he commands as he grabs my wrists in his, turning me as he pulls me into the warmth of his body. "This is crazy."

"No, what's crazy is you telling me time and time again that I should trust you and here you are, again, trying to steal my case. *My case, Wes.*"

"You know you shouldn't be on this case, Claire," he whispers into my ear as he holds me tight to him, my back to his front. To anyone else, it would look like he's comforting me, but we both know there's no comfort here, only restraint and deceit.

"Let me go," I plead.

"Your emotions are too close to the surface, Claire. You're heading for a crash and we can all see it."

"I don't see it. I only see you taking one more thing from me, Wes. Tell me, when will you have had enough?"

He rears back as if I have slapped him. And then the shutters slam down behind his eyes. Gone is the boy who went off to the Navy that I once knew and loved. Here is the SAIC hell bent on ruining my career and my life.

"Okay," he sighs running his hand over his face. For a split second he looks tired. "I thought you'd be reasonable . . ."

"Ha!" I interrupt.

"But if you can't then I will arrest you for interfering in my investigation."

"You wouldn't dare," I growl.

"Try me," he snaps standing nose to nose with me.

We're both breathing hard. Huffing and puffing like the big bad wolves we are. Either one of us could come out on top but I won't give Wes the satisfaction of arresting me in front of my officers. With one false move I could not only lose my case to this asshole, but hand him the ammunition he and Liam need to end my career once and for all.

I see the ME loading up the body into their van. Emma winks at me. We women have to stick together in this sausage fest of a profession. I have always wondered if she and Liam had a thing but that's neither here nor there right now.

Emma is silently telling me she'll hold the evidence for me to see first. That will go a long way toward my keeping the case where it belongs—with me. I take a deep breath and a big step back. I roll my shoulders back and throw down the gauntlet.

"Well, I guess we'll just see about that." I smile sweetly.

"I guess we will," he smiles back.

"No one touch a damned thing until you hear from me, do you understand me? Not one damned thing!" I shout before I head to my SUV and jump in.

The drive back to the station is not a fun one. I spend the entire time working up a plan to protect myself and keep my hold on the case, and my job. Both are not looking so good. Worst of all, I know that Wes is somewhere behind me actively tearing apart my life.

I pull into the parking lot and head inside. I take a deep breath, I'm not going to go off halfcocked and act like an asshole. I will not give Liam any ammunition. I will not lose my job. I say those things over and over again in my head like a mantra as I walk down the hallway and knock on Liam's door.

"Enter," he hollers.

I push his office door open and cautiously walk inside. "Can I talk to you for a minute?"

He sighs, "What is it now, Claire?"

"I need you to call off your dogs, Captain," I say as I take a seat in the chair facing his desk.

"I don't have time for your stupid fight with Wes, Claire," he grumbles. "Maybe you guys should just fuck it out and be done with it."

"That's not what I'm talking about. Your special friend threatened to arrest me at a crime scene this morning."

"I can't imagine what you did to warrant the FBI's interest," he says blandly.

"What makes you think it was something I did?" I can't believe he would side with Wes over me. Actually I can. Bastards. "I didn't do anything wrong. I was working my crime scene and Wes showed up late and tried to pull rank."

"He does out rank you," Liam adds.

"That has nothing to do with it!"

"It could. What case was he trying to take over?"

I sit silently with my hands folded in my lap while I wait for Liam to catch up. I see his eyes widen slightly with a sparkle to them that I do not like one bit as the lightbulb goes off over his head.

"You don't say?" he mumbles.

"Don't even think it, Liam," I bark.

"You know that I'm right," Wes says quietly from behind me. I close my eyes. I feel the weight of defeat on my shoulders, but I'm stubborn enough not to give up until I'm dead. You know what they say about pride and the fall . . .

"It's still my case. I'm getting closer."

"You're no closer than you were two days ago. The only difference is now the boy is dead," Wes says. I feel the guilt already. It's thick and suffocating.

"He's dead?" Liam asks.

I just nod.

"Turn it over to me," Wes pleads.

"No," I whisper.

"You're too close to it, you know that."

"No."

"When were you going to tell me that the Donovan boy is dead?" Liam thunders.

"When we had a positive ID," I answer. "He's with Emma now."

"It's time to pull in the FBI, Claire, officially," Liam says calmly.

"Over my dead body!"

"It might be if you don't give on something," he shouts back. "Look at you. Are you eating? Sleeping? Because you don't look like it."

"Gee thanks, asshole."

"The dreams are back, aren't they?" Wes asks, outing me at the same time.

"What dreams?" Liam asks.

I just stay silent.

"Claire . . ." Wes calls softly. Quietly ordering me to lay all my secrets out into the light.

"No."

"No, they're not back or no?" he betrays.

"What dreams?" Liam thunders.

"She has nightmares about her abduction," he says softly to Liam. "She always has."

"I didn't know," Liam pains. "Why didn't you tell me?"

"It wasn't my story to tell."

"Bullshit!" My brother roars. "Claire?"

I don't answer, I just sit there staring at the wall just over my brother's shoulder, unable to look at him or Wes as my world unravels. My vision swims and I feel the hot tear as it burns down my cheek.

"Claire! Answer me!"

"No!" I scream as the thin thread of my control snaps. "You don't get to know all the little bits of my life so that you can use them against me."

"Is that what you think?" He looks stricken.

"Can you honestly tell me that you're not thinking about how you can use the information to pull me from the case?"

"What about a task force?" Liam changes tack.

"No," Wes and I both stay at the same time.

"She's off the case and the FBI is taking over," he demands.

"I'll work it alone if I have to."

"I'll ban you from the case if I have to," Wes threatens.

"Over my dead body," I snap.

"I'd prefer to be over your naked body."

"How can you say that?" I snap. "Like I would take the flotation device's sloppy seconds."

"Jealous much?"

"Not at all," I say sweetly. "One of these days that nasty dick is going to rot right off."

Wes just smiles. The fucker knows that he's gotten to me. I'm too tired, too emotional to not be jealous of the idiot that spent the night in his bed with him. How sick is that? And he ruined my favorite bar. I can never go back there after seeing that.

"You're too close to the case, Wes is right," Liam interjects.

"And Wes isn't?"

"It's not the same and you know it," he barks.

"How is it not? We were all there."

"You were taken for six days, baby," Wes says softly from behind me. "You're right, I live with that. It burns to know that I played a part in it, but I wasn't the one who had to escape hell," he says as he brushes hair back from my face.

"I did escape hell, so let me use that to do my job."

"It's going to take you down if you don't start taking care of yourself, Claire, and you know it." He's right. The job takes down too many who can't leave their cases at the station. Whether it's stress and bad diet or the bottle and a bullet, we don't have longevity on our sides.

"I won't give up my jurisdiction for a dick."

"But it used to be your favorite dick," Wes circles back to his favorite topic.

"It was never my favorite dick, it's short and crooked," I lie.

Wes just laughs. "Liar," he winks.

"Well, what I do in the back of vans these days has nothing to do with you or your dick," I shout. There goes my temper again.

"That's not fucking funny, Claire." Liam jumps to his feet.

I shrug. "And you two threatening my job at every corner is?"

"That's not what we're doing."

"Isn't it though? If you loved me, you'd let me do my job," I implore.

"Liam don't cave to her," Wes barks.

"You don't get to control me either, Wes."

"The hell I don't. I'll take you over my knee if I have to once and for all," he barks.

"You don't have it in you. You don't have the balls."

Wes pulls his handcuffs from his back pocket and swings them around his index finger, smiling away like a loon all the while. Liam just laughs.

"I gotta go," I shout as I race out the door.

I barely make it out the door when Wes nabs me around the waist and pins me against the wall in the hallway. He brushes the loose strands of my hair out of my face with the tips of his fingers.

"So beautiful," he says absent mindedly. "That's all I could think of the morning after we slept together. That you were so beautiful and your life was almost over before you got a chance to live it."

"Wes . . ."

"I made love to you and then you screamed in your sleep about that man touching you. Years after he took you, he was still taking from you, from me, from us. *I couldn't stand it.*"

"Wes . . . stop." I shake my head, I can't hear anymore.

"So, I pushed you away," he whispers, his lips hovering just over mine. "I can't stay away."

"So . . . don't," I whisper just before his mouth crashes down on mine.

Wes kisses me like his life depends on it. His hands crushing my body into him. I open my mouth under him and he plunders. Gone is the gentle young man who made love to me twelve years ago and in his place is a man tired of waiting.

I dig my fingers into his shoulders and kiss him back with all that I am. I rake my nails down his back hard enough to leave marks through his clothes. He groans into my mouth. And pulls back.

Wes tips his forehead to mine. We're both breathing heavy. I squeeze my eyes tight. Again, he brushes my hair back from my face before trailing his hand down the side of my face and running the pad of his thumb over my swollen bottom lip.

"Claire," he calls softly. "Don't make me lose you again."

"That would imply that you already have me," I whisper back.

"Don't I though?"

"No, I'm not anyone's to have," I say softly. "That girl died a long time ago when she had her heart broken by the only boy she ever loved."

I can't let the hurt look on Wes's face stop me. History shows he won't stick around. I need to make sure my job is protected for when he leaves. And really, everything I said to him is true. We all have to live with the mistakes we make. He's paying for his now.

"Claire, don't do this," he pleads.

"I have a murder to solve," I say as I duck under his arms and walk away.

I hear a fist hit the wall and his deep voice cry out my name, but I just keep walking. I'm already gone and like I said, I have a murder to solve.

chapter 12

nightmare

I WALK INTO THE station earlier than usual the next morning. Last night I left the station and Liam and Wes behind, or so I thought. I went home and when I walked through my front door, the first things I did were lock up both my sidearm and my drop gun in the safe. Then hid the key from myself. The last thing I need is to do something I couldn't take back—in the permanent sense—when the demons creep in. Just like I knew they would.

I kicked off my boots and dragged myself into the kitchen where I climbed on top of a kitchen chair to acquire my emergency bottle of whiskey. And it was an emergency. I poured myself two fingers and shot it back, cringing at the delicious heat that burns its way down my throat and through my chest.

I added ice to my glass and poured myself two more fingers. And then I ordered more fried rice from my favorite place around the corner. Bobby is the kid who delivers for them and he knows the drill on nights like this: bring the food, take the money, and leave ask no questions. He follows directions to a tee.

After Bobby leaves, I placed my bounty of little foldy take out containers on the old battered coffee table. My mom is dying to pick out new furniture for this place, but honestly, why bother, I'm barely ever here. I strip out of my jeans leaving me in my t-shirt and panties. I still don't know where my bra is and I don't care.

I carry the bottle with me back to the living room where I turned on the tv. That was a mistake. Not my first mistake of the evening and definitely *not* my last. I sit down on the couch and watch the news.

"And the top story tonight, what is believed to be the body of a missing local child was found at the falls late last night by a group of high school students celebrating last night's win against Ben Franklin High School . . .

"This is believed to be the body of six-year-old Anthony Donovan who disappeared from his George Washington Township home three days ago. It is our understanding that no ransom was ever recovered."

"That's correct, June. And here comes the late statement from the local police precinct and the FBI . . ."

"Good evening everyone, my name is Captain Liam Goodnite with the George Washington Township Police Department, I'm here with Special Agent

in Charge Wesley O'Connell of the FBI and we will be answering your questions to the best of our abilities without compromising an ongoing investigation."

I set down my Chinese and pick up the bottle of whiskey. Maybe I shouldn't have hid the key to my gun after all . . .

"Is it true that the body of Anthony Donovan was found late last night?"

"We cannot confirm or deny that the body found belongs to Anthony Donovan as it is currently pending identification," Liam says clearly.

"When will you know for sure?"

"We hope to have a clear identification or rule out that it is Anthony via fingerprints and dental records as early as tomorrow afternoon."

"Is it true that your sister, Claire Goodnite, is the lead detective on the case, Captain?"

"I will not confirm the activity of any of my detectives or officers, not now or ever, as it compromises the safety of the officer and the integrity of the investigation," Liam says. His eyes narrowing just slightly in his frustration.

Someone leaked the discovery of Anthony's body to the local news. I'd be more pissed, but he was found by a bunch of scared teens who were already up to some mischief last night. I'm sure someone sold the story for some quick cash. I can only hope is that it pays for college and not crack.

"Is it true that she is the same Claire Goodnite that famously escaped captivity by a deranged child molester and murderer?"

"We are not here to comment on ancient history, only the facts as they pertain to the discovery of a body at 12:42 this morning," Wes comments.

"So, it is the same Claire Goodnite! Would she be willing to do a follow up interview on her case? I would love to do a 'Where is she now?' story and tie it in with her investigation of the missing boy," a reporter in the crowd chirps enthusiastically.

"Ma'am, this is an open FBI investigation, there will be no interviews of any sort until the case is closed. Thank you for your time," he smiles a feral baring of his teeth before walking back into the station with Liam on his heels.

As much as I hate him right now, he's still handsome. I still want him even though I know that I shouldn't. Those assholes took my case away from me and publicly threw me to the wolves. It's all out there now. My past, my involvement with the case, all of it. And then they took it all away.

"We can confirm that Detective Claire Goodnite of the George Washington Township Police Department is in fact the daughter of retired Police Captain Callum Goodnite and sister to current Captain Liam Goodnite.

"As you remember, Claire was kidnapped on June 8, 1997. She was six years old at the time. Her family, with the help of the police and the FBI searched for six

days before she was found dirty and malnourished in the woods mere miles from her family home.

"It is believed she was held by an unidentified man in a shack in the woods for the duration of that time. While the family and law enforcement have remained tight lipped for decades, it is believed that she suffered sexual and physical abuse at the hands of an unknown assailant who was never identified or subsequently tried for her kidnapping . . ."

I close my eyes tight. I can't hear any more so I switch off the tv. My dinner sits cold and untouched on the coffee table. I don't have the stomach for it now. Even my whiskey earned a certain ambivalence from me. Part of me wants to drink it all and let the darkness come for me, and the other half knows that I shouldn't.

There's a knock on the door while I sit debating whether or not to finish off my drink. I pick it up and knock it back with a shaky hand when I hear his voice call through the door, "Claire, let me in. Please . . ."

On unsteady legs, I stand and make my way to the door, the locks tumble and I pull open the door. Wes stands there with weary eyes and stubble overgrown on his cheeks. He looks hesitant . . . and then he reaches for me.

The culmination of the last few days, this case, the kidnapping, the ghosts of the past, it all comes rushing out as I pull Wes in the door and slam it closed. He's on me before I can say boo. His mouth greedily claiming mine and I lay my own claim to him right back.

Twelve years ago, Wes took everything I had to give and then walked away leaving me broken hearted. Now, I'm a big girl and I know exactly what I'm getting. And I'm going to give it just as good right back. For twelve years, every man after Wes left me aching and wanting, not completely fulfilled so I'm taking this one night for myself. Tomorrow, I'll go back to my life the way that it was . . . or at least I'll do my best picking up the pieces.

I rip at his shirt, the buttons popping everywhere as I nip and kiss and bite at his mouth. There's an aggression here that wasn't there twelve years ago. Wes slips his hand down the front of my panties and into my core. I let out a hiss as his fingers stretch me, the burn both beautiful and tortuous.

I tip my head back against the door and hold on to the open sides of his shirt as I ride his hand, taking everything he offers me and more. It feels so good and I'm so close. Just a little bit more, I'm almost there.

"Give it to me, Claire, it's mine and you know it," Wes growls in my ear as he adds his thumb to my clit. Swirling around and around. The delicious pressure is exactly what I need and I come on his hand with a keening cry I don't recognize as my own as I rock harder and faster against him. "Yes, take it!" he shouts as I cling to him as my heart races and my climax barrels through me.

I hear his belt buckle hit the floor and the rasp of his zipper and that is the only tell that Wes is about to give me his cock. My heart still blasting from my orgasm as his rips my panties down the center.

Wes grips my thigh in his strong hand and pushes it up against my side. The stretch and burn of my over-taxed muscles is welcome. And then he enters me in one full thrust.

Wes buries his face in my neck and groans as he begins to move. Harder and faster than I think either me or my front door can take. It rattles on the hinges as he pumps into me. His cock thick and hard.

I'm going to come again. It's upon me before I can even brace for it. I'm not sure I'll survive an orgasm of this magnitude. By the way the muscles and tendons are corded on Wes's neck I think he feels the same way.

His thrusts grow wild and erratic as we both race towards the edge. Harder and harder, faster and faster he powers his hips into mine. I bite my lip until it bleeds in my mouth. When he sees the red drops, he sucks my lip into his own and groans at the coppery tang we both taste.

I tip my head back and he buries his face in my neck again. I scream and Wes calls out my name as we both barrel over the edge at lightning speed. And then I can't breathe.

I open my eyes and it's not Wes I see, but the monster who took me when I was six years old. He has his hands wrapped around my neck and his knuckles turn white as he tightens them around my neck, cutting off my air.

I close my eyes again and when I reopen them, I

realize I'm standing at my front door. I'm paralyzed by what lies on the other side. There's a pounding that shakes the door on its hinges.

"Claire!" Wes screams from the other side of the door.

This was all a daydream. There was no moment of passion. There is no scent of sweat and sex lingering in the air. This was all a daydream.

"Claire! Let me in, God damn it," he pains. "I'll knock it down if I have to."

"Just go, Wes," I say as I place my palm flat on the door. I know he knows that I'm here. "I'm fine."

"You're not fine, baby. I heard you scream."

"I'm fine, Wes, just go home."

"No, I won't leave you like this. Don't make me leave you like this."

"Why not? You have before," I say. I know it's a low blow, but it has to be said. I need him to leave me alone with my demons.

"I was a boy then, I wasn't ready." He slaps the door again. "I won't leave. You won't let me in, that's fine, but I won't leave either."

I hear him lower his body to the floor and lean back against my door. It appears that Wes is settling in for the night.

I was wrong, it wasn't a day dream, this is a nightmare, a living nightmare.

I, too, lower myself to the floor and fall into a fitful

sleep in the entryway to my apartment. I know that I cry out for him in my sleep throughout the night. He cries back, begging me to let him in, to let him protect me, to hold me, but I can't. I can't let myself want something that I know will be ripped away from me in the near future when the next shiny toy with big boobs and spread legs comes along.

So here I am, dragging my ass into the station in the early hours of the morning. Wes must have gone home when he heard me turn on my shower. And that's about all I was able to muster enough energy for this morning, shower, coffee, jeans and a sweater.

He's waiting for me at our shared desks when I walk in. A cup of coffee in his hand and another one from the shop I love waiting for me on my desk. He's beautiful even with bloodshot eyes with dark circles under them and more stubble on his cheeks than one of those guys that lives in the wild on those tv shows. A little wild, a lot sexy, and if he keeps this up, I'll fall again, I know it. Fuck, maybe I already am.

"Thank you," I say to the spot just over his shoulder.

Wes just nods.

In my head, nothing has changed. I figure if they're gunning for my job, I might as well hand it to them on a silver platter with my own head. So, I sit down at my desk and unlock my file drawer and sign into my geriatric computer.

I flip through my notes again and again. At this

point, I'm starting to bug myself, but there's that little niggling in the back of my mind. I'm missing something, I know it.

"I know that look," Wes says rounding the desk to stand behind me. "What do you see?"

"Nothing," I snap. "I see nothing. But, I know that something's there. I just can't figure out what. You know?"

He nods, "Something's off."

"Yes! That's it exactly. And I'm going to find out what it is," I say as I stand up and lock my desk and grab my coffee and keys.

"Then let's go."

"Oh no," I growl. "I'm not going anywhere with you, Benedict Arnold."

"You either go with me or I tail you. Don't you think the great state of New Jersey and the US government would like to save on fuel costs and emissions?"

"Oh my God, I hate you. Get in the fucking truck. But. Not. One. Word."

Wes mimes zipping his lips and then follows me out into the cold with a ridiculously smug smile on his stupid, beautiful face. We climb in and head off to figure out what the fuck is going on here. I can't bring back Anthony, but I can get some fucking answers. And that's exactly what I plan to do.

chapter 13

a choice

I PULL OVER TWO houses down from the Ascher's house. For some reason, I feel like I'll find answers here. The ride here was silent, both of us lost in our own thoughts. Wes and I both step down from the car and our faces go blank. It's game time.

We step up to the porch and I ring the bell. *Nothing.* I lean back and look at the driveway. Mrs. Ascher's car is there. Mr. Ascher's vehicle is not present, but it's nine in the morning on a work day. I would assume he's at the office. Well, I assume he'd be with his wife since she was notified this morning that the body found is her six-year-old son, but what do I know?

"Oh, hello Agent O'Connell, Detective," Mrs. Ascher answers the door coolly. "What brings you here today?"

"We have a few more questions for you and Kasey, is she around?" I ask.

"I heard you're not on my son's case anymore, Detective, so I guess it doesn't matter if she home or isn't."

Well this is a new Elizabeth Ascher. *Interesting*.

"Detective Goodnite is still on the case," Wes lies smoothly. He's trying to earn points with me and I hate to say it but it's working. It's never glamorous to find out you have a price.

"Hmm," she says noncommittally as she holds open the door for us.

"Thank you," I say kindly. "We won't take up much of your time."

"Kasey," she screams. "The police are here to talk to you!"

Well, there goes the "we're just checking in" vibe I was hoping for. I chance a glance at Wes and see he finds the shift in the family dynamic here interesting as well. His dark brows are drawn over his eyes.

Kasey ambles down the stairs like the sullen teen that she is. She's not happy that we're here. I wonder why. Or she's not happy with her mother, which is probably more likely. Teenage girls aren't supposed to like their mothers.

I always loved mine, but I avoided her when she looked like she saw too much during my teenage crush days over Wes. In hindsight, I wish she would have told me what an asshole he'd turn out to be and save me some heartache. But she wouldn't have said that any ways. Mom always did have a gigantic soft spot for the big jerk.

"What do you want, mom?"

"The police are here to ask you some questions," she says giving her daughter the stare down.

By the twinkle in her daughter's eyes, I would say a challenge has been issued and accepted. *Oh shit*. I see her turn her creepy Lolita charm on when she notices Wes and her mom ever so subtly twitches. So, the teen flirt vibe doesn't sit well with mom? Interesting.

"Oh, hello Agent," she purrs. "I didn't see you over there."

I roll my eyes. Wes visibly tenses. He knows that I won't bail him out this time. Good.

"Hello," he nervously clears his throat. "Detective Goodnite wants to ask you some questions."

Thanks for throwing me under the bus, buddy.

"I'd rather you ask them," she says petulantly.

"Well Detective Goodnite is asking them."

"Over coffee. Wouldn't that be nice?" She coos as she runs her fingertips up over his bicep.

"No, I don't think so."

"Or dinner. I'd love it if you asked me out to dinner," she breathes her underage siren call. What the actual fuck is this?

"No."

"For fuck's sake, Kasey, stop acting like a little slut," Mrs. Ascher snaps.

"Don't be jealous, Mother, it ages you."

Oh shit. Are they fighting? Over Wes?

"You're a child!" her mother screams. "A man wouldn't find that attractive."

"That's not what he said last night . . ."

"Excuse me?" I ask.

"I swear, it's not me," Wes pleads.

"I know that." I cut my eyes to him. "I know where you were last night."

"Thank God."

"We're getting nowhere here. Let's go," I tell him.

"Thank God."

We leave them fighting in the middle of the living room. I don't know what to make of that. Of any of it. None of the Aschers seem like they're grieving. At all. I guess everyone handles grief differently.

Kasey's Lolita act is creepy as fuck. I wonder if I was that obvious when I was sixteen. I already knew that I was in love with Wes back then. I wonder if that's how he saw me. Like a little kid that made him uncomfortable. It still doesn't explain why he slept with me that night. Maybe I'll never know.

I beep the locks on the truck but Wes pins me to the side before I have a chance to climb in. He runs his thumb down my cheek, stopping at my chin. He tips my head back so I'm forced to look him in the eye.

"What's bothering you?"

"Mostly I was hoping that I was never as desperately obvious as Kasey when I was sixteen," I blurt out, cringing as soon as the words are out into the universe. I wish that I could pull the words back into my mouth but I can't. His eyes immediately soften.

"You were beautiful even then," he says softly. "But with a wild innocence I kept desperately hoping would be gone every time Liam and I came home."

"Why?" I can't help but ask.

"Because I knew when you offered it to me, I wouldn't be able to walk away."

"And yet you did." I smile sadly.

"And it was the worst mistake of my life. But I knew that with my workup and deployment schedule, I would never be able to offer you the kind of support and help that you needed to recover. That was abundantly clear when you had your nightmare," he says sadly. "Will you ever forgive me?"

"Probably." I sigh, disgusted with myself and my easy capitulation. "I really don't want to, but when you say things like that you just make sense and I have nothing to say to it."

I really don't want to. But maybe, I don't have a choice where Wes is concerned. Maybe I never had a choice at all.

"What are you thinking?"

"Mostly that I can't think when you're around. I'm going to need you to give me some space," I say gently to soften the blow.

"Nope."

"What?" Maybe I misheard him.

"I said 'no' as in no space," he says calmly. "If I give you an inch, you'll bolt again."

"I'm not going to bolt," I put my hands on my hips and square off.

Wes just raises an eyebrow.

"Okay, I might," I rally. "But you don't know that for sure!"

"Babe," he sighs.

"I just need you to give me the space that I need to do my job, Wes."

"No."

"Wes!" I snap.

"Baby, I can't," he visibly shudders. "I can't let anything else happen to you," he says, his voice gruff with emotion.

"You can't protect me for forever, Wes," I say softly.

"I have to try."

"At what expense, Wes?" My frustration leaking into my voice. "We'll never work like this and you know it . . . Plus, we'll both get fired and then we won't have money to eat or pay rent and I can't move back in with my mom and dad."

That makes him crack a smile.

"Well, it wouldn't win me any points with your mom if she found me in your bed," he smirks.

"Are we talking about the same woman?" I joke.

"She'd have china patterns and baby names picked out by dinner time," he laughs.

"It's my dad and Liam you have to worry about."

"I wouldn't be so sure about that," he says cryptically. Whatever that means.

"So, are we going to be okay?"

"Yeah, baby. We'll be okay."

"And you'll let me do my job?" I need to be sure or Wes might as well take his toys and go home. But I can't help but feel like things are changing.

Wes growls. "I won't stand in the way of your career, babe. I'm more man than that," he rumbles. "But I won't stand back and watch you get killed either," he barks just before he crashes his mouth to mine.

His kiss is like a tsunami, all-consuming as it rolls in. He's fierce and dominating as he plunders my mouth. Our teeth clash as we both kiss and bite, lick and soothe the wounds we keep inflicting on each other. It won't be long before I let his storms consume me, I only hope this time I'm a strong enough swimmer to survive.

"I can't go back," I whisper against his mouth.

"I'm not that boy anymore," he says one more time.

"Oh no, now you're all man." I swallow as I feel his erection press against my belly, his hold on me still firm.

"I'm glad that you noticed," he smirks before regaining his composure. "I swear to you that I'm the man you need me to be. I won't run or let you scare me off."

I'm about to tell Wes that I might be ready for him to prove it, prove to me that what he says is true, but our heart to heart is cut off by a blood curdling scream emanating from the Ascher's house. We both take off running.

chapter 14

fucking run

"**Y**OU STUPID BITCH!"

Mrs. Ascher can be heard from the street. The neighbors are all coming out of their houses. Screams and fights in the late morning hours are not part of the everyday norm for this sleepy suburban town. Missing children aren't either for that matter.

"You better hurry," the next-door neighbor hollers from her front porch. "Something isn't right over there. I just can't put my finger on it."

You and me both, I think but don't say out loud.

Wes and I race down the street and back up the walk of the Ascher's house. My hand moves to the handle of my sidearm as the screams get louder and louder. I hear glass break.

"I hate you!" Kasey screams, then grunts as if something hits her.

"Police! Open up!" I shout as Wes pounds on the door.

We both stand off to the sides of the door just in case. He pounds his fist again. Nothing. You can still hear the furniture toppling over and the screams as Mrs. Ascher and her daughter beat the shit out of each other.

I look at Wes and nod. It's time to kick the door in. I take a step back to make room for him. His hand still on his service weapon in its holster. He leans back, puts his pretty shiny shoe to the door and kicks it in off the hinges. Both women scream as we move through the door.

"FBI!"

"Police!"

"Hands where I can see them," Wes says his voice ringing with authority.

The women jump and walk away with their noses turned up. They sit on opposite couches as if nothing had happened. What the fuck is going on here? I eye Wes and he raises his eyebrows. My guess is as good as his.

"What brings you back, detective?" Mrs. Ascher asks casually. Big words seeing as how the lower floor of this house is in shambles.

"Funny you mention it," I start. "We were about to go interview some more of your neighbors, but heard a commotion in this house and came right back."

"I have no idea what you're talking about," she says indignantly.

"Really?" I roll my eyes.

"We don't have time for this shit!" Wes booms from behind me. For a minute, I had forgotten that he was there.

"She started it!" Kasey snaps petulantly.

"Kasey!"

Wes shoots Mrs. Ascher a withering look. I feel bad for her.

"What did your mother start, Kasey?" he asks gently.

"She's jealous, that's all."

"That's enough, Kasey!"

Kasey shoots a mean glare at her mother. Her eyes are cold. The neighbor was right, there's definitely something wrong going on here. And I think it's about to blow up in our faces.

"What is she jealous of, Kasey?" Wes asks, giving her his full attention.

"Me, of course," she preens. Mrs. Ascher pales.

"How is she jealous of you?" I ask.

"Isn't it obvious?" She snarks. "I'm young, beautiful, and know how to keep a man happy. She's old and doesn't." She shrugs her narrow shoulders.

"You're both young and beautiful," I say to her and she relaxes a bit. "What makes you think your mom can't keep a man happy?"

"Well daddy left, duh." She rolls her eyes.

"And you know how to keep a man happy," I say repeating back the words that she chose to use. They taste funny, foul even in my mouth and I don't want them there anymore. Wes stays quiet but watches.

"I do . . . I do all the things men like that older women can't or won't," she says looking straight at Wes.

He scowls, his dark eyebrows drawn. It doesn't take a rocket scientist to tell that she's implying her sexual prowess over mine. I have a sinking suspicion that they weren't fighting over a teenage boy.

"Shut up, Kasey!" Mrs. Ascher screams.

"You're just jealous that Jonathan comes to me every night and not you!" She volleys back at her mother.

Oh fuck.

I had a feeling this is where their fight was headed. Now that it has flopped in my lap, I can't help but wonder what the fuck. I'm glad I don't live in the suburbs.

"You bitch!" Her mother screams before launching at Kasey again. "You slept with my husband!"

I notice Mrs. Ascher isn't furious that her husband has been molesting her sixteen-year-old daughter, but is instead more concerned that her daughter seduced her husband. I kind of want to throw up.

"I did. And I'll do it again," she screeches. "Did you know that his throat makes this little catching sound in the back right before he . . ."

"Don't you finish that statement!"

"And that he loves this thing that I do with my mouth . . ."

Mrs. Ascher unleashes a battle cry worthy of an ancient warrior but I grab her from behind before she can renew her assault on her daughter.

"Enough!" Wes shouts.

"Kasey," I whisper, but she just takes a haughty tone with me.

"I could take him from you too," she snaps. "They all want me. All the while, their wives and girlfriends don't know that he's giving it to me every Tuesday, Thursday, Friday . . . On my back, on my knees, any way they like it."

"Yeah, no, Kasey, a real man doesn't have sexual relations with girls," Wes snaps.

Just then the door opens and Mr. Ascher walks in. He takes one look at his living room, his wife being restrained by the police, and the disgusting smile on his teenage stepdaughter, and the smile on his own face slides right off.

"Mr. Ascher, you're under arrest on allegations of child molestation, statutory rape, and . . ." Wes starts but doesn't get to finish because Jonathan Ascher turns on his heels and runs. "God damn it, why do they always run?" Wes shouts as he bolts after our suspect.

I pull my phone out of my pocket and call in for dispatch, "This is Detective Goodnite, SAIC O'Connell and I responded to a domestic at 1312 Orange Drive, I have two I need brought in for questioning. SAIC O'Connell is pursuing a suspect northbound on foot. Requesting backup."

"Request for backup acknowledged, officers are in route."

"Thank you." I hang up.

It's not long before we can hear the sirens and Mrs. Ascher groans. Yep, this will be a fun filled little reunion down at the station.

Jones and his partner walk in through the broken front door. The blue and red lights of their cars flash through the opening. The sirens are silenced. They take Mrs. Ascher and Kasey out through the open entry way and into the waiting police cars.

I follow them out onto the lawn and see Wes half a block down hot on the heels of Mr. Ascher, whose fatal mistake was pausing to look over his shoulder. It gave Wes the opportunity to jump and take his runaway to the ground.

"When I say, 'stop running,' stop fucking running!" Wes shouts as he handcuffs Jonathan Ascher.

He looks up and sees me. I bite my lip to stop the laughter inside but I'm losing the battle.

"They always fucking run," he shouts.

I lose it. I bend over, clutching my knees as I laugh. Wes tries his best to wipe the grass off of his fancy ass suit and I laugh even harder.

"I didn't see you running," he pouts.

"Why should I when you were doing just fine." Another laugh bubbles up from my chest.

Wes just groans as Jones reads Mr. Ascher his *Miranda Rights* and then loads him into the back of the second police car. Wes and I stand there and watch as they pull away from the curb and head towards the station.

chapter 15

doomed

"**W**ELL, THAT WAS FUN," I sigh, wiping a stray tear from my eye.

Wes just grunts.

He holds out his hands for my car keys. I know what he's asking—demanding really—but I refuse to cave that easily. That's not me and we both know it. I raise an eyebrow.

"Give me this one thing, Claire," he growls.

"What would that be, Wes?"

"Claire."

"Oh fine, you big bully. You can drive." I cave.

I pull the keys from the front pocket of my jeans and hold them up in front of us. Before I can blink, Wes snatches them from my fingers and turns on his heels, marching back down the street towards my department SUV. I can't help it, I let out a little snicker.

"I heard that!" He shouts over his shoulder.

I follow Wes down the drive and climb into the passenger side of my truck. The ride back to the station is quiet. Not just quiet but silent. A lesser woman would be bothered by it, but I'm not a lesser woman.

We both quietly climb from my car and head up the walkway towards the front door of the station. Wes gets there and pulls the door open for me and that is exactly where the silence dies.

A brutal keening can be heard throughout the building right before Mr. Donovan, who I had forgotten was supposed to come into the station this evening for an update on his son's case, rushes Mr. Ascher taking him to the ground where he proceeds to beat the shit out of him.

"You hurt my baby," he screams. As he hits him again and again. Mr. Ascher's face is swelling and covered in blood. "You raped my daughter!"

There are a lot of brothers and fathers that work out of this station. Lots of women are loved by the men who work in this building. I can see them all sit there and watch Mr. Donovan get just enough licks in before they separate them. It may not be the right thing to do, but it's also not wrong.

Mrs. Ascher comes running around the corner, "You beat up my husband, you animal. I'll kill you for this!"

"I slipped once, Elizabeth. Once," he growls, shaking out his hands. "You have been punishing me for one stupid mistake for two years now. You split up our family. You kept the kids from me, and all for what? Our son is dead and your husband has been raping our daughter. Are you happy now?"

"You don't know what you're talking about," she looks away.

"Oh, I think I know plenty, Elizabeth. You'll be hearing from my attorneys. It'll be a cold day in hell before you see your daughter again."

"Do you think I want to?" She screeches. "She tried to steal my husband!"

"Do you even hear how disgusting you sound?" He shakes his head. "I can't even stand to look at you right now."

I chance a glance at Kasey. She's standing in the corner, away from everyone else. She looks like a lost little girl as she watches her mom and dad duke it out. Her bottom lip quivers.

"Come on, Kasey, let's go," he says to his daughter.

She hesitates a moment and looks back at her mother.

"Go, why would I want you," Mrs. Ascher says, not even bothering to look her daughter in the eye.

Something passes through Kasey's gaze but it's gone in a blink of an eye. And then she follows her dad out of the station. She's got a long road ahead of her, my only hope is she gets the therapy I know she's going to need.

Jones leads Mrs. Ascher to an interview room. A few uniformed officers haul Mr. Ascher to booking. They're both going to get to sit for awhile. There's nothing else we can do here.

"What's next, Detective?" Wes whispers in my ear. His voice tickles the shell as he brushes a strand of hair back from my face.

"Now we let them implode all on their own and hope they tell us who killed Anthony."

"Sounds like a great time to get a bite to eat," I can hear the smile in his voice.

"I'm not hungry," I say just in time for my belly to growl.

"Want to try that again, maybe with the truth this time?" He smiles as he catches me in a white lie.

"I could eat," I shrug. Wes just laughs.

"Great, let's go to *Mama's*," he says as he leads me out to his own car. I love *Mama's*. It's the best Italian place in the area, maybe even the state. My belly growls again at the thought.

When we walk into the restaurant there are the same potted ferns hanging from the ceiling and the same white taper candles in the chianti bottles in the middle of the tables, that provide most of the light in the room, that there has been for the last fifty years, or so I'm told.

"Wesley!" Mama coos when we walk through the door.

Figures he's loved here. Everyone loves Wes. He and Liam were the darlings of the area. They took our football team to state, they got scholarships to college, joined the Navy, became war heroes, and came home to follow in their father's footsteps. Me, on the other hand, no one really knows what to do with me.

"Hello, Mama," he smiles that heart melting smile. *Bastard.*

"And who have you brought with you tonight?" She asks before getting a good look at me. "Oh, it's you," she deadpans. Wes just laughs.

"You remember Claire," he says politely.

"Yes," she clips. "You know, you don't have to scrape the bottom of the barrel, my granddaughter, Gianna, is still single."

"That's kind of you to think of me, but I'm spoken for these days," he semi-lies. At least he better freaking be talking about me or he's a dead man.

"Oh, who is the lucky lady?"

"Claire."

"Really?"

"Pretty sure."

"I'm right here, guys."

"Just think of Gianna," she pleads.

"I hear Liam is single these days," he slips in coolly.

"He always was my favorite," I snicker.

"Abby will see you to your table," she says no longer involved in the conversation.

We're lead to a quiet table in the back. Candles flicker from the table top. Music plays softly through the room. It's romantic as hell even if I did have to hear Mama try and steal Wes away for her crazy granddaughter.

Wes pulls my seat out for me. Such a gentleman. I thank him as he pushes the seat in for me. Who is this man and what has he done with the Wes that I know? Wes shoves my chair in a little harder. Whoops, that part might have been out loud and I smile sweetly at him.

He takes his seat next to me, not across from me and Abby hands us our menus. Nothing at *Mama's* has changed in fifty years so locals already know what they want. She scurries away and hurries back with water glasses and a basket of breadsticks.

"Are you ready to order?" Abby asks softly. I look at her, she's maybe all of eighteen and seems to have a little bit of a crush on good old Wes. Spoiler alert, me too, Abby. Me too.

"We are, we'd both like to start with the house salad, followed by the linguini in clams and a bottle of the pinot grigio please," he says politely.

"I'll have that out right away, Sir."

I would normally be mad that he ordered for me, but the big bastard ordered my all-time favorite meal and wine. I lean back in my chair and fold my arms over my chest. I raise one eyebrow. Well played, Wes, well played.

Wes just smiles at me, his eyes twinkling with mirth. Abby brings out our salads as the bartender follows with our bottle of wine—denoting Abby's young age—before uncorking it and pouring us each a glass of the cool, crisp wine.

"Thank you for joining me for dinner," Wes says with so much meaning that I set my fork aside and look up at him.

"Of course," I say honestly.

He's looking at me with so much emotion in his eyes that I want to look away. Wes is usually so cool and collected. Totally unflappable. It's unnerving to see him laid bare for me like this. It makes me . . . want things. Things that I swore were better left alone twelve years ago.

As our meal is served, Wes reaches for the salt and pepper, accidentally brushing the side of my breast. My skin heats at the contact. My face burns with the knowledge that he still affects me. Out of the corner of my eye, I see him smile, he knows it too, *fantastic.*

My main dish is a perfect mix of garlic, cheese, and pasta. I love it. I pop a bite in my mouth and moan as the flavors burst on my tongue. I chance a glance at Wes as he squirms a bit in his seat. It looks like I'm not the only one affected by our heat. Perfect.

I'm sipping my wine as Wes pats his mouth with his napkin and then drops it on the floor. He bends over to grab it but slides his finger up the outside of my thigh on his way back up. I choke on my wine, his bold hands surprising me. His husky laugh fills my ears and my nipples pucker against my t-shirt. Wes slaps me on the back a couple of times before I stop coughing.

I look to Wes and smile. I notice he has a tiny bit of sauce on the corner of his mouth. I lean in almost like I'm about to kiss him, but I stop inches away and use the pad of my thumb to wipe the missed sauce away.

I suck the tip of my thumb into my mouth and hold his gaze with mine as I lick all the sauce away. I scrape the last bit with the tip of my teeth and smile at poor, sweet, *doomed* Wes and the look on his face. Two can play this game. Wes wants to play with me, that's okay, I'll play right back.

"Check, please."

chapter 16

everything to him

I HAVE MY BODY wrapped around Wes as we walk up the steps to his house. My cheek is pressed to his chest sweetly as he unlocks the front door. I'm sliding my hand up and down the bulge in his pants, making the task of opening the door as difficult as possible.

But he succeeds. We go flying through the front door and as soon as it's closed with the lock clicked into place, Wes pins me to the door, my back to the wood, his mouth punishing mine. He licks and bites and soothes as he goes. His hands gripping the sides of my face.

His hardness presses into my belly and I do my best to rub against it. I need some kind of friction. My body heats to unnatural levels. Whether it was the wine and the candles or just Wes, I don't know and I don't care. I have never wanted anyone the way that I want Wes, then or now, the thought is unnerving, but I don't let it get to me.

I pull on the knot of his tie. I need him naked. *Now*. I push his suit coat off of his shoulders and let it drop to the floor. He toes off his shoes and I do the same with my boots as I press my lips to his. I open to him and let him lick in. I suck his tongue into my own mouth and he groans.

Wes unbuttons my jeans and the sounds of the zipper sliding down echo through the entryway of his home. He puts his palm flat against my belly, his fingertips pointing down, and then he slides it down into my panties and straight to the promised land.

I tip my head back and close my eyes as he slides a finger through my wetness. Back and forth, before swirling it around my clit.

"Is this for me?" He asks, his voice rough.

I nod.

"Tell me," he purrs as he slides a finger in deep before pulling it back out and swirling it again around my clit.

"Yes," I gasp. He slides two fingers back in and I try to wiggle, to gain . . . *something*. Anything. "It's for you, it's all for you," I get out before he crushes his mouth back down on mine.

Wes swallows my cries for more as he pumps his fingers in and out of my pussy, his thumb circling my clit. No one knows how to play my body like Wes, no one. Others have tried, most have failed, but Wes has always known how to make me come. I should hate him for it, but right now I can't.

I feel my skin flush again, heat rising and pooling all over, I'm close, so, so close. He knows it too as he increases pressure on my clit. I grind my hips down, riding his hand and he growls against my mouth. I clutch at his shirt, my fingernails digging in and then I'm spiraling down, down, down.

I close my eyes again and lean against the door as Wes pulls his hands free. He gently pushes my jeans and panties down my legs and I step out of them when he taps my ankles one at time. And then he's lifting me up into his arms. Wes carries me to his bedroom like I weigh nothing, but as though I'm everything to him.

He stands me in front of his bed while he pulls the covers back. Then he gently pulls my t-shirt over my head and drops it to the floor. With hooded eyes, he watches me as I unsnap my bra and slide the straps down my arms before tossing it down on top of my shirt.

"Get on the bed, Claire," he growls low and a shiver racks over my body as I crawl into his bed.

When I'm on my hands and knees moving towards the center of the bed, I look over my shoulder at Wes. His hands are frozen on the buttons of his dress shirt as he watches my naked body move across his bed.

I roll over and lay back in the middle of the pillows. Wes snaps out of it and pulls his shirt from his body. His eyes are locked on me as he unbuckles his belt and lets it fall to the floor with a clank.

I decide to see how far I can push Wes as he unbuttons his slacks. I run my hands up my sides and feel the weight my heavy breasts in my hands. I hear his breath catch in his throat as he stops to undo the zipper and push his pants to the floor.

He pushes his boxer briefs to the floor and has to squeeze the base of his cock in his hand when I pinch my nipples. But it's when I trail a hand down over my belly that he comes unglued as I part my knees and swirl a fingertip in my own wetness.

Wes dives for me on the bed. I scream a little in surprise and then laugh. But my laughter dies in my throat when he buries his face between my legs and devours me. Taking as much of me in his mouth as he can and rolling his tongue over my clit. My orgasm hits me like a freight train and I scream as I come.

In a single breath, Wes is over me and driving in deep. I clench around his cock as I continue to pulse and the movement seems to drive Wes wild. He pumps harder and harder, faster and faster, his movements are wild with little to no finesse, but I don't need it. I dig my nails into his back and arch my back as I continue to climax, or maybe I come again. I don't know and I don't care.

Wes drives his cock into me once, twice more before burying his face in my neck and groaning as he follows me over the edge. He rolls us to the side so that I'm no longer taking all of his weight, but I'm still wrapped in his arms, his body still joined with mine as we drift off to sleep.

I wake before the dream can fully grip me. I'm not sure how I did it, but the department shrink would probably call it a break through.

I look around and realize that I'm not in my bed, but Wes's. He's asleep beside me, his face looks younger when relaxed by sleep. I wonder what would life have been like if he had never witnessed my night terror and ran. But then I remember, I can't get used to this. I have hoped for this life before and it always leads to devastation. Not to mention, hope is a real bitch and this isn't my real life, so I quietly slip from his bed and dress in the hall gathering my clothes as I go.

When I'm done, I call a cab and wait outside. The older man eyes my disheveled appearance but wisely says nothing as he drives me back to my apartment across town.

When he pulls up, I quickly toss him the last of the cash in my pocket and race up the steps to my apartment. I head straight for my bathroom, strip off of my clothes, and crank up the heat in my little shower.

I step in and let the steam surround me. I tip my head under the spray and shampoo my hair, rinsing it until the water runs clear. Then I tip my head under the spray so it falls over the back of my neck and shoulders, bracing my hands against the smooth surface in front of me.

I gasp when steel bands wrap around my body and

a very long, very hard cock presses into the small of my back. He smells like sweat and frustration, like sex and my Wes.

"Don't. Run," he growls.

I open my mouth to respond but he quickly covers it with his hand. Feeling him shaking his head no over my shoulder so I hold still. His cock is behind me reminding me of what I missed by not staying in his bed, so I squirm and wiggle my ass back against it. He groans and drops his head to the spot where my neck meets my shoulder. And bites.

I widen my stance and tip my hips back. His cock slips between my legs and I rock back and forth sliding him through my wetness. My fingers turn white with the pressure as I grip the shower wall.

"You want me," he says as he nuzzles my neck while I ride his cock.

"Yes," I gasp.

Wes has my upper body pinned with an arm firmly wrapped around me, holding my back to his chest. He glides his other palm down my belly and straight to my center where he cups me before pushing my hips further back.

"I think I should teach you a lesson on why you should always stay with me," he whispers in my ear as he slowly feeds his cock into my body.

"Yes," I moan.

I'm so full. From this angle, he's so tight, I can feel

every inch as he slowly pushes in to the hilt and then pulls back out. Wes slides back in and we both groan. He's going so, so slow, it's torturing us both.

His fingers find my clit and he is not gentle. I'm so sensitive from fucking him last night. His touch borders on painful. But it's so good. I want it. In this moment, I want all of it.

Wes takes a step back and slides me back with him, but my hands remain on the shower wall. The movement bends me forward and deepens his reach inside me. He pushes me forward with a hand between my shoulder blades. He slowly pulls out and the thrust back in.

"Are you going to run from me again, Claire?" He growls as he painstakingly pulls back out and then pumps in again.

"No!" I shout, his torture almost unbearable.

"Promise," he growls as his fingers dig into my hips.

"I promise."

"Tell me you're mine," he slides back out.

"I swear it!" I scream as he thrust back in.

"You are mine, Claire," he chants as he pumps into my body.

He's so hard and stretching my body. The punishing rhythm he sets is about to be my undoing. I can't keep up. It burns. I burn. I'm burning up as Wes thrusts harder and faster. And then through all the hurt and the anger, we come, together.

I lose my grip on the shower wall and we both fall to the shower floor. Wes surrounds me with his body trying to take the brunt of my fall. As our breathing slows back down he holds me in his arms tenderly, reverently and I hope against hope that I'm not falling in love with Wes, but like I said, hope is a real bitch.

chapter 17

fix me

"WE'RE GOING TO HAVE to talk tonight," he says as he touches his mouth to mine and lets his cock slide from my body.

"I have no idea what you're talking about, Wes," I say as I stand and start to wash my body.

Wes stares at me for a moment. He blinks once, twice, before he begins to shower himself. We turn off the water and towel off side by side. Wes handed me a towel before grabbing one for himself. Sometimes he's so damn considerate, tender even, that I forget that I want my life just the way that it is and start playing the what if game. But that game has never lead to anywhere good before.

One look at Wes's face tells me he is not pushing the conversation issue right now, but that he's definitely going to push it later. *Yay me*. I am not going to be available for this conversation about who knows what.

"Claire," he says softly.

I'm lost watching him dress. I stand there for who knows how long, watching him pull one of his tailored fed suits from my closet. He does up the buttons on his white collared shirt and my skin flushes at the memory of my removing a similar shirt from his body last night.

One night. It was supposed to be one night with Wes to tide me over for the rest of my life, and now he has a suit hanging in my closet. What the hell is happening here.

"Claire," he calls again.

"Did you have a suit hanging in my closet?" I ask and instantly regret it.

His smile goes lazy, "Yeah, baby, I brought it with me this morning."

"Why?"

His smile turns predatory. "Because you seem determined to be here and I'm determined to be with you. So, I brought some things . . ." He trails off.

"By 'some things' what do you mean exactly?" I ask still standing in nothing but a bath towel and Wes is fully dressed for a full day as a federal agent. This revelation is annoying.

"Just that. I brought some things to keep here. Later, I'm taking some of your stuff to my place," he tells me coolly as I start to throw things around in my closet.

As I toss on a light green lace bra and panty set and I notice Wes's eyes grow dark. He takes a step towards me, but we don't have time for anymore shenanigans so I quickly skirt him, snagging jeans and a wine colored long sleeved t-shirt. His eyes twinkle with humor at my expense so I pointedly ignore him and his sexy twinkle while I pull on socks and my tall brown boots.

I feel the heat of his eyes track me as I walk through the apartment to brush my teeth and put on a little makeup. I tag my badge to my belt and holster my sidearm next to it before looking back at Wes. He leans against the door jamb, his long body stretched out and his feet wide as he watches me.

"You ready to go?" I snap.

"Yeah," he breathes as he straightens his body to full height. "I'm ready for anything you want to throw my way." That doesn't sound good.

"Oh, okay . . ."

"Today or any other day. You want to avoid me for twelve years, I'll wait for you. You want to run head first into a sketchy situation, I'm at your back. You want to run the first chance you get after I have my dick so deep in you that we both forget our own names, I'll chase you down. But if you think you're going to run and hide and avoid me when we have so much shit to talk about after the first time I get in there in over a decade? You. Are. Wrong. You can't shake me babe, so get used to it."

I don't know what to say to that other than *well, fuck,* so I just nod my head once and turn on my heels to walk away, but I don't get the chance because I'm tagged around the waist and hauled back up against Wes's hard body.

"One more thing, baby," he says and I can hear the laughter in his voice.

"What?" I snap.

"Kiss me," he rumbles next to my ear. I turn to look at him over my shoulder and freeze. His eyes are hooded and crinkle at the corners. Before I can get my wits about me, he drops his head close and kisses me in a way that scrambles my brain for the foreseeable future.

"Okay," I whisper when he leans back to look at me.

"Great!" He says cheerfully. "Glad we got that all cleared up. Let's get coffee on the way to work. I'll drive."

With that he walked out the door of my apartment, holding it open for me. What else was I supposed to do but follow? So I do.

"Goodnite. O'Connell, my office. Now," Liam shouts through his open office door the minute my boots are through the front doors of the station.

I hang my head and sigh, "How does he do that?" I ask my shoes.

Wes just laughs. Asshole.

We make our way back to through the station. Everyone is watching. There are virtually no secrets in a room full of detectives. We're paid observers, so I know that everyone in this room sees exactly what there is to be seen. Wes has a stupid grin on his face as he swaggers through the station behind me. I roll my eyes. I see others smile at their paperwork or bite their lips to quell their laughter and look away.

I could fucking kill Wes. Although fucking Wes seems to be the problem. I hope these assholes don't think I'm available now. I'm not dating anyone. *Ever*. Well . . . I might have accidentally started dating Wes. God damn it! He has me so jumbled in my head.

"You wanted to see us, boss," I ask as we walk through the door of Liam's office.

Liam's gaze seems to burn as he takes us both in. His lip twitches as he avoids a smile that he knows will piss me right the hell off. "I see you've worked out some of your differences."

My spine straightens and my eyes harden. Wes hooks me from behind for the second time that morning and hauls me back against his body.

"I would go easy on her, Lee." Wes laughs. "She'll be out for blood by lunch time."

"Is it that obvious?" I snap.

"Let's just say I have an overwhelming urge to punch Wes in the face and then pat him on the back and welcome him to the family."

I throw my hands up in the air. "You've got to be kidding me!"

"Nope," he says as he leans back in his stupid fucking chair and crossing his arms over his broad chest, smiling like the dumbass that he is before turning to Wes. "Like I said, welcome to the family, brother."

With his arm still binding me to him, Wes laughs. So, I do what any woman in my shoes would do. I deliver a slight open palmed slap to his nuts, effectively cutting off his laughter as it turns to choking.

Liam starts laughing so hard, he falls out of his rolly office chair. He's hysterically rolling around on the floor and cackling like a loon as he clutches his stomach. Since Wes dropped his hold on me when he bent over to check his junk, I round Liam's desk and see him still rolling around, so I do what any younger sister would do in my shoes, I land a soft, swift kick to his nads. His laughter turns into howling.

My work here is done, so I turn on my heels and walk towards the door. One of us might as well get some work done while the two of them are horsing around like little boys.

"God damn it, Claire!" Liam thunders from his position on the floor.

"Don't be a dick and you won't get kicked," I snicker.

"You are such a bitch," he growls.

"You can't call me that!" I yell, whirling around to face him head on. "You take that back or I'm telling mom."

"You're such a baby, Claire," he rolls his eyes and

groans.

"You know what, fuck you both. I don't need either of you guys in my life," I snap

"Thanks ever so much for your help, buddy," Wes quips from his spot on the floor.

But I don't care. I step out the door and slam it to. Fuck both of them. Fuck everyone in this room. I. don't. Care. I'm just going to do my job and go home. Actually, I can do my job from home. I go to my desk and unlock the flash drive with the video footage and head home.

I make it to the parking lot in time to remember that Wes drove this morning. I sigh and feel my shoulders sink in defeat. I could go back inside and wait for him to forgive me and get to work. Or I could wait for another officer or detective that I know to head out and see if they can drop me on the way. Or I could call an uber. *Or . . .*

Or I could tap into the skills of my misspent youth and hotwire a federal vehicle. Yes. Yes, I think I will.

I look over my shoulder and make sure no one is watching or milling about the parking lot not minding their own fucking business. Then I march over to his stupid nondescript town car. If there was ever a vehicle that said *Federal Agent*, it's this one.

I reach down the neck of my shirt. There's a little tear in the corner of this bra. I had forgotten about it when I put it on this morning, but it's been bugging me since we left for the station. I use my fingernail to widen the tear just enough to pull the underwire out. Those little mistresses of torture are such a pain in the tit. Not for the first time, I wish I had smaller boobs. One, they get in the way on the range, and two, underwires are a real bitch.

I insert the long strip of plastic in between the seal of the driver's side window and the pane of glass like a slim jim. Sometimes spending so much time with criminal types has its perks. The lock pops and I pull open the door.

I feel eyes on me and turn to search out the interloper as I slide into the driver's seat. Nothing. I see no one. I shake off the weird feeling that making the hair on my arms stand on end like a static charge.

I need to get this show on the road.

I pull off the plastic panel underneath the steering column and pull out the wiring harness connector. I reach into my right front pocket to pull out my swiss army knife. It's pink and sparkly. Mom bought it for me as a present when I graduated from the academy. Though I'm not sure this is how she intended it to be used.

I pull free the battery, starter, and ignition wires that are bundled together neatly. Thank you, Ford manufacturing plant, for making this so freaking easy.

I strip about an inch of the rubber coating off the ignition and battery cables with the blade of my pocket knife and then twist them together. The dash lights up. Yes! I'm almost there.

I let those two dangle while I strip part of the starter wire. This is where things can get a little dicey. If I remember this shit wrong, I'll electrocute myself.

I put my foot on the brake and hold the bundled wires in one hand and the stripped starter wire in the other. I hear someone shout my name just as I tap the exposed wires together.

"Claire!"

Shit!

I look up towards the front of the station. Liam and Wes are running out of the door and are headed straight to me. Shit! I don't want to get caught stealing a federal vehicle. I mean I am caught because those two clowns are watching me do it, but if they reach me before I have a chance to get away they'll never let me live my life the way that I want to. Plus I'm pretty sure that's jail time. Normally, I wouldn't think my brother would turn me in, but he's not real happy with me right now. And he doesn't want me on my chosen career path.

I tap the wires again. I get a little bitty spark but the engine doesn't turn over. God damn it! I see them stalking towards me like big feral cats. Fuck. *Tap, tap, tap*. Jesus Christ, I'm sweating.

"Come here, Claire," Wes calls out. I shake my head and tap the wires together again. I get a little bit more. But still nothing.

"God damn it, this isn't funny, Claire," Liam barks.

I tap the wires together one last time, they're about fifteen feet away now, and the starter catches, the engine turns over. *Fuck yes!*

I feel a maniacal smile stretches over my lips as I put the car in reverse and back out of the space. They're running towards me, but they won't catch me, we all know it.

I throw the car in drive and peel out of the parking lot. I roll the windows down and crank up the radio to *Born to Run* as I hold my middle finger up out of the window. Childish, yes, but it feels oh so good.

I let the wind float through my hair as my favorite station plays some choice cuts. I feel free. It's nice to best them every once in awhile knowing that they think I'm not capable.

I pull into one of the visitor spots at my apartment complex and kill the engine. I neatly tape up the wires and roll them back up into the column. I replace the panel and use my pocket knife to tighten the screws that hold it in place. I open the glove box and pop the trunk before stepping out of the vehicle.

I run upstairs and unlock my apartment. That big bastard should feel a little of the humiliation that they've made me feel. This is why I don't date. Anyone. I don't want the other officers to know my business. It's bad enough that the local news put it all out there for the world to see and Liam basically confirmed it all at his weasley little press conference.

I march straight to my closet and scoop up all of Wes's clothes and shit. As much as I can in one go, then hustle back down stairs and dump it all into his open truck. I have to repeat the process once more. I slam the trunk closed and march back upstairs, throwing all the locks closed. Including the chain. Good riddance, fucker.

The weather has cooled down a bit so I strip out of my jeans and boots and into a comfy pair of fleece leggings and thick, cable knit socks. I sit down on the couch and open my laptop. My home screen opens when I put in my password. I insert the flash drive and wait for the grainy black and white footage to load.

I wait for what feels like hours, when my stomach grumbles. I look at my watch, it's noon. I don't want to stop watching the footage and I don't want to risk running into Liam, Wes, or any other agency that might currently be looking for me. So, I pause the video and pick up my phone.

Oh whoops, I have thirty-six missed phone calls. Two are from my mother, the rest are pretty equally divided between Wes and Liam—the *traitors*. I ignore all of the voicemails and text messages and call my favorite Chinese place for an order of Mu Shu chicken and some eggrolls.

I resume the video and see a white van. Holy fuck there was a white van! It has no markings on it and I can't see a full license plate. Fuck. I finally catch a break and I have nothing to go on with it. I write down on a sticky note the two letters in the middle that I can make out. No matter what I try I can only get two freaking letters, not that I have superior computer skills, because I don't. And those two freaking letters are in the middle so I'll never be able to figure it out.

The doorbell rings. I sigh and pause the video and close my laptop. I'm breaking enough rules working from home, I don't need to let the Chinese delivery kid see what I'm looking for.

I look through the peephole, Bobby stands there with the bill of his ball cap pulled low over his face, but I can tell by his jaw that it's him. He's holding a white paper sack.

I reach down and tag my jeans from the floor and pull out a twenty-dollar bill before opening the door. He smiles at me when he sees my face.

"Here's your usual, detective," he says as he hands me my lunch. Apparently, I'm a creature of habit.

"Thanks, Bobby," I smile back. "What's new with you?"

"Oh, nothing much," he smiles a smile that I'm not completely comfortable with. I'm kind of hoping Bobby hasn't developed a little bit of a crush on me, I'd hate to have to change Chinese places. I'm also aware that this makes me sound completely shallow.

"Oh good, well, I better get back to work. Thanks for this," I say holding up the bag as I hand him the twenty. "Keep the change."

"Thanks." He waves as he turns and walks back down the stairs to a white delivery van. I shrug. I guess they're more common than I thought.

I settle back in on the couch and open my bounty on the coffee table. I crack open a can of coke and shove an eggroll in my mouth before opening my laptop again. I eat as I watch the various surveillance videos until my belly is full and my eyes burn. I can barely keep them open.

And then I can't.

There's a ringing in my ear. Why is there a ringing in my ear? I slap around by my head to silence the disturbance when I realize it's my phone. I swipe my finger across the screen before putting it to my ear. I never open my eyes.

"Hello?"

"God damn it, Claire, you're late for dinner!" My mother shouts.

I sit straight up on my couch. My back and neck are killing me from falling asleep here.

"Dinner?" I ask knowing that I'm screwed. No one is ever late for dinner at my mother's house.

"Yes, dinner," she snaps. "I left you two messages about it."

"I'm not really feeling up to it, mama," I whisper. I can feel her softening towards me, giving in, but at the last minute she shores up her reserves and shuts me down.

"You're fine. Be here in ten," she barks as she

hangs up.

"Shit!" I jump up and start running around.

I have no time to change or make myself present-able, so I grab my black Ugg boots and exchange my socks for them. I throw my coat on over my burgundy t-shirt form this morning. I'm almost to the door when I taste something awful in my mouth. It's bad Chinese.

I wonder if there was something wrong with my mu shu. I shrug. I'm still breathing so it couldn't be that bad. I run to my bathroom and swish some Lis-terine really fast before spitting it back into the sink. I grab my keys and head out the door.

I climb into my SUV and notice that Wes's crappy fed car is gone. I shrug. There's a small pain searing through my chest at the thought of his walking away so easily after all of his bluster. I brush it aside as I put my car in gear and head for my parent's house.

The drive is not long. Liam and I both live rela-tively close to the house we grew up in. The woods surrounding the historic neighborhood welcome me home. I'm sure a lot of people would find them creepy, but I'm not a lot of people. I'm running so late, know-ing how mad my mom must be I don't even notice the other cars parked at the curb of our family home as I rush inside.

I pull open my mama's front door and hang my coat up in the entryway closet. I smell her lasagna and I can't wait. It's my favorite dinner. Actually, it's every-one's favorite dinner I think as I round the corner. Dad,

Liam, me and even Wes love mama's lasagna.

"I smell a rat!" I shout as I take in the sight of the aforementioned rat. Wes stands in front of me with a small smirk playing on his full lips. Liam, on the other hand is out and out grinning.

"Don't be rude, Claire Ann," Mama chastises. Liam's grin turns into a maniacal smile.

Shit!

"Well, say hello to our guests," Mama chastises.

"Hello, Wes," I growl. It's then that it dawns on me, she said, "guests" as in plural, more than one.

I turn around and there sitting on the sofa are Wes's parents. They look anything but thrilled to be here looking at me. Oh. Shit. *Double shit.* Wes's mom is my mom's best friend. And she has never liked me. I mean never. Mostly because she could see how much I was in love with Wes and felt I wasn't good enough. That I would never be good enough.

"Hello, Claire," she says softly with mean eyes.

"Hello, Mrs. O'Connell."

I freeze. I'm frozen with my eyes wide, unbelieving my personal misfortune. I'm stuck in her old lady powers. It's like I'm twelve again and she's telling me why riding my bike in the mud isn't befitting of a lady. How I'll never be a lady. How I would never be good enough to be an O'Connell was definitely implied.

"Hey, babe," Wes whispers in my ear as he puts his arm around my shoulders and draws me in close.

I cringe. That was the wrong fucking move, Wes. Wrong. Fucking. Move.

"So, it is true," she huffs.

"No," I shake my head vehemently. "Nope. No. No, ma'am."

"Then why does my son have his arm around you?"

"He's just joking. Always the joker this one," I jerk a thumb over my shoulder. Shit. I'm panicking. I always babble when I panic.

"Really? Because I've never know my son to be a practical joker," Judge O'Connell says softly. Shit!

"It's not a joke, mom," he says and I choke loudly. "I have feelings for Claire and I want her in my life." I cringe.

I have feelings for him too but not all of them are nice. My head is swimming. My forehead is sweating and my pits are gross. I bet everyone can smell me. Smell my panic. My fear. Mrs. O'Connell hones in like a rabid dog. Perspiration dots my upper lip and my knees shake.

"Are you okay, Claire," Wes asks, but he's at the end of a tunnel. A long tunnel. Underwater. The Holland Tunnel.

"Claire?" Mom leans in and tips her head to the side looking at me.

"I-I'm not feeling so well," I whisper.

"Sis?" Liam says from somewhere, but I don't see him because the lights are dimming. Everything goes dark.

"I can't believe you impregnated that girl!" I hear Mrs. O'Connell shriek.

"The fuck?" My dad barks.

"Dude, you knocked up my sister! I have to beat the shit out of you now. It's a rule," Liam growls.

"What rule?" Wes asks. "This afternoon you were all welcome to the family."

"I said that I wanted to welcome you to the family after I punched you in the face, but before Claire punched us in the dicks. At least now I know why."

"That's my girl," dad cheers and I can hear the pride shining in his voice.

"Your father is a sitting Judge, Wesley. How could you do this?" His mother wails.

"Melanie, it'll be alright," Mr. O'Connell comforts. "I always kind of wanted to be a grandad."

"Me too," my dad sniffs.

"My baby's having a baby," my mom sniffs.

The feeling is starting to return to my limbs and I'm able to flutter my lashes a bit but not quite open them.

"I think she's coming around," I hear Wes say softly.

And not a moment too soon. What's with all the baby talk?

"Baby? Are you there?"

"Of course I'm here, dipshit. Where the fuck else would I be? The moon?" I growl with my eyes still closed.

He crushes me tight to his body. "You had me worried there for a minute, you okay?"

"Yeah," I gasp unable to breathe his hold on me is so tight. "No, I can't breathe . . . I think the Chinese food I had this afternoon gave me food poisoning."

"Babe, the shit in your fridge is disgusting," he admonishes.

"No, Bobby brought me fresh."

His body goes taut, "Who the fuck is Bobby?"

"Language, Wesley!" His mother barks. I just roll my eyes.

"He's the sixteen-year-old kid who delivers for Szechuan Gardens." His arms loosen around me. Wes looks at me, his eyes soft and full of care and concern.

"Food poisoning is bad for the baby, Claire," my mom says softly, the concern weighing heavy in her voice.

"There is no baby, mom. We've had sex like twice," I shrug.

"Like four times if you count twelve years ago," Wes adds unhelpfully.

"You had sex twelve years ago!" His mom screams.

"She was like seventeen," my dad growls.

"She was eighteen," Wes defends.

"Barely," I add. Take that fucker.

"Not helping, babe," he whispers in my ear.

"It's like you want me to beat the shit out of you, buddy," Liam wades into the fray.

"But why is there no baby?" Mom shouts obviously grasping onto the idea of a grandbaby in the future. Danger! Danger! DANGER!

"Because I'm on like nine kinds of birth control, Mom," I say softly. "It's not like we're getting married."

The room goes quiet and the air takes on a weird charge.

"Why wouldn't we?" Wes asks. Uh oh.

"Because we have way too much going on. What with a murder to solve to even go on a date. We've never been on a date," I grasp onto that idea and run with it. "So, we can't get married."

"I took you to dinner last night, then to my place and made love to you all night."

"There was that . . ."

"Gross, dude, that's my sister," Liam moans. "Now I think I'm going to be sick.

"Shut up, Liam!" We both shout.

"So why can't you guys get married?" My mom

asks. Shit.

"Mom," I whisper looking into her eyes and hoping she sees what I'm trying to show her. I can't get married. Ever. I can't saddle someone to the baggage that I have been carrying since I was six years old.

Mom sees and she gets it. She bites her bottom lip and then looks away. Tears are glittering in her eyes. As a mother, it hurts her that her child is stuck in this weigh station in life. Unable to move on, unwilling to go back. She nods once but doesn't look back at me.

Wes's whole body is tight. He sees the byplay between my mom and I and he knows. Wes knows that I can't marry him or anyone. And it kills him. He wants a life that I can't give him. Even if I did, one day, he wouldn't be able to take it anymore. One day he would look at me the way that he did twelve years ago. One day, Wes would know that he cannot help me and he will never be able too. And if we were too far down the line he would not only take himself from my life, but the home that we would have built together, the babies we would have had. I can survive a lot, I already have, but that one we both know, would kill me dead.

"No," he growls pushing up from beside me. "No! I refuse to accept your bullshit reasonings to push me away. So that you can run and hide because you're scared."

"You know that it's not bullshit, Wes," I say softly.

"It is!"

"It's not," I take a deep breath. "You think right

now that you care for me enough to fix me, but there's nothing to be fixed, Wes. So, say we keep on the way that we are, we get married, and we have a ton of babies. Then one day you can't stand the night terrors . . ."

"What night terrors?" My mom asks but I keep on.

"And you can't stand the screaming in my sleep . . ."

"What's happening? What is she talking about?" Judge O'Connell asks.

"And you can't stand to look at me anymore because you know that I'm broken and you can't fix it. What then, Wes? Do you take everything away from me?"

"Why wouldn't he be able to look at you?" Mom asks.

"Because he can't. He thinks he can now, but in the long run, he'll see that I'm not the same girl that he thinks he married. He'll walk away."

"I would never—" he starts.

"You already did."

He drops his eyes to the floor because he knows that it's true. Every last bit of it is true.

"What are you talking about, Claire?" My dad asks.

"I'll tell you later, Pops," Liam says quietly.

"I should go," I say not looking anyone in the eyes. It's tough to be such a Debbie Downer but the truth would come out sometime. "I'm sorry I ruined your dinner party, mama. I told you I wasn't feeling well."

She takes me into a fierce hug and kisses my cheek. When she lets me go I stand on shaky legs and head to the front door. When I get there, I turn back and see Wes is still looking at the floor. Liam, my dad, and Judge O'Connell are all looking at him with scowls on their handsome faces.

I feel bad for him. I'm not sure when that happened or why. Maybe because I have loved him my whole life. Maybe because I've known for just as long that he was never meant to be mine. He hurts and we all know that he deserves some of it because what he did twelve years ago was not nice, but the other part of me doesn't want Wes to hurt at all, ever again.

I grab my coat and wrap it around my body. I pull my keys out of the pocket and pull the door open. The biting wind stings my cheeks as I step out onto the stoop.

Just before I close the door, I hear voices. One of them sounds like my dad's and I swear I heard him say, "Now it's my turn to beat the shit out of you."

But that can't be right. My dad is a great guy. A big teddy bear. He wouldn't hurt a fly. Liam and I get our tempers from our mother.

I close the door behind me and jump in my car to head home. The drive is quick and quiet, but I don't like the voice in my head telling me that I was too cold, too brutal back there. I hurt too, damn it. But there's nothing I can do about it.

When I get into my apartment, I take as hot a shower as I can stand, but part of me thinks I will never be warm again. I dress in sweats and climb under all of the covers and wrap them tight around my head and hope that as sleep claims me I will feel better in the morning. But I know not to count on that either.

chapter 18

any other way

"**C**OME OUT OF THE closet, baby."

"No," I whisper, tears hot on my face and snot stuffing up my nose.

Liam and Wes were right, I'm just a baby. A big kid wouldn't be crying in the dark corner of a closet hoping it'll all go away if you just wish hard enough. I bet Wes never cries. I know Lee doesn't.

"Come out now, Claire. Playtime is over."

"No," I cry louder. "Please don't make me."

"Now!" He growls as the closet door rattles. I gasp.

"Leave me alone!"

"Get out of the fucking closet, Claire!" He roars.

"Please no," I cry harder, my body shaking with each sob.

"When," he kicks his hard boots against the closet door and it shudders.

"Please."

"Are you," he kicks it again.

The doors are the kind with the slats that fold sideways. We have them at home and mama says I always pinch my fingers in the accordion. Whatever that is.

"I just wanna go home," I whisper.

"Gonna," he kicks again.

"I just want my mommy," I sob. "Please. I just want my mommy."

"Fucking," the boards snaps and I scream.

"I just wanna go home, please," I beg.

"Learn!" he shouts as he kicks the broken boards out of the way. He leans down and grabs me by my upper arms.

"Please," I wheeze but my words are cut short when he slaps my face hard. So hard I taste blood in my mouth and it's so yucky I feel sick. I'm going to throw up from the yucky taste. I try as hard as I can not to. I know that if I do, he'll punish me again. I don't want that. Anything but that.

"You are home, baby," he coos right before he slaps me again. I cry out again, falling to the floor with his last hit. It's so strong he knocks me down with it. "And I thought I told you to call me daddy," he says as he lands a hard kick to my back.

"You're not my daddy, you'll never be my daddy,"

I whisper. "My daddy is a nice man. He would never hurt me. You'll never be my daddy," I say again but the bad man can't hear me, he already walked away. I have nowhere to go, but one thing is for sure, I have to escape.

I sit straight up in my bed, gasping for air. My heart is beating a million times per second. That can't be good for my health. The *beep . . . beep . . . beep* of my alarm is pounding through the room in tandem with my close to explosive heart.

I press my hand to my chest willing my heart to slow. I try to hold my breath, forcing my heart to slow down when it won't. Sweat has the old academy t-shirt I wore to bed plastered against the skin of my shoulders, back and chest. My hair is also matted with sweat.

I have to use the breathing they taught us at the academy to slow my breathing, my heart. I take a deep breath in, not letting it out, then another in, still not letting it out, then one more, a third breath, but this time, I slowly let them all out. Like a light switch that someone flipped, my focus snaps into place. My eyes no longer blink wildly around. My heart no longer feels like it will blow out of my chest at any minute. It hurts, it will for awhile, but I'll live. It's a sign of my mortality. The blood that pumps through my heart keeps me living, grounded to the earth. My lungs sear with the oxygen I can finally absorb.

I hug my knees to my chest and drop my head to them. I have to gather my thoughts. My sanity. The dreams never fully leave me, but they also never happen this often. It scares me. I'm running towards a precipice, a cliff, I can feel it coming. But I can't stop it. I only hope someone will be there to catch me when I fall. Maybe Liam was right after all, but I can't go back now, I have come way too far for that.

I pick up my phone from the nightstand next to my bed. The metal and glass, cool from the night air, stings my overheated palm. I stare at it for a moment before coming to the same conclusion that I always do. I wish I was stronger. I would give anything to be less weak, but I am weak. I can't stop the nightmares no matter what I do. They seem to be getting worse and worse, building to something, but I don't know what. I wish I didn't need this so badly, but I do. I won't ever be right if I don't. That much I know is true. That much I can admit to myself.

I stare at the little black lifeline in my hand and swipe the screen bringing it to life and dial the one number I know better than my own.

"Hello," she answers on the first ring. A sign that she sleeps as little or less than I do. No wonder we're friends.

"Hi, Anna," I whisper.

"Is everything alright, Claire?" She asks in her shrink tone. I have come to know this one well over the last couple of years.

Imagine my surprise when Liam demanded that I see a department shrink before I could sit for the Detective's exam. And that bastard would not budge one freaking inch. So off I trotted to the department shrinkey dink. Turns out she was a pretty cool chick and we both find Liam exhausting, so we joined forces. It's not often you find another woman in our field. Double points if she's not a raging bitch trying to prove she's tougher than everyone. News flash, we all have to prove we're as tough as the boys. You don't have to take out the rest of the women on your road to the top. As it turns out, Emma, Anna, and I are the cool kids. And just maybe the troublemakers too.

"No, doll," I answer her. "No. I'm not." With Anna and I, there is no bullshit, no prevarication. Which is probably really fucking stupid on my part since she could end my career with a snap of her fingers if she ever decides I'm more broken than I claimed to be.

I listen to her breathe into the phone while she processes my words. Too often, I tell her that I'm fine. It was no big deal. I'm great. I love my job, my life, the string of men I don't tell my name to. Whatever lies I happen to be telling everyone including myself that week. This is the first time I have ever told the truth. And that is, I am not okay.

"You had another nightmare," she wisely surmises.

"Yeah," I answer as I pull my knees to my chest and tuck my face into the sheets that cover my legs. I wish I could hide from it all.

"You're remembering." I have maintained that I

don't remember anything for twenty-four years, but Anna and Wes have always believed the dreams were memories. And they are. But I will never admit that. Not even to Anna, my closest friend. Too bad she's so damn annoying when she's right. I sigh.

"We don't know that."

"Are you sure about that, Claire?" She asks zeroing in on my lies.

"Absolutely."

"What happened this time?" She asks after a long pause.

"I begged to go home, he beat me, told me I was home. Lather, rinse, repeat." I shrug into the darkness. Into the nothing.

"You know you don't always have to be so indifferent, Claire," she whispers. I can hear the hurt in her voice. She wants me to be more honest, more open with her, and I am. But not completely and she knows it.

"This is who I am, Anna. I can't be any other way, honey," I say softly into the phone hoping she understands I don't mean to hurt her. I just can't.

"I disagree," she says firmly.

The doctor is back *in situ*. I sigh.

"Do you think they're right?" I ask, my voice small and I hate that. It fucking kills me. But there's a part of me that wonders if they're right. I'm not cut out for this job. I'm too weak.

I'm always too weak.

"Liam and Wes?" She asks, obviously surprised by my question.

"Yeah," I whisper.

"No," she says firmly, so much it scares me a little. "Not at all. I think you're hurting. I think the case is bringing up old ghosts you should have laid to rest years ago. And I do mean years! But I do not think they are right. This is where you were meant to be, Claire. Besides if you quit, who are Emma and I going to torture those moronic apes with?" She laughs.

"This is true," I murmur. And it is. I'm the best at taking the Neanderthals down a peg or two.

"You know it is." She laughs. I can hear her voice relax. I know that I do that to her.

"Alright." I sigh. "I think I'm okay."

"I think you're getting there," she says going back to business. "But I would like to see you in the office this week. I have heard great things about a new hypnotherapy that I think can really help you regain those memories," she says excitedly.

Whoops. Time to go.

"Well, look at the time, I really must be going now . . ."

"Don't you dare hang up on me, Claire!" She shouts. "I know where you live!"

"What's that *kussshhhhh* . . . you're breaking up . . . *kkkuuuusshhhh* . . . I think I'm losing the connection," I lie just before I hang up.

I peel the sweat soaked covers back and toss them in the washer in the hall closet. I peel my sweatpants and t-shirt off of my body and step into the shower. I stand there for a minute just letting the hot water wash away the dreams, the memories, I'm not sure which they really are anymore. The water eases my sore muscles.

I soap up my body and shampoo my hair. It's not lost on me that twenty-four hours ago, I was in this shower with Wes. His hot, hard body here with mine. He worshiped my body, me even, time and time again, I threw it back in his face. One day, Wes will realize that I'm not a sweet kitten but a mean rattlesnake. I ruin everything I touch. Today, I'm here alone and it's no one's fault but my own.

I turn the water off and squeeze the residual moisture out of my hair. I grab the towel that Wes dried my body with yesterday, sensuously wiping all the moisture from my skin while creating heat—a burn—in other places. Today, I dry myself with a brutal economy.

I walk to my closet and pull on plain cotton panties and a jog bra. I do not feel sexy or worthy of worship—by Wes or anyone. Today, I am just a broken toy, long forgotten. I grab jeans and socks, pulling my favorite brown boots on after. I pull a sage green, long sleeved henley over a white tank top and add a brown leather belt to the loops of my jeans. That's all she wrote.

I walk back into the bathroom, most of the steam has dissipated from the mirror over the sink. I take a black hair band and a handful of bobby pins, pinning my hair up into a messy bun on top of my head. I brush my teeth feeling loads better than I did the night before. Well, my stomach does, my heart, not so much.

I slap a bare minimum of makeup on my face. Just because my life has taken an epic shit doesn't mean I have to look like it's taken an epic shit. So, I slap a little light pink blush on my cheeks and black mascara to my lashes. My lips are dry and cracked from a night of being ill so they get a swipe of my lip balm. Glamorous, I know.

I head down the short hall to my kitchen. I see all of the Chinese takeout containers on my coffee table that were abandoned in my mad rush to get to my mother's house for dinner. Then forgotten in the throws of my food poisoning and heartache. My stomach rolls at the thought. I grab a garbage bag and quickly scoop them all up to take them out.

I holster my sidearm and drop gun to my hip and ankle. I pin my badge to the front of my jeans. My cell phone goes in my pocket. I grab my coat and wrap it around my body before pulling open the front door and locking it behind me.

I drop the trash bag into the dumpster and wipe the imaginary bad food germs on my jeans before brushing my hands together before a shiver wracks up my spine.

"Someone must have stepped on my grave," I mutter to myself. At least that's what my grandmother would have said.

I take a quick look around. The hair at the back of my neck standing on end. But my scan of the parking lot comes up empty. I shrug. This case can't close soon enough. I'm starting to jump at everything. And I refuse to live my life like that damn it!

A crow caws and flaps its wings somewhere. I hear a piece of gravel roll on the blacktop, but I could have sworn there was nothing here to have knocked it loose. It's official, I'm losing my mind.

I beep the locks on my SUV and climb in. I start the engine and I could swear, that someone's watching me. I hit the button on the door for the auto locks and then casually check my mirrors for any sign of someone somewhere that they shouldn't be. To the casual observer, it would simply look like I'm a careful driver, when in reality, I'm anything but. Really, I'm looking for something . . . anything, but there's nothing to be found.

I pull into my spot in the parking lot of the station. I grip the steering wheel tight in my hand and drop my head for a minute, shoring up my courage before I kill the engine and step from the car.

I pull open the big glass front door and buzz myself into the back with my ID. Wes is standing in front of my desk. His sexy ass rests against the edge of the table. His strong arms are closed over his powerful chest and he holds a paper coffee cup in his hand. His brows are pulled low over his eyes.

I notice a similar paper coffee cup on my desk waiting for me. Taunting me. I take my jacket off and hang it over the back of my desk chair. We stand there, silently staring at each other for what seems like years when Wes finally raises his dark eyes to mine. I gasp at the look on his face, not to mention the black eye that makes him look a little bit like a panda bear. It's so clear and open, Wes, who is normally closed off completely, which happens when you go to work for agencies with letters, is open for me to see everything.

"Bad news," he says.

chapter 19

here you go

"I'M NOT SURE I can handle any more bad news, Wes."

"Couple of things," he says as he straightens. "Last night did not go great."

"You think?" I snap.

"But I will not be deterred by you, your past or anyone else."

I sigh, "Wes."

"Now for the bad news," I suck in a breath. If dinner with our families wasn't the bad news, then we are completely and totally fucked. "Jonathan Ascher was found dead in his cell early this morning."

"What?" I bark.

"They think he was poisoned sometime last night."

"How? He was locked up in a jail!" I'm shouting.

"Sit down and lower your voice," he quietly demands. "I don't know if this is an inside job or not. Don't give us away yet," he whispers against my ear. His hands hold me tight by my hips. To anyone else, it would look like a couple of lovers having an early morning chat before work picked up. We are and we're not.

"Okay," I whisper. "Tell me."

"Last night, he was complaining about a stomach ache after dinner. He said his head hurt, he was tired and sweating profusely. When asked about it, he said it was probably just a bug and he needed to sleep it off. So, the deputies at county left him alone instead of taking him to medical."

"Shit."

"Yep," he agrees.

"What now?"

"Now he goes to the M. E. for an autopsy because it seems a little fishy to me."

"Obviously," I snap.

"I don't think you're understanding me, baby," he says softly in my ear, still holding me.

"What's to get? Someone killed him because of his affair with the daughter. The list isn't long, Wes. If she was my daughter, I would have probably killed him too."

He sighs, "Don't you think it's just a little bit odd that Jonathan Ascher exhibited the exact same symptoms that you did last night at dinner? Right before he died?" I feel my eyes widen.

"But I had food poisoning . . ." I justify.

"Maybe," he says nodding his head. "Then again, maybe not."

"Shit."

"My thoughts exactly."

"Shit!" I shout.

"Babe, we covered that already."

"No, I threw out the containers this morning because just the sight of them made me want to yak all over again," I shout. "We have to go find them. The lab can tell us if there's something other than botulism in them."

"You need to go to the hospital, Claire."

"No," I say adamant that I keep up on this case. The pieces are swirling in my brain and I know that I won't settle until they all find their places where they fit.

"I can't let anything happen to you, baby."

"I'm fine," I reassure him. "Take me to the lab."

"Okay. Get in the car, I'll drive."

I roll my eyes. I would argue with him about his being a big bossy bastard this early in the morning but we don't have fucking time. So, I race out of the station, hot on his heels. We jump in his Federal issued sedan and take off.

It should be said that Wes can drive when he wants to. And how sick is it of me that we are on our way to grab evidence that I was poisoned last night, along with a suspect in a high-profile murder case, and I'm sitting here thinking about how sexy he is when he drives like he means it. I groan.

"What is it, babe, still feeling bad?" I feel my eyes widen a bit in panic.

"Yeah, that's what it is. Exactly that."

We pull into the parking lot of my apartment complex and Wes heads towards my actual unit. He's smart to figure that I would throw away my garbage close to where my unit is so that I wouldn't have to schlep it all over. He knows for a fact that I park close as well.

"That one, over there!" I shout pointing at the big dumpster in the far corner just feet away from the stairs to my apartment.

Wes barely has the car in park before we are unbuckling our seat belts and throwing open our doors. Energized by the possibility of a lead, I race towards the fence that surrounds the dumpsters. I hear Wes's feet beat the pavement behind me.

I already know that they keep the dumpster gate locked to keep animals and vagrants out so I don't even try it. Without breaking my stride, I push off of the ground with my back foot and land my front foot on the wall pushing upward. I follow the upward momentum and grab the top of the fence with my hands and pull myself up and over to drop down on the other side. Sometimes it's good to know I still got it.

I immediately start sifting through the bags looking for the one from my apartment. I use a specialty trash bag because I hate germs. And spills and the disasters that come from garbage bag tears. So, the ones from my place are a light robin's egg blue, like the color of hospital scrubs.

I climb over garbage bags and the other detritus of human life, tossing bags back and forth. It's not here. Shit. I climb over more shit, some literally. Mrs. Fratelli's dog is possibly the most disgusting dog in life. Adorable, don't get me wrong, but the shit that comes out of that dog is truly disgusting.

"Shit!" I shout one more time for good measure. "It's not here."

"I figured that out," Wes calls. I look up and he's standing there swinging the evidence bag holding the remains of the broken padlock in his gloved hand so that I can see it.

"Broken or cut?" I ask.

"Definitely cut," he says. "I'm calling it in." I just nod.

I climb back out of the dumpster and this time walk through the gate with the broken lock. Wes and I stand together waiting for the Crime Scene Unit to come and collect evidence. I wish I had gone back to my apartment to shower and change clothes, but I didn't and I will regret that for all time.

The CSU van pulls up and a bubbly blonde with

personality traits which can only be described as sorority girl or Chihuahua on crack hops out and bounds.
Yes, bounds like a goddamn Labrador, up to Wes.

"Hey, Wes," she breathes. Oh yes, *breathes*.

He does his best not to cringe but it's there and
I see it, so yeah, that's fantastic too. I try to remind
myself that this is what I wanted, what I always knew
would happen. Wes would move on. Although by the
way she was slithering all over Wes, I'd say he had
moved this particular direction before we were ever on
and she's not so thrilled to be put aside.

"Hey, Sarah," he responds with a tight-lipped
smile. "We need fingerprints from the gate, the lock,
and anything else you can find to tell me who broke
in here this morning after Detective Goodnite left for
work."

It's at this moment that she looks to me and gives
me the up and down. Maybe it was department gossip.
Maybe it was how close to me Wes is standing. I don't
know, but whatever it was it made her give me an as-
sessing once over and by the look on her face she finds
me sorely lacking. Or maybe it was the banana peel on
my shoulder. Who knows.

"Oh God, what is that smell?" She asks with a
twinkle in her eye.

I smirk. It's cute she thinks she can embarrass me.
She obviously doesn't know who I am. Or that I don't
care. Ever.

"What were you guys looking for?" A man asks as

he steps around the van towards us.

"A blue green trash bag," Wes looks to him.

"Gross, why would you do that, babe?" She tries to draw herself back into the conversation. I roll my eyes. The other man snickers and we have a moment. It looks like he doesn't like her either.

"It's evidence in an ongoing investigation."

"That little boy, right?" She asks as she lays her hand on his chest. He looks down at where her hand is pressing into his suit. "That's so sad. I'm glad the FBI finally got the case. Too bad you couldn't get it before that poor boy died," she adds helpfully. *Bitch.*

"De we have access to a control sample of the bag?" The other man asks.

"Yeah, I can run and grab you one," I answer.

"Thank God, you're disgusting. Not to mention in the way." She turns her sharp gaze to me. "I mean can you do anything right?"

I have to bite my bottom lip hard and hold my breath to keep from strangling the bitch. I get that she wants him and she thinks I'm in the way, but damn, does she have to be so awful. I mean power of the sisterhood and all. I take in a deep breath and turn to the other guy and smile.

"I'll go run and grab that for you," I wink at him to let him know there's no hard feelings toward him. "Do you have gloves and an evidence bag?" I ask.

"Sure do," he answers before handing me clean

gloves and a bag.

I take both with a quick, "Thanks," and then jog across the lot to my building.

I do not stop and look back even though everything in my belly is telling me that I should. I just can't bare to see them together at work. Being without Wes will hurt, but I know that it's better for us both.

"What a bitch," I mumble as I step through my front door.

First things first, should I take a quick shower and change my clothes? Or do I stay in the garbage stink and show Mr. $800 Suit how different we really are? Part of me wants to show Bubbles that I am easily as pretty as she is, but that would be defeating the purpose of trying to shake Wes off my tail.

I stand with my hands on my hips in the entryway to my apartment while I debate the merits of showering or staying in the stink of garbage filth. I'm not going to let Bubbles get to me. No, I think with a maniacal glee, I'm going to make them suffer. I mentally brush my hands off. Well, that's that.

I walk into the kitchen and pull open the drawer where I keep the trash and sandwich bags. I pull on the latex gloves and shake open the evidence bag. Then I drop one of my funky green trash bags inside and seal her up.

I point my nose in the air and sniff. I have to admit, it's not great. I see some of those strings that come from bananas stuck in my hair and shrug. Oh well. I can't help the smile that spreads across my face as I walk back to the front door and pull it open with my free hand, making sure to turn the lock before it closes behind me.

I take my sweet, sweet time as I walk down the stairs and head back across the lot to the dumpster. I wouldn't want either Bubbles or Wes to think they run my show. No, that job is for me and me alone.

"Any day now," she snaps at me from her spot cozied up to Wes. I smile brighter.

"Sorry it took so long, I had to remember where I stuck the rubber gloves you gave me," I wink at Bubble's partner. He smirks.

"For God's sakes you put them in your pants pocket! Even I noticed."

"Awe, isn't that sweet," I croon. The other man snickers at my game. Wes pulls his eyebrows down low in a deep scowl.

"Here you go," I smile as I hand over the bag.

"Jesus, I was hoping you were showering with how long you took," she spits. "It would have done us all a favor." I just smile.

"It's not like we have all day, you know. Parker, Wes and I are very busy people." Oh so Wes is busy but I'm not. I see how it's going to be. I mean I knew, but still.

"No, I had no idea," I smile. "I do apologize. I was busy running a murder investigation."

She bristles at my comment. I'd like to stay and appreciate pushing her every last button and all that it entails, but Wes grabs me by my upper arm and hauls me away. My feet are dragging and running at the same time to keep up with his long, angry strides.

"Hey!" I call out. "I was working."

"No, Sarah and Parker were working, you were doing your best to be you," he growls. My spine turns to steel and I pull my arm from his grasp.

"Excuse me?"

"You heard me, you just can't help yourself can you?" He shouts at me as he grabs me again and resumes dragging me back to my apartment. I'm sure Bubbles is just loving this.

"Let me go!"

"No."

"I'm not a child!" I shout trying to pull free again.

"Then stop acting like one."

"You just did not!" I shout back.

"I did!" He barks back as he reaches into my pocket and deftly pulls my keys out, opening my front door and then giving me a good shove into my humble abode.

"You just had to push, didn't you?" He asks as he shoves me gently back.

"Stop shoving me," I snap, but Wes keeps pushing me back, further and further until I'm in my bathroom.

Wes crowds me into the small room and reaches around me, switching on the light. Then he keeps crowding me back and back, more and more, until my shoulder blades hit the wall. He reaches in and turns the water on. His dark eyes look me up and down. I shiver. It feels like his gaze burrows under my skin and see right through to my soul. Every last thought and feeling laid bare to him.

"Strip," he commands.

"What?"

"I said, strip," he barks out. "You can do it now or I'll do it for you."

"No." I cross my arms over my chest as I dig my heels in.

Wes does not answer me. Instead, he slides his suit coat down his arms and folds it neatly before placing it onto the bathroom counter. He unknots his tie and then, again, neatly folds it, placing it on top of his coat. Slowly, oh so slowly.

"Wh-what are you doing?" I rasp.

"I already told you, you could strip, or I would do it for you," he looks me dead in the eye. There's a cold-ness behind his that I haven't seen before. I shiver.

"And I said no."

Wes watches me huff out another protest but doesn't say another word. Slowly, methodically, he unbuttons the cuffs of his shirt and rolls them up his forearms. Can forearms be sexy? If so then Wes's are. They are strong and muscular with veins that pop out travelling up the inside to his elbows.

When he's done he takes a step towards me. I put my hands up to block his chest. I expect him to grab my arms again, but he reaches for my belt. Before I realize what he's doing, Wes has divested me of my badge and holster. Because that's not embarrassing. He sets them on the bathroom counter.

My t-shirt is whisked over my head and my button and zipper are undone by his quick, efficient movements. He nods towards my feet. I sigh loudly and toe off my boots. Wes surprises me by dropping to his knees in front of me. He glides his hands down the outsides of my thighs on his way down before putting the sole of my right foot on his strong thigh and pushing up my pant leg. He removes my ankle holster with little fanfare.

Wes uses his hands to push my jeans and panties down my legs. He picks up one foot at time, freeing my legs from my clothing. He then stands on his powerful legs and it's the first time I see him for the predator that he is. How did I forget about the SEAL? I couldn't look past the suit and now I'm about to pay for my mistakes.

"Get in the shower, Claire," his voice rumbles.

I look up at his beautiful face and see the seriousness in his eyes. I could push him, but I wouldn't like the outcome, that much is obvious. It's clear now that

Wes has been keeping his temper on a tight leash. And Crime Scene Sarah was a trigger. Who knew?

I always knew Wes had a past. I never once doubted that it was littered with women of all shapes, sizes, and occupations with the only common denominator being that they were beautiful. Hell, I never even thought he would be interested in me again. I never planned for any of this.

Wes pursued me. He chased me down. As early as this morning he told me that he wouldn't give up on me, on us, that he wouldn't let me chase him away. Turns out he didn't need me to chase him away, he just needed Bubbles to wave her magic twat around in the air. I guess I wasn't that important after all.

I'm angry. I'm really, really angry. But most of all, I'm hurt. It hurts to know that I'm so replaceable. That Wes could fuck me and then bail on me. Twice! He is the king of the hit it and quit it.

I don't want him to see my cry. The tears are burning up the back of my throat. I look at him one more time and bite my lip to stop the quiver. God damn it! I am tougher than this. So he broke my heart? So what? I never should have let him get close enough to do it again, this one's on me.

I nod once and then open the door to the shower stall and step in. I close the door behind me and turn to face the steam. The heat and mist envelope me as the water beats down on me. I drop my head so that the stream hits my shoulder blades.

His phone rings and he answers it with a clipped, "Yeah," he sighs. "Alright, I'll tell her."

And I no longer care. I don't care if he's still standing there. Nor do I care if he hears me cry or if it bothers him. The sob bubbles up from my chest and tears free. I press my palms to the tile wall in front of me and let the tears run free, unchecked.

The shower door bangs open and his heat wraps around me instantly. Wes turns me into his body and tucks my face into the crook of his neck. He strokes my hair gently and coos in my ear.

"It's okay, baby," he soothes. "I'm sorry. I'm so very sorry." But for the life of me, I can't figure out what for.

Then it dawns on me, he must be apologizing for his feelings for Crime Scene Sarah. I sigh and try and pull from his embrace. His arms tighten around me.

"Not yet, baby, I need this too."

"It's okay," I whimper. "I'm sure you'll be very happy together."

"What?" He stiffens.

"You and Bubbles. You'll make a lovely couple," I choke back another sob. "I didn't mean to make you that angry."

"Bubbles?"

"Crime Scene Sarah," I clarify.

"Babe," he sighs again. On further thought, Wes seems to sigh a lot around me.

"What?"

"There's nothing going on there?" I ask narrowing my eyes.

"No."

"So, you've never slept with her?"

"I didn't say that," he says softly. I pull from his arms.

"Claire," he warns. "I told you not to pull away from me."

"Why don't you go pull out of Sarah instead," I snap instantly regretting my words. Wes smiles a smile and it isn't nice.

"Yes, I slept with her. So has half the department. So has your brother," he growls.

"Oh,"

"Yeah, oh."

"Gross," I shudder.

Wes sighs and pulls me back into his arms. He brushes my wet hair back from my face and plucks out a few banana strings, shaking them off of his fingers.

"It's you that I want, Claire."

I just nod because I don't really know what else to do. We seem to be on this carousel and there doesn't seem to be any stopping it. We just go around and around as one or both of us get our hearts broken along the way.

"I don't know what to say to that," I whisper.

"Don't say anything, just be," he shakes me a little as he emphasizes his words. "Just be."

"I don't know if I can."

"We're a swirling storm, baby. You can either ride it out and hope something good comes from it, or we can let it drown us. From the little taste of us that I've had, I can already tell that we're headed towards something special."

I stand there and stare at him. How I wanted those words or ones like them twelve years ago. I would have given anything for him to want me then like he says he does now. Is he right? I feel the attraction between us, there's no denying it. I'm just not sure he won't drown me when this is all over.

"I can't make you any promises," he says softly. "But I will take care of you. I have a right to be mad when I find out you've been poisoned by a suspect and I don't even know which fucking one!" He thunders, the rumble of his voice in his chest shaking me where my head rests against him.

"Oh."

"Now, let me wash you up because you positively stink," he says and I can hear the smile in his voice.

Wes gently washes my hair, massaging my scalp as he goes. He pours body wash into his hands and then rubs it into my body, taking a few liberties along the way. When he's satisfied that I'm all clean and banana garbage free, Wes shuts off the water and opens the shower door.

He grabs a towel from the rack and wipes the water droplets from my body before wrapping it tightly around me. He snags the other towel and quickly dries off. He takes his towel and wraps my hair up in it, squeezing all the water out.

Then Wes scoops me up into his arms like a princess, like I'm everything and carries me to my closet. He pulls a bra and panties out of my drawer and quietly dresses me. He snags a pair of jeans and holds them out for me to step in. I let the towel fall to the floor and do just that as I watch his eyes darken as he takes in my body. Then he grabs a red, long sleeved vee neck t-shirt and pulls it over my head.

Satisfied with my dressed form, he moves to put his clothes back on quickly and I mourn the loss of view if his hard ass and long cock. Even if we're not meant to be forever, I can still appreciate his form whenever possible.

Wes walks back towards me with long, even strides and stops in front of me. He holds his hand out to me, palm up and in it are my badge and holster. The gesture means everything to me and I show him. I let Wes see the emotions that I would usually keep locked away play across my face. His own face softens as he looks at me. The view is even better than his perfect ass and you could bounce a quarter off that for sure.

I grab my ankle holster, clean socks and boots. Then we're ready to go. Wes holds his hand out to me and I take it. Without thinking, I take his hand and his partnership on this assignment. And I take a little more of what he's offering. I don't know if it's forever. I don't even know if it'll last longer than the week. But for this minute, right now, today, I'm taking it.

chapter 20 ⊹

for all to see

"WHAT I WANT TO know is, why you?" Wes asks as we power down the highway back towards the station.

"What do you mean, why me?"

"Why poison you?" He rephrases his initial question. "You know something. You have to. We just don't know what that is yet."

"We have to go back."

"We have to go back," Wes parrots my words back to me.

I can't help but think he doesn't mean Orange Drive where the Donovan-Ascher's live. I can't go back. I won't. Whatever Wes has up his sleeve, I will avoid it at all costs. I'm hanging on by a thread as it is. I will solve this case without trudging up the past. Even if it kills me.

Wes takes the next highway exit and angles us towards George Washington Township Savings and Loan, where Jonathan Ascher was a Vice President until this morning when he bought the farm. There is something . . . *off*. I just can't put my finger on it.

Wes pulls into the parking lot of the bank. I unbuckle my belt and step from the vehicle. Wes is by my side as we walk through the shiny glass front doors. Badges in hand we walk up to a pretty young thing sitting at the front information desk. She takes one look at Wes and I swear the top button on her collared shirt pops open revealing even *more* cleavage.

I roll my eyes.

Wes clears his throat and I stop my eyes mid motion. There's a sexy smirk playing about his stupid face and I find it incredibly irritating. I hate that he sees me so clearly. I hate that he knows I get jealous and I really freaking hate how much he seems to be enjoying it.

I clear my throat, "I'm Detective Goodnite, George Washington Township PD, and we have a few questions regarding Jonathan Ascher."

"And you are?" She preens to Wes. If she was a bird in the wild she would be ruffling her glossy feathers. Fuck my life.

"Special Agent O'Connell, FBI," he smirks again. She's reeled in and he knows it. This makes me irrationally angry.

"I've never met an FBI agent before," she says all breathily like when Marilyn Monroe sang "Happy

Birthday" to JFK.

"Here we go," I mutter under my breath.

"Well, here I am and I sure would like to ask you some questions about Mr. Ascher," he shoots her his panty dropping smile.

"Oh brother."

"I'd do anything for the FBI," she says as she places her hands on her desk and leans forward, her breasts hitting the desk with a plop. "I mean anything," she says as she looks up from under her lashes.

I sigh. *Heavily.* It's five o'clock somewhere, right? I am going to need a bottle of whiskey to get me through this witness interview.

"I was wondering if you could tell me a little bit about Mr. Ascher and what it's like to work for him," Wes says calmly,

"He's a great man," she says and it dawns on me that they don't yet know that he's dead. "He's always been really nice to me," she blushes.

Uh oh.

"I bet he was," Wes says softly. "How nice was he?"

"He always buys me coffee when I run out to get him his. He takes me to lunch sometimes or buys me dinner if we have to work late."

"How often do you and Mr. Ascher work late into the evening?"

"Oh, about once a week," she blinks into Wes's

eyes.

"Did anything inappropriate ever happen during those times?" She visibly bristles at the question.

"Did you ever have a relationship with Mr. Ascher?" I ask softly. She blinks before turning her gaze to me. "I know what it's like to love someone that you shouldn't," I whisper as I touch a fingertip to the top of her hand.

"Yes," she whispers. Bingo.

"Does it bother you that he's married?" I ask softly.

"No," she says a little stronger as she looks around to make sure no one is listening. "I don't think he ever really loved her. Elizabeth is so . . . old and stuffy."

"Then why do you think he married her?" Wes asks.

"I don't actually know. He never wanted children. Everyone knew that. Then one day, he's married with two step kids living in his house. It was weird."

"Do you think anything is off in that home? What is their family dynamic like?"

"I don't think there really was much of one, you know? A family dynamic." She takes a deep breath and then continues, "I think there was the family of Elizabeth and her kids, and then I think there was the couple of Elizabeth and Jonathan, and I think there was an image of what they wanted everyone to see."

"What do you mean?"

"I don't think he had anything to really do with the

kids. He and Elizabeth go out all the time and the kids are never with them."

"Where are the kids when they go out?"

"I assume with a sitter if Elizabeth's teenage daughter isn't watching the little boy. I know they preferred her to babysit as much as possible."

Interesting. So, the perfect family was all an act. I already knew that they were a disaster but hearing someone else say it only adds to my theory.

"I just don't get it, you know?" She babbles.

"What don't you get?" Wes asks.

"What did he see in her? Before they got married, he dated women a lot younger . . . and prettier. Sexier maybe," she adds.

I'm not touching that one with a ten-foot pole. I'm sure they'll all find out soon enough what Jonathan Ascher was up to. And it wasn't nice. I only hope Kasey can get the help that she needs to move on from this sad time in her life.

"I think we have all we need," Wes says. "Thank you for your time."

We turn together and head for the door. Wes puts his hand on the small of my back and it burns my skin through my clothes. He's protecting me, claiming me for all to see, but at the same time, respecting me to do what I need to do to run my life and my career. The promise of this particular side of Wes is almost too good to pass up. But I'm still not sure. *Only time will tell.*

chapter 21

trust

"WHAT'S GOING ON HERE?" Wes asks when we climb in the car and shut the doors behind us.

"I have absolutely no fucking idea but I'm going to find out," I say as I buckle my seatbelt.

"I couldn't agree more, babe."

Wes puts the car in gear and we head out, once again. Hopefully find something, anything, to piece this puzzle all together again. I know that I won't be able to rest until I figure out what happened to Anthony and by the look on Wes's face and the set to his shoulders, he won't either.

The phone clipped to Wes's hip rings and he answers it with one hand while driving. Men. I roll my eyes as he talks to whomever is on the phone.

"O'Connell," he answers. "I see . . . We'll get right on it . . . Thanks, Jones," he says before hanging up.

"You can't have Jones, he's mine," I snap.

Wes just raises one dark eyebrow before ignoring my outburst completely.

"It seems you and Jonathan Ascher had something in common," he starts. I just raise my hands out, indicating that he should continue. "You both had shit Chinese for dinner."

"What?" I whisper.

This can't be a coincidence. It just can't. But why would someone want us both dead? Thoughts are swirling through my head as Wes pulls a u-turn and heads back towards my neighborhood. I'd ask him where we are going, but I already know. And I may never be able to eat Mu Shu Chicken again. God damn it. I love Mu Shu Chicken. I don't want to live in a world where Chinese takeout is dangerous to anything other than the size of my ass.

Wes exits the highway and traverses the old, narrow streets of our home town. He pulls into the parking lot of my favorite place, *Szechuan Gardens*. Chinese and Italian places are a dime a dozen in George Washington Township, but this one has been my favorite for as long as I can remember. It appears Wes remembers too.

I look at him, his strong profile in view. His angular jaw covered with dark stubble. He bites his full bottom lip between his teeth but doesn't look at me. Is he afraid of what I will say? I have to say, I'm a little surprised he bothered to pay that much attention to me over the years. I always figured he saw me as little more than a nuisance. It seems there is more to Wes than meets the eye.

He turns the car off and pockets the keys before stepping out. I scramble to catch up to him, but he just stands there waiting for me. Whatever this might be between us, he won't sacrifice my safety over his pride. That is probably the most surprising part of him yet.

Wes pulls the door open for me and the smells of hot and sour soup and fried dumplings fill my nose. I take a deep breath and my belly rumbles loudly. Wes turns to look at me and raises an eyebrow.

"Really, Claire?"

I glare back.

"What? I love Chinese food," I shrug.

Wes just shakes his head like he can't believe that I would go back to eat at a place that should have killed me. Like that is the craziest thing I have ever done in my life. I snicker to myself. Poor Wes. He should really know better. He thinks he wants all of this, well he should figure out sooner rather than later that all off me is a veritable shit show.

Bobby is loading up take out containers in paper sacks as we walk up. I smile brightly at him and wave. If I had to put a name to the emotion that just blew across his face for a split second, I would say it was surprise. To see me? That's weird. I eat here all the time. Well, I order delivery from here all the time. I almost never eat in the restaurant.

"Hey, Bobby!"

"Hey, Claire. What's up?" He asks. "Back for more Mu Shu Chicken so soon?"

I cringe at the mention of my favorite dish, the dish that almost killed me the other night. Although, I should really be thankful because it saved me an evening of torture with Wes's parents. If anything, Judge and Mrs. O'Connell are the biggest reasons that I shouldn't be with Wes. As much as I loved him as a kid, and how hot he is in the sack, they're still major assholes. Wow, it feels good to get that off my chest.

"No," I shudder outwardly. "Not yet."

"I'm Special Agent in Charge Wes O'Connell and I'd like to ask you some questions," Wes starts with his whole title like an idiot. Although, if I had a ridiculous title I'd probably throw it about all over the place too.

"I was just on my way to make a delivery," Bobby says holding up a brown paper sack.

"It won't take too long. I promise," Wes narrows his eyes and probably lies. Somehow, someone here slipped both me and Jonathan Ascher deadly dinners.

"Oh," he hedges, shifting from foot to foot. "I guess that would be ok." Clearly Bobby is uncomfortable, but why?

"Is there somewhere we can go to talk more privately?" I ask.

Bobby turns to look at me full on and really study me. I take the opportunity to do the same. Bobby is about eighteen or nineteen years old and tall. Not as tall as Wes, but Wes was always built like a mack truck. He took after his dad in that way even though his mother is tiny. Bobby, also like Wes, has some bulk on him. His face has the hard planes of a man and the round cheeks of youth. His brown hair, gone just a little too long between trims hangs over his forehead shading kind brown eyes. Bobby is on the cusp of manhood, stuck between a child and an adult. He's a man cub and my friend who delivers me delicious Chinese food.

Bobby leads us to a booth in the back corner of the restaurant. Wes and I sit on one side, Bobby on the other. I slide in first towards the wall and Wes slides in after me. His large, muscular thigh is pressed up against mine and the heat of his body, a body I have come to know every inch of over the last few nights, sears through his pants and my jeans, burning me, branding me as his. My body knows who owns it and there is not one thing I can do about it, for better or worse. But I can't think about that now.

Water glasses sit on the table in front of us and I pick up mine and sip it, letting Bobby know through my actions that this is a casual question and answer. I want to show him that he has nothing to worry about. Bobby and Wes follow suit. We sit silent, not talking as we drink fucking water. Part of me wants to get the show on the road. That's the part with no patience. And the other part of me wants to be as gentle as possible with this sweet kid.

Finally, Wes clears his throat.

"Can you tell me where you were last night?" Wes asks.

"I was working," he stammers. "Here. Why?" He asks but Wes sallies forth.

"On a regular work night, do you ever handle the food?"

"Sure, everyone does," he answers and I hold my breath. "What's this all about?"

"Did you deliver a meal to Detective Goodnite last night?"

"Yeah," he says before looking to me. "Claire, what's this about?" He asks but Wes redirects his attention back to him.

"Did you help prepare the meal that you delivered to Detective Goodnite?"

"I didn't cook it but I boxed it up," he snaps. "What's this all about?"

"Did you deliver a meal to the George Washington Township Police precinct last night?" Wes asks.

"Yeah, why?" He asks. "Tell me what's going on."

"And who did you deliver that meal to?" Wes pushes on.

"A woman," he says. "I can't remember the name. I can look at last night's tickets though. Why?"

"You don't remember the name of the woman?"

"No, why?" Bobby asks.

"You don't remember what she looked like?"

"She was stuffy. Wore one of those button up sweaters with the matching sweater shirt underneath like grandmas wear."

I want to laugh at his description, but I know that he's describing Elizabeth Ascher so I hold my breath. I sit tight and clench my hands into fists on top of my thighs under the table while Wes continues to question Bobby.

"Did she say anything to you at all?"

"No. Yes. Maybe?" He questions. "I don't know. I didn't know I should be paying attention. What's going on, Claire?"

"Did anyone else handle the food that you delivered last night to Detective Goodnite or the meal you brought to the precinct?"

"I don't know. Everyone in the building could have touched it. What's going on?" He asks one last time before losing his cool. "Damn it! Tell me what's going on?"

"Last night, the meals that you delivered to Detective Goodnite and a woman whose husband was in custody contained enough poison to drop an elephant."

"What?" Bobby asks. "It wasn't me! You have to believe me."

I want so badly to tell him that I do. That I don't believe he would ever do anything like that, and I don't, but I need to let Wes handle the questioning. As much as it pains me, I am no longer impartial. But make no mistake, I will nail the bastard to the wall.

"Have you ever seen this child before?" Wes asks as he slides a picture of Anthony Donovan across the table. Bobby looks at it for a second.

"Is this the kid from the news?" He asks.

"This is Anthony Donovan. Have you ever seen him before, other than on the news?"

"No."

"Have you ever seen this man before?" Wes asks sliding Jonathan Ascher's driver's license photo across the table. Bobby again looks at it before sliding it back.

"No."

"Are you sure?" Wes prods.

"Yes."

Again, a one word answer.

"And this woman?"

"That's the woman who ordered the take out last night," he says. "What's this all about?"

"You don't recognize the woman?" Wes asks. "You've never seen her before last night?"

"No, why?"

"You mentioned seeing the child on the local news?"

"Yeah, so?"

"But you've never seen his mother and stepfather before last night?"

"So?" Bobby asks clearly agitated. "What are you

getting at?"

"Nothing," Wes says. "Stay available."

"What does that mean?" Bobby snaps.

"Don't leave town."

Wes unfolds out of the booth like a cheetah stretches. The big cat knows he is the top predator here and has nothing to worry about. I find the movements equal parts annoying and sexy. Annoying because I'm a predator to damnit. But my lady bits are all tingly and can't wait to see his muscles up close and uncovered again. Fuck.

I scrape my hands down my face. This is why I don't fuck coworkers. It's never a good idea to shit where you eat. And now I can't get my head in the game. The realization has me feeling dejected. I should call Anna but I'm afraid one day she'll decide that I'm so fucked in the head that she has to report me to Liam. That would suck, so . . .

I push up out of the booth and follow Wes to the glass doors at the front of the restaurant. He pauses at the entryway and holds the door open for me. I mock curtsey, holding my imaginary dress out wide in my hands. He rolls his eyes at me. I toss my head back and laugh before walking through the door.

"So, what now?" I sigh after we climb into the car and close our doors behind us. I'm feeling down and it shows.

"What's got you down, babe?"

"I don't know," I shrug. "I mean it takes a lot out of a girl getting poisoned and all."

"How about we go to dinner?"

I shrug again, "I don't think I feel up to it."

"How about we go back to my house and order take out?" He asks me.

I raise my eyebrow. "You really think offering take out to a gal who was just poisoned by delivery is a good idea?"

Wes shrugs, "I did not think about that until right this second." I sigh. "How about pizza instead of Chinese?"

"I don't know." I do know. I love pizza and Wes knows it the dirty rat.

"I'll show you my murder board . . ."

"You have a murder board?" I shout.

"Uh huh."

"And you never told me!"

"Nope."

"I don't think I can trust a man who doesn't share his murder board with me," I say petulantly as I fold my arms across my chest.

Wes, the bastard, just throws his head back and laughs. And then drives us towards his house. He better have a fucking murder board. Oh shit. I bet he doesn't!

"You better have a murder board," I glare at him out of the corner of my eye.

"I do," he laughs. "Don't you want to see it?"

"Of course I want to see it!" I snap. "But it better be an actual murder board and not your 'etchings' that you want to show me. Read: your penis."

I didn't think Wes would laugh any harder, but I was wrong. He can. And he did. The bastard. Wes laughs his sexy ass off all the way back to his house. He better show me his murder board. And after that, maybe I'll be interested in seeing his penis again.

chapter 22

don't move

BY THE TIME WES pulls into his driveway the sun is setting and I'm nervous. I don't know how I keep ending up here. With Wes. I keep saying I'm done, that I'm not coming back, but here I am again. This is embarrassing, not just for me, but for women everywhere. I'm being ridiculous and I know it but that doesn't mean I'm about to stop.

"You sure you're alright, Claire?"

"Of course. Why wouldn't I be?"

Wes knows that he can't say because this case is too close. This isn't the first time someone has slipped me a substance that shouldn't have been put into my body and we both know it. I should have died last night, but I didn't. I'm actually alright. But Jonathan Ascher is not.

"Come on," he says as he steps out into the cool evening air. "Let's go figure this out before you think yourself to death."

I roll my eyes and follow him up the front walk to his house. I am careful to keep my distance as he unlocks the door. I need space to keep my head clear until I can't. Wes keeps me confused, my thoughts fuzzy and unfocused. More than anything I want to solve this case. Even more than I want Wes. And I do want him.

He opens the heavy wooden front door and I follow him in. Wes shuts the door behind me and the lock clicks loudly. I have to steel myself not to jump when I realize that he's right behind me.

"Should we order a pie?" He asks, his lips right next to my ear.

"Yes," I whisper as I leap away from him, desperate for distance.

We both know that I am going to fall back into his bed tonight. It's inevitable, but at the same time, I need this moment. To be able to work beside him and get our jobs done before anything else happens. And I think on a deeper level, Wes understands that as much or more than I do.

Wes takes a deep breath and then pulls his cellphone out of his pocket and calls in my favorite pie. First, he knows my favorite Chinese place. Then how I take my coffee and where I get it from. Now he knows my favorite pizza. I'm not sure I can handle how observant Wes has been where I am concerned after all these years.

I wonder if Liam or my dad know. And how they would feel to find out that Wes has been watching—

closely—maybe even a little too closely. Although it's probably all water under the bridge now. Liam and dad have all but physically given me to Wes and I'm not sure how I feel about that. Hell, Liam even welcomed him to the family.

"Well, shall we go see my murder board while we wait?" Wes asks me as he pockets his phone and turns to me.

"Yes, we shall. And this still better not be code for your penis." I link my arm through his elbow which he holds out for me like a gentleman. The action makes me think of the ungentlemanly things he has done to my body over the last few days and my nipples harden. "Well, we better go see this murder board."

He laughs and then walks me down the hall. At the end we could go left towards his bedroom or right towards another set of rooms. Wes turns right. He pushes open the door and there are rows and rows of full bookshelves. In front of that sits a massive, old, oak desk. It must have been his father's from their old home. To the right is a large stone fireplace. Wes tosses in a match with a well practiced hand and the logs ignite. And to the left is a giant whiteboard. The kind that you can roll around and stands on its own. I gasp when I see it.

"I've never seen anything so beautiful." I fake cry as I wipe away an imaginary tear with my fingers.

"You are such a pain in my ass, beautiful," he shakes his head. "You're lucky I know what else you can do with that mouth besides drive me to drink."

"Ugh," I groan. "You just ruined it."

"You want to see it or not?"

"Are we still talking about your murder board or have we switched to your penis?" I ask sweetly. "Because yes to the murder board, maybe but leaning towards probably not for your penis. You're being annoying and I'm over it."

"Over it?" He laughs as he tackles me from the side. We land on a tufted leather sofa that I didn't realize was hiding behind the door.

I let out an embarrassing squeak when Wes grabs me. Some tough chick I am. I land with my back to the sofa and Wes on top of me, his lip crushing down on mine. I can't help it. I kiss him back. My mouth moving under his.

"Why do you fight it?" Wes asks when he tears his lips from mine. "Why do you fight me?"

"I can't," I say as I pull him back down to me. "I can't fight anymore." I kiss him again. I press my body to his. "I can't."

Wes presses his hips into mine. He groans when I buck against his hardness. His body provides the friction that I need in all the right places. I gasp when his cock rubs against me one more time and Wes uses that to his advantage, moving his mouth down to nip at my earlobe. He then drags his lips and scrapes his teeth down my neck where he bites, then soothes my skin with his lips and his tongue.

I pull at the buttons of his dress shirt. Wes sits back

on his heels and undoes the rest of the buttons. I laugh when he pulls his white dress shirt free from his body only to realize that his blue tie is still tied around his neck.

"You think that's funny, do you?" He asks with a sexy smirk playing on his lips.

"Uh huh." I nod. "I do. I really do." I laugh only to moan when he rocks his hips again and his hard length hits me in all the right places.

"Still think it's funny?" He growls.

"Yes," I rasp.

Wes reaches forward and pinches my nipple through my t-shirt and my bra. I arch my back pushing my breast into his palm. The movement presses my core against his cock and we both hiss at the contact.

"Still funny?" He asks as undoes the button on my jeans and pulls down the zipper. I hold my breath as he flattens his palm against my belly and slides his hands into my wet panties against my heat. "Well?"

"Yes," I pant as I rock against him.

Wes slides two fingers deep inside me and I toss my head backwards and arch my spine. He curls his fingers in a come here motion and I am about to come undone. I'm about to come. Wes plays my body like he owns it and I'm beginning to think that he actually does.

"Is it still funny, Claire?" he asks one more time.

"Yes," I buck against his hand. It's not actually

funny but all I can say is yes to Wes as my body shows me truths it has always known. It was always Wes. It will always *be* Wes.

"See, I don't think it's funny when you play games with me Claire," he says his voice rough as he continues to fuck me with his hand. My heat pours between his fingers betraying how much I want him and how much control he actually has. "Do you think it's fun to play games with me, Claire?"

"Yes," I cry out but the words are wrong. He pulls his fingers out just enough that he's not hitting the good spots anymore, but his other hand, flat against my belly, holds me still so I can't use him to find my own completion. "No!" I wail.

"What is it, Claire?" He asks as he swirls his thumb gently against my clit. It's just firm enough to make me moan, but not enough to get me anywhere.

"I'm not playing games!" I cry out, desperate to have him, his fingers, his mouth, his cock, any which way I can have him again.

"When are you going to learn that you can't lie to me, Claire?" He asks as he thrusts his fingers back in, curling them as he goes, but he immediately pulls them back out. "Your body knows the truth. Feel how wet you are for me?" He asks as he wipes his fingers against my inner thighs.

"Please," I beg.

"Please, what?" He commands. "Are you ready to stop fighting me, Claire?" He gives another gentle

228 | jennifer rebecca

swirl to my clit.

"Yes!" I scream as he thrusts his fingers back in, this time adding his thumb to my clit.

I grab the tie that still hangs around his neck and pull it. It anchors me and is something I can hold onto while my world spins wildly out of control.

"That's right, baby. Take it. Take what's mine to give you."

"Fuck! Wes—" He pumps his fingers again and again and then I arch my back and squeeze my eyes tight as I come.

Before my world starts to right itself and I can flutter my eyes, Wes grabs me by my hips and stands me at the arm of the sofa. My legs are still Jell-O and I flop around like April the giraffe's baby. Wes quickly puts a hand to my back between my shoulder blades and arches me over the arm. My hands cushion my fall.

He uses his foot to spread my feet wide and I hear the telltale clink of his belt buckle and the grind of the teeth of his zipper. He still has his hand on my back and it burns my skin. Wes uses his fingers to circle my core. I look back over my shoulder at him and I see the proof of my climax glisten on his fingers. Wes sees me watching and circles my pussy again before holding his fingers up to the light.

"Do you see this?" He asks, his voice rough.

"Y-yes," I stammer. I have to clear my throat before I can answer him clearly. "Yes."

"This is mine, Claire," he says. "This is for me and no one else. Not some asshole from the bar or one of the guys from the station. This is mine and mine alone. Do you understand?" He circles me again. He shoves his finger in deep when I hesitate and I groan.

"Yes," I buck against his hand but he pulls his fingers free and swats my ass. Hard. "Yes! I understand," I cry out when he slips his fingers in one last time.

I look over my shoulder again as Wes locks eyes with me. He swirls his fingers one last time before slipping them from my body. I watch with rapt attention as he raises his hand to his mouth and licks his fingers clean. His eyes roll back in his head and he moans. I could come from watching his face alone.

And then he opens his eyes.

"I always knew there was sweetness hidden in you somewhere, baby. I should have known it was in your tight pussy."

I narrow my eyes and open my mouth to bite back because really, he deserves it but he takes the opportunity to thrust his cock home. We both groan as he circles his hips. This angle makes me take him deep. Wes could go deep before, but Wes like this is a beautiful thing. So beautiful that I forget my earlier irritation.

He circles his hips again and I feel my ass press up against his lower stomach. Wes runs his hands up and down my sides before they come to rest on my ass. He squeezes a cheek in each strong hand before pulling his cock out to the tip and slowly driving it back in.

His fingers bite into my ass as he pulls back out only to slowly slide back in. He does it again and again. It's so slow it's painful. I'm so turned on I need him to fuck me, hard and fast but he won't. I grip the couch cushions in my hands as he glides out again and slowly drives back in.

Wes's grip on my ass tightens as he pushes my cheeks up and separates them. He holds them there, tight. I look back again and watch him as he watches his cock slowly sink into my body over and over again. The look on his face of pure pleasure and passion has me completely undone. And now I need to undo Wes.

Wes pulls back again, but this time I'm ready, with my hips pressed as tight against the sofa as possible. When he moves to glide his cock back in, I use my hands on the cushions to leverage my weight back and impale myself on his hard cock.

Wes's eyes darken and he growls. I lean forward and then thrust back onto his cock again. I repeat my move once more before his grip on my hips tightens and he meets me thrust for thrust.

"Is this how you want it?" He demands.

"Yes," I moan as he pumps hard into my body.

"You want it hard, all you have to do is ask, baby," he croons as he thrust into my body. "And I might see fit to give it to you that way."

"Wes," I plead as he stops to circle his hips.

"But if I want to take my time and watch my cock sink into your sweet pussy, I'm going to," he says as he thrusts home, hard. I whimper and arch my back tipping my hips up, hoping that he'll give in and give me what we both want. "And if I want to fuck you hard, that's what I'm going to do," he says as he pushes all the way in in one quick move.

"Yes," I call. "Wes!"

"Hold on, baby."

"Yes!" I scream as he pumps harder and harder, his cock hitting all the right spots over and over again. I push my hips back against his cock.

"Yeah, baby," he groans and he picks up his pace pumping faster and faster. My climax is barreling at me full speed ahead. I clench around his cock. "Fuck yes, take it! Take my cock," he shouts as he moves faster and faster.

My feet are slipping against the carpet on the floor as the sofa moves just a little bit more with each of Wes's powerful strokes. But I don't care.

"Wes," I plead. It's so strong I don't think that I can take it. I need him. I need Wes. I need his body. I need his strength. And with overwhelming clarity, I know that I need his heart. "Please."

"Come for me, baby," he chants as he pumps faster and faster. "Let go." And I do.

"Wes," I cry as I find my release. Wes thrusts once more before planting his cock deep and following me over the edge, calling out my name as he does.

Sweat rolls down my naked back. Wes's hard,

chiseled chest is flush against my back and his cock is still mostly hard and deep within my core. His face is buried in the crook of my neck and he groans as I clench around his cock once more as the aftershocks still wrack my body. There is so much to say and I don't know how to say it.

"Wes," I whisper.

And then the doorbell rings.

"Saved by the pizza guy," he laughs as he pulls out of my body, pausing to look at my nude frame slumped over the arm of his sofa. "Don't move," he says the smile evident in his voice as he does up his slacks. I realize now he never even bothered to take them off. Something about that is very sexy. "Definitely don't move."

I roll my eyes.

I definitely do not stay with my bare ass on display. As I stand and stretch out my overtaxed muscles, I watch the muscles play in Wes's bare back as he walks down the hall towards the front door.

Once he passes through the room, I scoop up his shirt from the floor and do up a few of the buttons. I leave the cuffs open and loose. I'm just plucking my panties up off of the floor when I hear a throat clear behind me. I peer around my legs as Wes walks in and catches me. He has a large pizza box tucked under his arm and a ridiculous grin on his face.

"I like this look, babe," he says as he sets the pie down on the desk and runs his calloused palm up the back of my thigh and over my bare ass cheek. "I'll be taking these though," he laughs as he snatches the underpants out of my hand.

"Hey!"

"What?" He laughs. "You won't be needing these."

I sigh and walk on over to the pizza box. I pull the lid open and inhale the scent of tomato and basil. My favorite. I pull off a piece and take a huge bite. The hot, melty cheese pulls free and a string catches on my chin.

"Classy," Wes laughs.

I growl and chomp another big bite off to Wes's raucous laughter. He grabs his own piece and a napkin before plopping down onto the sofa. The very same one we just used. I raise my eyebrow but Wes just snuggles in deeper into the cushions.

"This might just be my favorite couch ever," he sighs.

I roll my eyes.

chapter 23

stop

"I JUST DON'T GET it," I say as I crumple my napkin into a ball and toss it into the wastebasket next to Wes's desk. I miss and have to walk over to scoop it up.

"Well, let's figure it out," Wes says as he slams the lid down on the now empty pizza box. He crumples his own napkin and tosses it in the basket . . . and makes it.

I glare.

Wes just laughs.

"Sometimes I really hate you."

"Let's start at the beginning," Wes says seriously, ignoring my competitive outburst.

I roll my eyes again and walk over to where he stares at the murder board. I have to admit, I'm a little jealous. I want my own murder board for my apartment. Why didn't my mom get me one as a housewarming?

Why didn't my dad or Liam for that matter? Oh, that's right, because they don't want me in this field. I sigh to myself. I should have been a teacher or a waitress. They probably would have been pleased as punch if I went out for New York Fire, but I didn't. Tale as old as time . . .

"Alright," I sigh. "Let's start at the beginning."

"On Thursday, Anthony Donovan left Adams Elementary School with his older sister, Kasey Donovan, and returned to the residence at 1312 Orange Drive that they shared with their biological mother, Elizabeth Ascher and her new husband, Jonathan Ascher, now deceased," he recites.

"Kasey Donovan, sixteen years of age, is the oldest child of Elizabeth Donovan Ascher and Anthony Donovan, Senior. Older sister to Anthony Donovan, Junior, age six years old."

"By all appearances, Kasey is the perfect teenager. Babysits her younger brother regularly. Gets good grades in school. She's picture perfect," he adds.

"Yeah, right," I snort.

"I said picture perfect, not that she is!"

"Yeah, Lolita is definitely not perfect," I say snidely, but the minute I think of her stepfather abusing her I sober. All my earlier humor lost.

"You didn't know, Claire," Wes says softly.

"I know, but I do now. Moving on."

"Kasey Donovan is perfect at face value, but behind closed doors, she's engaging in an inappropriate relationship with her stepfather, Jonathan Ascher."

"And let's not forget illegal. Speaking of Jonathan Ascher, forty-two years old, works for GWP Savings and Loan. He was newly married to Elizabeth Donovan Ascher after her divorce from Anthony Donovan."

"And even more newly dead," I add helpfully.

Wes rolls his eyes but the smile on his face is indulgent, loving even, and softens the blow of his annoyance.

"Married to Elizabeth Donovan Ascher," Wes talks over me, obviously ready to move on now.

I sigh, picking up where he left off. "Elizabeth Ascher, forty years old. Previously married to Anthony Donovan, Senior. Mother to Kasey and Anthony Donovan. Previously worked for GWP Savings and Loan," I add.

"By all evidence, looked the other way while her husband was molesting her teenage daughter," Wes snaps. Obviously angered by how awful her mother actually is.

"Showed signs of jealousy over her husband's relationship with her daughter."

"We witnessed an altercation between mother and daughter over the stepfather," Wes adds.

"We also witnessed an altercation between the father and stepfather over the illicit relationship Jonathan Ascher was engaging in with Kasey Donovan," I said using finger quotes over the word altercation.

"Wouldn't you be pissed if she was your daughter?"

"Oh yeah, I would have kicked Ascher's ass WWE style," I laugh.

"That brings us to Anthony Donovan, Senior, forty-six years of age. Previously married to Elizabeth Donovan Ascher. Is an executive for Kline Mini Blinds. Biological father of Kasey and Anthony Donovan."

"Was visibly distraught over the disappearance and murder of his son," I chime in.

"The rest of the immediate family was oddly . . . *not*." Wes runs a hand over the stubble on his jaw as he turns over the information in his mind.

"Mrs. Ascher said Kasey was too upset to be interviewed the day that Anthony disappeared."

"But then you were poisoned."

"And Jonathan Ascher got dead," I add. "Kasey wouldn't do that. She claims to love him," I shudder.

"Elizabeth Ascher claims to be in love with him as well," Wes comments. "So, I doubt she would poison him either. But I think she would poison you."

"Thanks ever so much, dearest," I narrow my eyes on him when he laughs. "Anthony Donovan would kill Jonathan Ascher."

"But he is still in lock up," Wes shoots down my easy answer. "And the kid at the Chinese place identified Elizabeth Ascher is who he delivered the take-out dinner to."

"Bobby," I remind him.

"Who?"

"Bobby, the boy who delivers for the Chinese place by my apartment," I say and shudder. God damnit, I love Mu Shu Chicken! And I can never eat it again.

"You close with him?" Wes barks taking me by surprise.

"What?" I ask back. "No. Of course not. Well, kind of. I mean he delivers me take-out Chinese like twice a week. Maybe more."

"He did know your preferences. Should I be worried?"

"Don't be ridiculous," I roll my eyes. "So, he knows what I like," I shrug my shoulder in a so what effect.

"I know what you like," Wes says in a super douchey come on and I laugh. I laugh until he tackles me to the floor in front of the fireplace.

I let out an eep as we fall to the floor. Wes moves his body to take the brunt of the fall. I land on my back with Wes on top of me, he keeps his weight on his knees so that he doesn't squish me. His hips are between my thighs which instinctively open for him.

I laugh. Playful Wes is one I could use more of. He is so serious most of the time that it's nice to see him be able to cut loose once in awhile. Especially in the middle of a tough case.

"I think it's time I take possession back of my property that was wrongfully acquired," he says seriously as he begins to unbutton the buttons on his shirt. Wes pushes the two sides open, parting them, and grazes the outer sides of my breasts with his fingertips. "So beautiful," he whispers, almost to himself.

"Wes," I whisper as I take notice of the adoration in his face. For so long as a girl, I wanted Wes to notice me, to look at me this way, it's almost too much to hope. I think he has finally worn me down. "W—," I start but I don't get the words out because he presses his lips to mine.

This kiss is different. This time feels different. As Wes gently touches his mouth to mine, I can't help but feel like everything is changing. Is it possible to get everything you once hoped for?

I can't help but open my mouth to him under his lips and Wes gently licks in, his tongue tangling with mine. He moves his hands over my collarbone and down to my breasts where he holds them, weighs them in his hands. Wes skates his thumbs over my nipples and they harden under his touch.

He sits up on his heels in between my parted legs and softly tugs on one of the sleeves of the shirt I'm wearing until my arm slips free. Then he repeats the process with the other side before tossing the shirt aside. I fight the urge to cover myself as he sits and silently stares at my naked body.

I finally give in and wrap my arm over my breasts. I turn my head slightly to one side and avert my gaze, but it's when I try and close my legs that Wes finally stops me, pulling my arm back to uncover my breasts before placing his palms to my thighs and gently opening my legs for his inspection. My face heats at his attentions.

"Don't hide from me, Claire," he whispers. "Not ever."

"Wes," I say feeling the weight of the moment.

"I could look at you forever."

I open my mouth to say something but Wes moves like a big cat, all graceful sudden movements. He folds his body over mine and silences my words with his mouth. And what a mouth it is so I leave those words unsaid. For now.

As it always is with Wes, my body heats and is primed with just a few kisses. He knows this too so when he runs his fingers through my wetness he is not surprised and just groans against my mouth. One hand holds his body up, hovering over mine, while the other opens the fly on his slacks. His mouth touched to mine with his eyes open and trained on mine the whole time.

Wes slides his hard cock through my arousal before plunging all the way in. I lift my legs high on his hips and wrap them around his waist. He slides out of my body all the way to the tip and I wrap my arms around his neck pulling him close to me. This time I need close. I think Wes needs it too.

Wes glides effortlessly in and out of my center as I cling to him. I need to be as close to him as possible. The base of his cock rubs against my clit as I wiggle against him, making me try to force Wes to go faster but he continues to keep his pace slow. I growl and he smiles against my mouth. Wes doesn't pick up the pace, but instead swivels his hips so he grinds against my clit as he hits all the right spots.

And then it builds. The burning starts in the pit of my belly. A fire lit when I wasn't even paying attention. But Wes knew. He always knows me. He has always known me. What I wanted. What I needed.

"Wes," I gasp as it washes over me like gentle waves in a bay.

"I'm right here, baby," he says as his own climax washes over him. "I'm always here."

And he is.

We lay here on the plush rug in front of the fireplace. The sweat cooling on our skin. The look in his eyes as he brushes the hair back from my face is one I want to remember for the rest of my life. I want to hold onto this moment and whatever may come, no matter when or where, no matter how hard times may be, I can pull out the memory of this tender moment with Wes. And I know that I will.

"It's time, baby," he says softly his voice rough.

"What time?" I ask smiling up into his handsome face.

"We have to talk about it."

And I know he doesn't mean the Donovan case. Wes wants to talk about my case. My own disappearance and kidnapping. And I know that I cannot. I will not. My body goes tight. Wes's does too and I know that he has registered the change in me.

"I don't know what you're talking about."

"You do," he tells me. When I don't answer he pushes on. "You were six years old when you were kidnapped."

"Wes," I plead.

"Liam and I were both sixteen and didn't want to be saddled with a little kid so we pushed you away, told you to leave us alone so that we could talk about girls like Kira McIntire and her early developments."

"If by that you mean her bra stuffed full of Kleenex," I snap. "Then, yes."

"So, you do remember?" He asks me with a raised eyebrow.

"I don't want to talk about it."

Wes strokes my cheek with his fingertips before speaking. "A man in a white van took you, drugged you."

"Stop."

"He abused you," Wes chokes out.

"Wes, stop." But he doesn't.

"We looked for you. For days, Liam and I got all of our friends to help search the woods for you. For so many nights I thought, 'Will tomorrow be the day that we find her body in the woods?'" His breath catches in his throat.

"Wes."

"I thought, 'it's all my fault. If we had just let her follow us around one more day. If we'd of just been a little less selfish, none of this would have happened.' But it *did* happen. And I carry that guilt every day, Claire."

"Well, you shouldn't," I snap.

"Don't you have any feelings you want to share with me about that time, baby?" He pleads. Wes is begging me to open up to him and I want to, but I just . . . *can't*. So, I lie.

"I don't honestly remember anything from that time Wes. So, put your guilt aside. I'm fine," I lie through my teeth. The look on his face says he doesn't believe me for one second, so I switch tactics and change the subject. "Besides, I'm hungry," I say as I roll over, gently nudging Wes over to his back.

I take his rising cock in my hand and gently run my fist over it. He begins to fill and harden in my hand. I squeeze him in my fist and his breath catches. I pump him in my fist a little faster.

"Claire, babe, we-we-we're not done here."

"I know, baby, we're not done here, not by a long shot," I say as I lean down, brushing my hair to the side over my shoulder, as I take him into my mouth.

Wes groans as I swirl the tip in my mouth before sliding down as far as I can take him before I choke. That is never attractive. I come back up and swirl the tip again, this time, pumping him in my fist as I go before sliding down again.

I rub my legs together like a cricket as I suck on his cock, turning myself on as I go, so I slide my free hand in between my legs. I moan around his length as my fingers find my clit.

"Claire," Wes growls when he sees me start to get myself off. "You better not make yourself come."

Wes pulls my hand out from between my legs, pulling me up, up, up, until he can suck my fingers into his mouth licking away my wetness. But he pulled me so far, I had to let go of his cock which is now throbbing against my center as I straddle his waist.

"I could probably meet all of your demands, Agent." I smirk as I rise up on my knees and sink down on his cock.

Wes's hips buck underneath me and I lean back, reveling in the fullness of him. I lift my head and look in his dark blue eyes. Then I rise up and slam back down. His fingertips dig into the fleshy part of my thighs. I rise up and slam back down again and again and again. Neither of us will last long this way and that's fine by me. I want—no, I *need*—Wes so lost to his lust that he forgets all about the questions he wants answered. Questions I will do anything to avoid, obviously. By the look in his eyes as we fuck on the floor, Wes knows it too. He always did see me just a little too clearly.

Sweat rolls down my spine as I rise up on my knees and slam back down over his cock. Wes watches where his body meets mine, letting me have this moment. His hips come up to meet mine thrust for thrust as I ride his cock.

"Claire," he says through gritted teeth. "I'm almost there."

"I know," I say as I move faster and faster chasing my own climax and his. I'm almost there. Almost. One more time, I rise up and slam back down. I rake my nails down his chest.

"Baby, I'm . . . I'm," he says as I rise up one last time and slam back down over his cock, taking us both over the edge, together.

I lay sprawled over his body, his cock still inside me, the mixture of our sweat making our skin stick together. Our breathing evens out and then sleep takes me. My last conscious thought is this is bliss.

It's dark. So dark. At night my mommy leaves a night-light on for me and my favorite piggy stuffed animal that I've had for ages to help me sleep. I hate the dark. Monsters only lurk in the dark. I want my mommy but I can't cry. If I cry, the bad man will come and he will hurt me again. He always hurts me. Even though I don't want him to, I know, he always comes, but this time I will be ready.

I was digging in the closet when I knew that he was asleep. I found a pile of old junk. He must have been too lazy to clean out the closet that has been my prison for I don't know how long. But his laziness is my win. In the corner under the pile of old stuff, I found a baseball and then a glove, and in the very bottom of the pile, I found an old metal bat. Just like the kind Liam and Wes used when they were my age.

Sometimes it pays to be the little sister. My whole life I've been following Wes and Liam around hoping that they would play with me. I even told Wes that one day he would marry me. He just laughed and said, "I'm not so sure about that, squirt." That's what he calls me. Squirt.

So, all the times, I followed them around when they played ball or walked in the woods finally is going to pay off even if Wes never wants to marry me because I learned how to swing a baseball bat watching them. I learned to run through the woods following them. I am going to run away from the bad man because of all that I watched them do.

So, I wait. And I wait and I wait and I wait. I almost fall asleep. Almost. I feel my eyelids getting heavy but then I hear footsteps and I know that he's coming. He always comes.

I sit quietly and try not to make any noise. I hurry to my feet and grab my bat. I crouch in the corner with the bat over my shoulder just like Liam showed me how to do. When I hear the lock that he keeps on the closet door open I know that it's time.

My hands sweat and I feel shaky all over.

"Wake up, Claire, it's time," he says as he pulls open the closet door. "What are you doing?" He asks when he sees me but I don't answer. I swing the bat as hard as I can, hitting him in his big belly.

When the bad man falls forward, I swing one more time, hitting the side of his head just like Liam and Wes taught me to hit a baseball when I finally got them to include me. And then I run.

I run out of the closet while the bad man screams my name. I run out of the ugly house that smells funny and then I run out into the woods.

I run and I run and I run.

I don't hear him, but he's a sneaky man, I have to be smart. I look all around me. The sun is just setting to my left. I close my eyes and hear water to my right. And then I know where I am. I turn a little to the right, towards the water, and I run as fast as I can.

But I'm slow. Slower than I can usually run. I'm so tired. I haven't slept since I woke up on the dirty blanket in his stinky living room. My belly hurts, he doesn't give me much to eat either. But I have to run. I have to get home to mommy and daddy and Liam and Wes. Even if they're mad at me, I have to get home. Away from the bad man.

My feet don't feel like they can go much farther, but I see the clearing up ahead. I know my house is just beyond those trees! So I push my legs and run faster and faster.

"What's that, Wes?" I hear Liam ask.

It's me! But I can't shout. I'm breathing too hard from running. I just break through the trees and I think I see Wes, but it's blurry, my eyes are blurry.

"Lee, it's Claire!" He shouts. "It's Claire! I got her, Lee. I got her!" He shouts.

I can hear his feet running on the grass and the dirt the twigs crunching under his feet as they eat up the ground to me. But when he sees me. He sees my swollen face and dirty t-shirt and panties his face looks awful. So awful I want to cry. I don't ever want to see Wes look at me that way again. But it turns out I don't have to because as he shouts my name, everything goes black.

"Claire!" Wes shouts and he shakes me. "Claire!"

Someone is screaming. It's me. I'm screaming. I can't let the bad man get to me again. He can't get to me again. He can't find me. I have to run home. I have to find my family.

"Claire!" someone shouts. "Claire wake up, you're dreaming," he shouts shaking me again.

It's Wes. I'm safe, I'm finally safe. I open my eyes, see a grown-up Wes, and remember where I am. Naked on the floor tangled up with Wes. I smile until I see the look on his face. It's the same horrified look he had worn the day I made it home. Wes doesn't know that I remember, but I remember everything. But I especially remember that horrified look I have seen on him twice before, three times including now.

The first time was the day I made it home, the second was the morning I woke up with him after bequeathing him my virginity at the ripe old age of eighteen, and the third time is now. Now when I finally realized how badly I wanted him, a life with him, how close within my reach it was, only for him to discover that I am just as broken as he always knew I was. The funny thing is I knew we would eventually get here, and yet, I was helpless to stop it.

"Claire," he whispers but I can't bare to look at him.

I jump up and grab his shirt pulling it on swiftly and wrapping it tight around my body. I start grabbing my clothes off of the floor of his study. I race around the room plucking them up as I go.

"Don't do this, Claire," he pleads as he jumps up and gets in my space, crowding me in.

"No!" I shout as I duck under his arms and race around him.

I run down the hall with my clothes balled up in my arms. I find a downstairs powder room and rush inside, slamming the door shut and locking it just as Wes reaches the door. He pounds on it with his fists so hard that the door shakes. He is pounding so hard I'm afraid that he will knock it off of the hinges.

"Don't do this, Claire," he shouts. "Let me in."

I turn on the water in the sink so I can't hear him.

I splash some water on my face to cool my overheated skin down, but I know it's the combination humiliation and the lasting effects of the dream that still have me in its clutches.

I leave the water running and pull on my jeans and t-shirt. Once again going without my bra and panties. God, I'm such a tramp. My mother will need to light thirty candles and I'll need to say two hundred hail Mary's just for this month alone. It's moments like this, I halfway wish the poison killed me.

"God damn it, Claire! Open the fucking door!" He roars.

I'm running out of time. I need to figure out what I'm going to do. I know that I can't go back out there and face him like this. I just can't. I know that I won't survive it.

"Lee, I need you," I hear him bark into his phone. "Something's happened . . . It's Claire."

I need to get out of here, but how? I turn around looking everywhere. Over my shoulder and take stock of the room. A mirrored medicine cabinet, commode, towel rack, sink basin and cabinet . . . and then I see it. There is a small window at the top of the wall perpendicular to the toilet. It's small, but I'll fit. I climb up onto the toilet seat and unlatch the window. The glass panel tips out smoothly. Hooray for Wes and his anal-retentive home repair schedule!

"Please, Claire," he pleads as he pounds on the door again. "Fuck! Let me in or else I'll break this door down and I'm rather fond of this fucking door."

I grab onto the window ledge and start to pull. Fuck I'm out of shape. No more beer and onion rings for awhile. Oh shit. I might have to start running. Actually, that sounds like a great idea. I think I'll take up running right now, just like the chickenshit that I am.

"One . . ."

I get my head and shoulders through the window. The only way I'll fit is head first. Fuck, sometimes I hate my life. My need for self-preservation is warring with my need for survival.

"Two . . ."

Self-preservation wins out as I dive head first into the bushes. Executing my best tuck and roll as I go. I'm barefoot and running down the street when I hear Wes one last time.

"Three!" He shouts and then I hear him clip out, *"Fuck!"* when he realizes that I'm gone but I keep running and running.

The icy cold sidewalk is burning the soles of my feet but I can't stop. Like that god damned fish in the movie, I just keep swimming. I just keep running a path of streets and turns until I'm sure that he can't find me. I'm not ready for him to find me even though I know that he eventually will.

I pause in an alleyway when I realize my jeans still have my badge and sidearm clipped to the hips. I have just been fucked hair, running makeup, and no shoes on my feet. My boots are back on the floor of Wes's study with my drop gun and it's ankle holster. In other words, I look like a crazy person.

That's when I realize that my cellphone is still in the back pocket of my jeans. I whip it out and dial the one number that I know by heart. The one person that I know I can turn to even though I know that I shouldn't. That one day, I will call this number one too many times and it will cost me everything.

They pick up on the first ring just like I knew they would and before they can answer I say, "Anna, I need you."

chapter 24

low blow

"GET IN, LOSER. WE'RE going shopping," she shouts when the wheels of her white Mercedes screech to a stop.

I sigh and open the door. "Really, Anna?" I question her.

"What?" She shrugs. "I love that movie." But the wide smile slides right off of her face when she sees me.

"Sometimes it's hard to picture you as a world renowned shrink," I say as I climb in her car and the door quietly closes behind me.

"Psychiatrist, I'm not a shrink," she sighs.

I pull my belt across my chest and then sit staring at my hands in my lap. I scrub at the dirt on my palms that only I can see. Anna interrupts my Lady Macbeth routine.

"What happened, Claire?" She asks. "You're scaring me," she says when I don't answer.

"It's all falling apart?" I whimper.

"What is?" She asks.

I look over my shoulder. "My case, my life . . . *me*."

"Claire, look at me," she softly commands.

"Can we get out of here?" I ask, still looking over my shoulder. I'm not ready to be found.

"Okay, babe. Let's get you out of here."

She drives us back through the quiet streets of New Jersey. The interior of the car is dark but the streetlights we pass give short glimpses of illumination. I would like to find some symbolism in that, but I know in my heart of hearts, there is none to be found. In my world, there can only be darkness.

Anna pulls into the driveway of her suburban home, an old Victorian. Not huge, not small, with one bathroom. Otherwise, it's perfect and very Anna. She shuts of the engine and steps out of the car. I follow her into the house when she unlocks the door.

Anna sets her keys and purse on the table in the entryway before moving through the house straight to the kitchen. I follow her in my dirty, bare feet. She pulls an old, well used kettle off of the stove and moves it to the sink to fill it with water. I watch as she sets it back on the burner while switching on the knob. She pulls mugs out of the cupboard above the coffeemaker and then a box of tea out of the pantry and sets them both on the island countertop that separates her from me.

Anna stops to take a hard look at me. I feel laid bare, like she sees everything I wish to keep to myself. The things I most need to keep hidden. Finally, she looks away, having taken the pulse of me and the situation, before she moves back to the small pantry and pulls down a bottle of bourbon from a top shelf, and slams it down onto the counter with the tea and the mugs just as the whistle blows.

"Well," she sighs. "How are we taking our tea tonight?" She asks as she pours hot water into the mugs before depositing tea bags in the steaming liquid.

I look her dead in the eyes. "With bourbon."

She sighs as she uncorks the bottle and pours with a hand so heavy that it reminds me why we're friends. Finally, she passes me a mug across the large marble countertop before grabbing her own.

"Let's go sit down and get the shit part over with," she sighs before heading into a comfortable living room.

It's a large yet cozy room with big windows and tan walls. There are big, squishy corduroy couches that could swallow you whole. A large glass topped coffee table sits in the middle of a multicolored rug over dark hardwood floors. I love this room.

Anna sits in the corner of one of the huge sofas and I sit as far away as possible on the other one. She sighs. Anna knows that this can't possibly be good if I need distance from her, but she never lets the hurt my actions cause show on her face.

I take a long sip of my tea and let out a huge breath. Anna is visibly frustrated.

"Are you going to tell me what the fuck is going on or what?" She finally snaps.

"How very therapeutic of you," I joke. "Is this a new method?"

"Not funny, Claire, and you know it."

"I do, I'm sorry," I whisper tears stinging my eyes. "I-I just . . . I'm just so overwhelmed and I don't know what to do."

"I do," she sighs. "You start at the beginning and tell me everything. As your friend, not your shrink."

"Okay," I say and then I do. I tell Anna all about the nightmares which really are horrible memories.

I tell her about little Anthony Donovan and how I can't tell up from down with his case and the guilt that I feel that I escaped, that I survived and so many kids don't. I tell her how I'm beginning to fear that Wes and Liam are right and that I have no place in law enforcement and how much that hurts because I love it more than anything. I love following in my dad and my brother's footsteps. I tell her all about Wes and how much I'm afraid to love him. I tell her about all of the amazing sex and how sure he's been that we were meant to be together right up until I had another nightmare when I was with him and it transported me right back to twelve years ago when he broke my heart. I tell her about the look on his face. How he pities me and how he now knows that I was right all along, that we could never really be together. And then I told her how I bolted in a panic.

Anna sits there wide-eyed staring at me for what feels like forever. Finally, she slowly blinks once, twice, and then slams back all of her bourbon doctored tea and slams the mug on the coffee table before looking back up at me.

She blinks. "Other than that Mrs. Lincoln, how did you enjoy the play?"

I slow blink.

I stare at her like an idiot for who know how long. Was she not listening? Does she not understand what a shit show my life has turned into? I continue to sit there and stare at her, not saying a word. My mug is cooling in my hands but the residual warmth keeps me grounded.

"Say something," she implores. "You're scaring me."

I shot the last of my mostly bourbon tea back and slam my mug down on the coffee table in front of me. I narrow my eyes on her. She throws her arms up in the over her head in a "well?" motion.

"Are you listening to me at all?" I shout.

"Yeah, so?"

"So? So? So my life is fucking falling apart!" I shout standing up.

"No it's not!" She stands, screaming in my face

258 | jennifer rebecca

right back.

"How so?"

"Okay, I'll tell you," she shouts. "One, you are not broken. Two, you are the toughest woman I know. Three, you are a survivor. You survived everything that you have for a reason. Hear me out," she says when I open my mouth to correct her. "You couldn't save this boy. I know that that hurts, but maybe he wasn't save-able."

"What?" I ask as she turns my brain around in a different direction than the one my thoughts were originally going in.

"You said it yourself the other day, there was never a ransom," she reminds me.

There's something niggling at the back of my mind, but before I can give it a chance to break free, Anna is back in my face throwing old shit at me. If I didn't love her so much, I would wonder why we're friends.

"And there is definitely something there with Wes."

I growl.

"Don't argue with me," she snaps. "I'm right and you know it. And it's more than just the past. That was then, this is now," she finishes triumphantly, pointing her index finger aggressively towards the carpet. Anna would make a great politician. Or third world dictator.

I sigh. "It's both. It's then and now," I say look at the ground, my hands still on my hips. "I don't want to want him. But I do," I whisper as my eyes fill with tears.

"I know, honey," she says as she moves towards me and wraps her arms around me.

I put my head on Anna's shoulder and cry. For the first time in a long time I don't feel so alone. I have a friend. In my heart I know that I'm not alone, but my head does funny things with the information. The truth is, I have a loving family and great friends in Emma and Anna, in my life if I let them.

"Thank you," say through a watery smile.

"For what?" She asks.

"For not making fun of me when I became such a whiny girl. I swear it was just for a moment," I laugh.

"Anytime," she laughs too. "Now, what are we going to do about this man?" She asks.

I sigh, "I have no fucking idea."

"I have one," she says softly, a knowing smirk playing on her mouth. I also know I don't want to hear what she has to say.

"I already told you, Anna, you're good looking but I'm not interested, I like a huuuugggeee . . ."

"Ha!" She scoffs. "Like you could get me into bed."

"Don't be jealous because you don't do it for me," I tease.

"I bet Wes does it for you," she says just under her breath.

"What?" I shout. "Low blow!"

"And I bet he's got that huge . . ."

"Low. Fucking. Blow. Anna!" I shout at the top of my lungs. She just laughs, the bitch.

"I'm just saying," she laughs. "Maybe you already found what you've been looking for," She shrugs.

"And what about you?" I ask.

"Maybe I already found it too but it slipped right through my fingers."

I look at Anna more closely than I have over the last year. Maybe there's more to her than I realized. Or maybe I'm a really shitty friend and I just never bothered to ask. Why is she even friends with me?

"Do you want to talk about it?" I ask.

"Not even a little bit," She looks over her shoulder.

"Well hello, Pot. It's nice to meet you, my name is Kettle," I say as I try to lighten the mood. When she rolls her eyes, I know that it worked.

She sighs heavily. "He decided undercover work was more important than me. Thought he could drop me like a bad habit for two years and I would be happily waiting for him when he surfaced. I don't even know if he's still alive." She shrugs. "I'm just saying, it's old news," she says before she visibly brightens and her eyes twinkle with wicked glee. Well, fuck. "Wes on the other hand, is breaking news."

"Ugh, don't remind me," I say as I cover my face with my hands.

"I take it you have seen the coverage your case is getting?"

"Speaking of old news . . ." I sigh. "And yeah, I did. I wish they would forget about it. I wish everyone would just freaking forget about it."

"Everyone else will move on when you have," Anna says softly.

"What makes you think I haven't?"

"Do I look like I'm new here?" She asks as she rolls her eyes.

"No," I concede.

"You'll get there," Anna assures me.

"I'm not so sure that I will," I say. "Too many things are bubbling just under the surface. I feel like I'm drowning and I can't pull myself out of it."

"Maybe you just need to reach for one of the hands that's been waiting to pull you out," she says softly. "We've all been waiting, Claire. All you have to do is reach out."

"I know. Maybe one day I will."

"You will," she smiles confidently.

"Can you take me to my car?"

"Yay! I love walks of shame!" She claps her hands with glee.

"Why do I keep you?"

"Because you love me best," she smiles brilliantly.

"That I do."

"Now say please and thank you and I will not only take you to your car, but I will give you my spare set of keys to said car and your apartment."

"Please and thank you!" I jump up excited. I had forgotten about my keys which are probably somewhere in Wes's house. "You're the bestest ever!"

"Thank you! What have I been trying to tell you all this time?"

chapter 25

how long

"NO BRA? CHECK," ANNA ticks off on her fingers as she pulls into a spot in front of the station.

"Anna."

"No shoes? Check."

"Anna."

"No wallet or purse? Check check."

"This is unnecessary."

"Do you want my spare keys or not?" She asks triumphantly.

"You know I could just shoot you, right?"

"You won't," she shrugs. I'm getting more and more frustrated by the minute as she dangles them just out of reach.

"Anna."

"Hair that says you've definitely just been fucked and well fucked at that? Check!"

"This is beneath you," I add.

"Your brother and Wes staring at you from the front door of the station?" She prattles on.

"What?" I look over to where she's looking and sure enough there they are. They look both worried and pissed.

" . . . Check!"

"God damn it, Anna. Give me the fucking keys!" I shout.

"Don't do anything I wouldn't do!" She cheers as she tosses me the keyring.

I snatch the keys out of the air and take off running barefoot towards my SUV. Wes and Liam see me and hot foot it in the same direction but they'll never reach me in time. I am significantly closer to the car than they are. And I'm faster.

"Don't do it, Claire!" Liam shouts.

"Claire!" Wes calls for me, but I can't look at him. Not right now. Maybe not ever.

"Not now," I shout as I beep the locks.

"Please! We have to talk," he pleads.

The minute my hand hits the door handle, my foot is on the running board and I'm jumping into the car. I hit the door locks as soon as the driver door closes. My hands are shaking so bad, it takes me three tries to get the key in the ignition. It causes me to lose precious time that I could be using to escape.

Wes pulls on the handle of the passenger door as he pounds on the window. I get the engine to turn over and put the car in reverse.

"Claire," he shouts as he pounds on the window. "Let me in, baby."

I shake my head no, looking straight ahead.

"Please, baby. You have to talk to me. We have to talk about this."

"No," I say quietly but I know he hears me by the way his pounding on my passenger window becomes more frantic.

"This is fucking crazy, Claire!" He roars. "Let me the fuck in. Now!"

"No," I say as I start to back out of my spot.

"Claire," Liam shouts from behind Wes. "This is ridiculous. Get out of the fucking car."

"No."

"Claire, baby, get out of the car," Wes goes back to pleading.

"Claire, I will fucking fire you if you don't get out of that car and talk to Wes and I right the fuck now," Liam barks.

I shake my head. I can't. I can't look at them and have them see me as weak and broken. They know that I am and so do I, but I just can't face it. I can't watch Wes shut me out again because of it.

I tap the gas again.

"Stop, Claire!"

"No," I say. "I can't."

I keep backing up. I'm almost out of the parking spot when Wes hits the window so hard I think he might break the glass.

"God damnit, Claire. I fucking love you!" He thunders, but it's too late.

"I'm sorry," I say as I drive away. "I told you you shouldn't," I whisper to no one.

It was always too late for us. It was too late when that man took me and it was too late for us when I stumbled into his arms when I escaped. It was too late when I gave Wes my virginity and he threw it all back in my face. And it sure as hell was too late now when he blew into my life like a hurricane and he'll blow back out leaving the same wake of destruction.

We were simply never meant to be.

The drive back to my apartment is not a silent one.

My phone rings over and over again from the cup holder next to me. It rings again. I pick it up and look at the screen . . . *Wes.* Again. I silence it and keep driving.

It rings again and I sigh, frustrated. I stop at another red light. I pick up my phone again and look . . . *Liam.* Fuck. I silence it and hit the gas when the light turns green.

I know that they will both be looking for me. They want to convince me, sway me around to their way of thinking. As I sit in my car, I realize that they always do. Liam plays the protective big brother who recruits our father when he needs to for his cause. Dad is ever so helpful when it comes to thwarting my plans.

And don't even get me started on Wes. Wes does not dote on me in an effort to force me into compliance. Oh, no. Wes fights with me and fucks me into his way of thinking. And he's good at it.

It is no secret that I was in love with Wes from the time I was a little girl. A harmless crush, that's what my mother had said. But over time it has blossomed into something more. I had thought that he would always be the one.

In my youthful naivete I thought that Wes would come home from the Navy to me. And in a way, he did. I was a newly minted eighteen-year-old when Wes and Liam came home on leave and for the first time, Wes had looked at me the way that I had always hoped for—the way I yearned for—and so I gave him everything I had. I gave him my body and my heart. Simply put, I had given Wes *me*.

And at the first hurdle, he turned his back on me.

But now he's back. This week, Wes returned to my life like an unruly storm over the sea and I was helpless to stop him. If I was being honest with myself—which I am *definitely* not—I would admit that I have never stopped loving Wes and he knew it. He seized upon it and made me feel like I had something to hold onto, something to believe in. Again.

Wes gave me his body, his magnificent body, which has only gotten better with time. He is no longer the lean twenty something, but a man bulky with muscle and lines around his beautiful eyes that show he both scowls and laughs and does both of them often, but in the sexiest of ways. And when he turned those eyes on me, I was hopeless. Oh, I fought, I did, but looking back now, I can see that he always knew I would fall to him, I would fall for him. Again. I probably always will. I can't say that this makes me feel good things for my future.

I pull into the parking lot of my apartment building and realize I can't park in my usual spot. Wes and Liam will see me at first glance and know that I'm back in my space. I drive right past my usual section and pull around back of the building and park there. I will have to walk a bit to and from my vehicle but it should give me at least one extra day before I have to deal with the two cave men. And possibly a third of slightly advanced age.

I step out of my department SUV and look back at it after I get a few steps away. I can't help but wonder if today will be the day that Liam manages to take it from me. To take everything away from me. It's not just the car, it's my job, my livelihood, my way of life, but all my hopes and dreams too. Why can't I be the one to catch the bad guy? Why does it get to be them? Because they have the dicks, obviously. Or they are dicks.

I sigh and beep the locks before heading around to the front of the building. The metal steps leading to my front door are so cold and icy that they burn my bare feet. But I can't rush them. There is a weariness that has settled in my bones and I can't seem to make my body move any faster. In my head I know that this is just the adrenaline let down after my last great escape, but in my heart I can't help but feel like everything is coming to a head and I just might not come out on the winning side.

I let myself into my apartment, quickly shutting and locking the door behind me. Not that it will stop Wes and Liam. I'm sure they could con my spare key from mom and dad in a heartbeat if they played the situation right. I'm pretty sure they could con the panties off of a nun with the intentions of a three way if they played the situation right, but that's neither here nor there.

My phone starts ringing again. This time I don't even stop to look at it. I just toss it onto the sofa after silencing it and keep walking towards my little bathroom, shutting that door behind me too. I turn the water to as hot as it will go which isn't much in this old building, but at this point, I'll take what I can get.

I strip off all of the clothes that I could manage to find over the floors and furniture of Wes's house, which is most definitely not a full set, onto the floor of my bathroom unceremoniously. I kind of want to dump them straight into the garbage, but those are my favorite jeans and I already lost my favorite boots this week.

Speaking of garbage, I can't help but turn my thoughts to the garbage bags that were stolen from the dumpster of my place. Who would want to cover their tracks badly enough to steal my kitchen trash? And for that matter, who would poison me? Besides Wes's mom, that is. I'm sure she wouldn't shed any tears if I left this world a little earlier than originally scheduled.

The scalding hot water sluices over my back and shoulders. The heat stings with a delicious bite, one that I need to keep me grounded in the here and now. Now, when I feel like I am on such unsure footing. My ground is shaking and the world is spinning. If I can't right myself, who will? The answer is no one. I can't rely on anyone to take care of me but me.

I soap up my loofa and scrape it over every inch of my skin. I need the sting and the burn. I need it to distract me from the ache in my heart. I suppose that I should be thankful Wes showed me his true colors sooner rather than later, but part of me can't let go of the anger that I shouldn't have had to. I knew all along that this was how it would play out, but Wes pushed and pushed. And now look where we are.

I scrub my skin harder at that thought, but the sting doesn't seem to take away the hurt in my heart, the sourness swirling in my belly, or the guilt that I feel over Anthony Donovan. At the thought of the little boy that I couldn't save, I realize I have failed.

Suddenly, my loofa feels like a coiled snake in my hands. I drop it to the shower floor and rinse the soap from my hands. I hear my phone ringing through the bathroom door, but I know longer care. I shut the water off and step out.

I pull on clothes and pin my hair up on top of my head still wet. I don't care that it's cold and icy outside. I don't care about anything except finding Anthony's killer. And I will, damn it. I will find them.

I sigh as my phone rings again.

I pull on soft, thick socks and my second favorite pair of boots. My drop gun, the small .38 that I like to keep in my boot for backup, is lost to Wes. I hope he treats it well. It was one of my favorites but I have absolutely no intention of seeing him again to get it back any time soon. Maybe in like five years . . . maybe eighty. Give or take.

I clip my badge and my sidearm to my belt. Until the day I die, I will never know how I managed to have foresight enough to grab those on my way out the bathroom window. But I'm thankful I did. The department frowns on losing either of those and I feel like *left them in a random man's house* is not a suitable excuse. But then again, Wes isn't just some random man and that's what makes this all the worse.

My phone rings again. I think for a minute that I should change my ringtone to something like a fire alarm or the dive horn from a submarine. Nothing says your angry ex-lover and pissed off big brother are blowing up your phone quite like a klaxon. *Ahh-ooohhhh-Gah!*

I exit my bathroom, walking towards the front of my apartment with nothing but coffee on my brain and then I stop in my tracks because sitting there on my battered sofa is my dad. His eyes, that same haunting shade of violet as Liam's, as my own, shoot lasers at me. I am clearly in trouble.

"Hey, Pop," I wave my hand lamely. The smile on my face falters because we both know that it's bullshit.

"Sit down, Claire." He gestures towards the other end of the couch.

"I was actually just leaving," I whisper. "I'm really in kind of a hurry."

"I said sit down." I sit down.

"How long, Claire?" He barks.

I just stare at him. I'm not sure if he's asking how long I have been having the nightmares or how long I have been fucking my brothers best friend. At this juncture I feel it behooves me not to answer.

"I'll make it easier for you. How long have you been having nightmares?" He asks answering my unspoken questions.

I look down at my hands in my lap. I feel the tears pool in my eyes and sting my nose. I don't want to answer this. I'll tell him anything—anything at all—but this.

His rough fingers tip my jaw up to look in him the eye. "Answer me."

"Always," I let out on a sob.

He immediately pulls me into his strong arms, holding me close and stroking my hair like he did when I was little and upset because the boys wouldn't let me follow them around.

"I'm so sorry, my sweet girl," he hums, his voice gruff with emotion. "I'm so, so very sorry."

I let him rock me for a minute while I cry. It feels good to let someone else carry my burdens for awhile. But I know in the end, I will take them back because they are mine alone to carry. I don't want my dad or anyone else to hold onto the guilt anymore.

"It's okay," I sniffle. "I'm okay," I say as I wipe my face and pull back to look at my dad.

"It's not okay, babydoll," he says as he looks me in the eyes. "You're not okay, but you will be," he finishes with a twinkle in his eye. Uh-oh.

"Dad," I hedge.

"So now, let's talk about Wesley."

"Dad."

"He's a nice boy."

"Dad."

"Your brother was a little miffed but they worked it out."

"You mean Liam got in a good hit?" I roll my eyes.

"Of course," he laughs. "That's how they've always handled their misunderstandings. Even when they were little boys. And I'm here to tell you that it'll only get worse as they become old men like me."

I sigh.

"He loves you."

"He doesn't. He just thinks he does."

"He does, babydoll."

"You don't see the way he looks at me when I have a nightmare. I disgust him."

"And you don't see the way he has always looked at you when you're not looking."

"I deserve to have someone who will fight for me, not with me," I tell him.

"That you do, my angel. That you do," he smiles at me with that twinkle in his purple eyes.

I look at my dad, really look at him and can see love and hope in his eyes, not fear or disgust. But he's my dad, he is always going to want the very best for me. No matter what.

"I'm broken, dad," I whisper, looking just over his left shoulder.

"You're not," his voice rings out, adamant. There is no swaying his mind.

"Dad—"

"You're a little scuffed and dinged up, but you're not broken, babydoll. I see too much fire in you. You get that from your grandmother," he laughs. "God help us."

"She's a pistol, for sure." I smile back.

"That she is."

"I need to get going," I say softly. "I've got bad

guys to catch."

"I mean it, Claire," he implores. "You're not broken."

I can't answer so I just nod as I stand up. My dad stands too and pulls me into his arms one more time for a dad hug. I don't know how he does it, but he always makes me feel a little better. Maybe not one hundred percent, but enough to feel like I can handle what life seems to be throwing my way.

My phone rings again as I walk to the kitchen to grab my borrowed keys from the counter. I look out at the sofa where it sits on the cushions face down. I could guess who it is or at least whom it might be, so I grab my keys and keep walking on by.

"You're going to have to answer them one day," he shakes his head.

"Yeah, but that day is not today, Pop," I toss over my shoulder.

He just laughs, "Just like your grandmother. Fuck us all."

I take a quick look through the peephole to make sure no one is lurking around my front door. With keys in hand, I exit the building keeping a watchful eye of my surroundings. Every time to exhibit this maneuver, I feel like an extra in *Charlie's Angels.*

The coast is clear so I carefully make my way back to the rear parking lot. I hold my breath hoping that neither Wes or Liam are waiting for me. I let it out in huge gust of air when it looks like I am alone. *For now.*

chapter 26

a small reprieve

MY DRIVE TO THE station is fraught with anxiety over seeing Wes. I hate that I ran. I hate that he makes me run. It's so unlike me. I'm a stand my ground, don't shoot until you see the whites of their eyes kind of gal, but Wes makes me feel weak and powerless. And I fucking hate that.

I feel the tension creep up my neck. I check my mirrors once more time before I circle around the station to park in the back, passing up my lucky spot out front. Later I would find out that I needed all the luck that I could get.

I climb out of my truck and head to the back door of the station. It puts me right outside of the Captain's office, but I'm hoping to use the opportunity to find out if the burrs in my bonnet are in situ before I reach the bull pen. As it turns out, they are not.

I do not stop to get coffee or visit with the other

detectives and officers. They read my mood, or more than likely, Liam and Wes have already blown through here and told the tale of my break with sanity to all who would listen. This is more likely since my own father showed up to give me shit—loving shit, but shit nonetheless—this morning.

Either way, they are leaving me alone. That's a good thing. I need my space to figure everything out. But I see the side eyes that my fellow officers are giving me. They know. Everyone knows it all. By the pointed looks that they're throwing each other and the looks they are not throwing me, I know. They think I sold out. And really, I did. I slept with a Fed and then I lost my shit. That's about as low as a cop can get. I know now without a doubt that I can't stay here. My mission is clear: get in, get what I need, and get the fuck out.

I sit down at my desk, unlock the drawers and retrieve my flash drives. I pick the locks to retrieve the ones Wes stored in my partner's desk as well. I know without a doubt that I cannot stay at the station. Not today. So, I quickly stuff them in my pockets and relock my desk.

I hear a commotion and mix of voices at the front desk so I make quick time of leaving through the back, my desk chair still spinning in my wake when I hear familiar voices and realize I was right to leave.

"Lee, look," I hear Wes say.

"Where is she?" He barks. "Dammit, Jones. Fucking answer me!"

I creep down the hallway towards the rear exit. I need to leave. Now.

"You just missed her," I hear him say as I push open the door and run for my car.

I jump in my car at record speed and peel out of the parking lot just as Wes and Liam bust out of the door. I can see them standing there with their hands on their hips watching me leave again in my rearview mirror.

I see Wes pull his phone out of his pocket and dial what I assume is my number, but I don't hear my phone ring. I didn't notice it's absence until now. I probably would have answered it if it was here. Wes has a way of wearing me down. But it's not with me so I get a small reprieve.

My drive from the station is filled with anxiety. Again. I can't help but wonder if I'm making the right choice. Should I be running from Wes, or should I be running to him? But I know that I can't. What I told my dad rings true to me. I need someone to fight for me, only then will I know that that man is worth it to me. Wes has only ever fought me. Over my career, my life, my abduction. He can't control those situations and therefore, he can't control me. But I'm not meant to be controlled. I have always been a free bird, at thirty years old, nothing has changed.

My belly rumbles loudly and I remember that I

skipped breakfast during my jailbreak this morning. I would normally get delivery from the comfort of my apartment but I don't want to go back there. I'll be restless until I can figure this case out. I can't sit still. I can't go home because I need to stay away from Wes. Wes clouds my head. I can't think clearly when I'm around him and that is a dangerous position to be in. Without a clear mind, someone could get hurt, or worse . . . *killed*.

My stomach growls again and I decide to stop for lunch. I briefly consider Chinese when I see the characters on the sign of my favorite place. My former favorite place. But the thought of being poisoned has my stomach turning sour and I decide against it. I will drive another block to a sandwich place.

I turn at the light and drive around to the parking lot where I pull into the first available space. The wind is cold and biting as I step from my SUV reminding me that winter is almost upon us. I pull my coat tight around me as the wind whips.

The hair on the back of my neck stands on end and I'm overwhelmed with the feeling of being watched. I stop and look over my shoulder but there is no one there other than the normal everyday lunch crowd. Still, I can't stop the feeling that something is not right. Someone out there is not the everyday lunch goer, someone is operating on malice and ill will. Could it be the bad man? Has he finally come back for me?

My face has been all over the news in conjunction with the Donovan case. Could that be what finally led the bad man back to me? The worst part is, of all I can remember, everything that I dream of, I cannot for the life of me, remember his face. The smell of his breath and the feel of his hand as it slapped my face? Every bit of it. But his face is veiled in shadows. Anna thinks my brain won't let me remember, that it's locked the information away to protect me from the horrors I experienced at his hands.

I look back over my shoulder one more time hoping to see something . . . someone. I don't know what. But there is nothing, not one thing, that stands out to me. But the feeling remains. Something is wrong. I pick up my pace as the rain and sleet start pouring down and I dive through the door to the deli with my hair soaking wet and chilled to the bone. The bell rings as I push the door open and the kids that work the deli counter look up at me and wince.

"It must really be coming down out there," the teenage girl says as I walk up to the order counter.

"It just started while I was walking across the lot," I say as I push my wet hair back from my face.

"Well come on in and get something good to eat," she smiles a white smile splitting her mocha face in half. "What can we get you?"

"A bowl of chicken noodle, with a huge hunk of crusty bread, and hot, hot coffee. As hot as you can make it, please," I smile back.

"Coming right up!" She says as she rings up my lunch.

I give her my money and take my number and my coffee mug over to the drink counter. Steam rises from my mug as the coffee pours from the big carafe and I can't help but sigh. I doctor it up just the way that I like it and find myself a table.

A shiver runs up my spine. My grandmother would say someone stepped on my grave. I can't help but hope that that is later rather than sooner. I scan the deli but don't see anything out of place. I'm lost in my thoughts when the young girl from the counter drops off my soup with an extra huge hunk of bread. I jump a little at the intrusion but she smiles sheepishly so I wink at her and offer up my thanks before digging into my meal.

As I eat and warm up I stare out the window, watching the ice and rain fall. I lose myself in my thoughts of Wes. If I'm being truthful with myself, I have feelings for him. But whether or not we have a future? I don't know.

What I need to do is lose myself in thoughts of this case. I can't help but be frustrated that it's taking me this long to figure it out. Although my focus has been lacking, the heart of the matter is a lost little boy who will never come home. Poor Anthony Donovan had to have trusted someone that he shouldn't have. I know from firsthand experience how dangerous that can be.

His family will never see him happy and alive again. I feel a twinge of guilt in my belly again at the idea that I survived and he did not. It's almost as if there can only be so many kids recovered and my taking a spot took one of them away for all of the lost kids to come. I know that it's an irrational thought, but when faced with the idea that a family lost their child, it's very real in my mind. But could one of his own be responsible for his death? As awful as it seems, it happens more than I care to admit.

Jonathan Ascher is out, mostly because he's dead. And whoever delivered him to the pearly gates tried to send me along for the ride. I'm trying not to cheer them on because he was molesting his stepdaughter.

Elizabeth Ascher is an odd duck. She was so upset when she found out that Anthony was missing and now that he's dead, she is fully removed. She would not let us interview her daughter, Kasey, and then turned on her when she found out she was sleeping with her husband. I can't figure her out. What's right and what's wrong? What's the truth and what is the lie?

Anthony Donovan, Senior was inconsolable when he found out that his son was missing and livid when he found out that his ex-wife's new husband was violating his daughter, rightfully so. But poison doesn't seem like his style. Especially given the way he laid Jonathan Ascher out in the police station.

Kasey Donovan is also a contradiction. On one hand she flirts with Wes in the most inappropriate ways. She was carrying on what she thought to be a romantic affair with her stepfather when she was only sixteen years old. But on the other hand, she was too emotional for us to interview her when little Anthony went missing, which makes sense since it was on her watch that he was taken.

My spoon scrapes the bottom of my bowl before coming up empty and sadly, I am no closer to solving this case than I was before. My only prize is that I am warmer and fueled up. What I need is to be on the street. I stand up and throw back the last of my coffee. I wave to the nice kids behind the counter and head back out into the ice and rain, but I don't care.

This ends today.

chapter 27

drive

I PUSH OPEN THE door to the deli, the tinkling bells are drowned out by the pouring rain. I beep the lock on my SUV and make a run for it but I'm soaked through again by the time I jump in.

I buckle my seatbelt and start the car as the rain pelts down all around me. As I pull out of the parking lot I'm lost in my thoughts. I drive down a small side street and get stopped at a light. There is something that I'm missing when it comes to the key players of this case. There has to be.

A white panel van at the cross-street drives through the intersection in front of me as lightning crashes and I am instantly lost to another time. Taken back to the last time I was truly lost and helpless.

I'm stomping through the woods behind out house.
I don't need those gross boys to have some fun. And
those boys are gross! They smell weird and put on too
much spray stuff when they think I'm not looking.

I just make it to the street on the other side of the
trees from our house when a white van pulls up next to
me. I hear my mom in my head telling me not to talk to
strangers. I feel my eyes going wide as he steps out of
the van.

"Claire!" He says and I wonder how he knows my
name. "There you are. I need your help!"

"What do you need help with?" I ask.

"I'm so glad you asked, Claire," he says my name
again like he says it all the time. It's weird but I don't
think too much about it. "My puppy, Millie, got out.
She's missing. Can you help me find her?" He asks.

"I don't know. I should probably go back home . .
." I say.

"No!" He shouts and it startles me. His eyes widen
when he notices my reaction. "I need you to look for
her while I drive around. I'll give you this candy bar
if you help me . . ." He offers, holding up my most fa-
vorite kind. I instantly grab for it, but he pulls it back.

"Okay, what does she look like?" I ask.

He smiles a creepy smile, but I open the front door
and get in the van. He hands me the candy bar and I
realize that I don't even know what his name is.

"She's little and fluffy and white . . ." He trails off

as I dig into the sweets my mom never lets me eat before dinner. Ever!

A horn beeps behind me pulling me out of my daydream. But it's not dream, it's a memory that won't let me be.

My palms and my hairline are sweaty but I'm chilled to the bone. I step on the gas and pull through the intersection. The light had turned green and I missed it because I was lost in my own head. I raise my hand to wave my apology to the driver behind me but my hand is shaking so I put it back on the steering wheel and grip it tight.

My head is pounding and the soup in my belly is threatening to make a reappearance. What happened? Am I finally losing it? I have never had a dream in the middle of the day—while I was awake. I have always had them while I was sleeping. Always. I'm scared. I don't know how to process this new development.

I pull into the parking lot of a strip mall. I need to get my bearings. Right now, I'm freaking out. My heart is beating wildly in my chest and I can't catch my breath. I throw my SUV in park and set the brake. My hands shake the whole time.

I need Anna. Anna is the only one who can talk me down from something like this. It feels like the walls of the car are closing in on me and sucking up all the air. I need Anna. I reach for my phone in the cupholder where I always stick it when I'm driving and realize I left it in my apartment when I was so mad at Wes for blowing up my phone and Liam for calling my dad in as back up in their war to get me off the job and barefoot and pregnant. Not. Happening. But I still need my phone. I need to talk to Anna. Shit!

Wait. I can do this. I can. I'm stronger than this I know it. I hold onto the steering wheel to keep me grounded in the here and now. I breathe in long and deep once, twice and a third time without letting any out, and then I slowly let it all out. I repeat the exercise they taught us in marksmanship training at the academy. It works to slow your heart rate and narrow in your focus.

When I open my eyes again, I feel calmer. The panic driving my erratic breathing and anxiety has lessened, but not left me fully. I take one more deep breath. I pop the brake and put my car in drive. I can and I will do this.

I like to drive to clear my thoughts. I always have. When something was bothering me as a kid, my dad would put me in the car and we would just drive around. While he drove us, we talked about anything and everything. By the time we got home, usually after a stop for the world's best ice cream, I felt better. Not one hundred percent, but enough to know that I could tackle anything.

To this day, I still love to drive when I need to work out a problem in my brain. There is no bigger problem that I can't work through than the disappearance and murder of Anthony Donovan. There are too many twists and turns, too many snarls along the way for me to be able to see clearly what happened. And truth be told, I have no ideas.

I drive for what feels like ages with no specific destination in mind. I drive through the neighborhood where Anthony lived with his parents, but the street is barren. No one is home, no kids are out playing and it looks like a ghost town.

It's such a pretty little neighborhood with tall brick houses and others covered with pristine white siding. The lawns are all carefully manicured, not one blade out of regulation length. The flowerbeds are perfectly tended with delicate rose bushes lined up like neat little soldiers. But it's the secrets that hide inside those houses that make this beautiful street ugly. Those secrets are sharper than the thorns on those rose bushes and can do way more damage than one little prick. It's my job to find out what they are and expose them.

I straighten my shoulders and firm up my resolve. I can do this. I exit the neighborhood and keep driving, thinking about secrets. What do those secrets have in common with Chinese food? Who would want to keep those secrets hidden so badly that they would poison both me and Jonathan Ascher with the same take out? That's what keeps getting me. The why and the who.

Elizabeth Ascher does not want me to expose her secrets, but by all accounts, she loved her husband and didn't want him to die. She sided with him instead of her daughter. But according to the teller at the bank, Mr. Ascher was just Elizabeth's meal ticket. That there was no love lost. No one even knew that they were seeing each other until they turned up married.

Anthony Donovan, Senior definitely wanted Jonathan Ascher dead. But I can't see him being so sneaky or underhanded about it. I see Mr. Donovan as more of a beat someone to death or give them a bullet to the brain kind of guy. Poison is so sneaky. And where does that leave me? What beef would he have with me that was large enough for him to want to poison me? I can't find one reason why he would want me dead.

Wes's mom, on the other hand, I could totally see poisoning me to keep me away from her precious baby boy, but even I have to admit that she wouldn't poison Jonathan Ascher. They didn't even know each other and besides, she's not the kind of woman to get her hands dirty.

Wes.

My mind will always go back to where it doesn't belong. I let myself imagine a life with Wes while I drive around. One where we both go to work in the morning, fighting crime like superheroes. Well, I'm the super hero, he wears wingtips for crying out loud. But I digress.

We would come home to each other every night. Wes and I would share meals and laughter. In my perfect world, he would hold me when I was sad or scared, but let me live my life like the independent woman I am and not like some china doll meant to be put up on a shelf where life passes her by. He wouldn't look at me like I was crazy, he would look at me like I was powerful and important.

Maybe one day, there would be a little boy with Wes's brown hair and my violet eyes and a little girl with black hair and green eyes chasing after him. Without a doubt, Wes's children will be beautiful. So smart and vivacious. I can see them wanting to know every little thing and bouncing around with excitement as they figure something new out, as they find other things in this world waiting to be discovered. And I find myself very much wanting those children to be mine. But it's wasted time dreaming of things that can never be.

I continue to drive around George Washington Township hoping that something, anything will jog my brain, but I stay locked in my thoughts about Wes and my past, unable to put those demons to rest until the radio breaks me out of my fog.

". . . This just in . . . We have it on good authority that the infamous Detective Claire Goodnite of the GWTPD has been released from duty, effective immediately. A statement was released from the office of Captain Goodnite also of the GWTPD. Whatever happened can't be good if your own brother fires you,"

"That's right, Marsha. As always, we will be following up on this story and all other news as it comes in. Now, what's new in sports . . ."

Fuck! I slam my palm against the steering wheel. Fired by my own brother. Not that I didn't see that coming a mile away, but still, it stings. I can't believe Liam had the balls to do it. I'm not going to be able to speak to him for a month of Sundays. God damnit! My job was everything to me. And I need this case. He knows it. He knows how much I need to solve this case.

And he didn't even call me. But then again, I left my phone at home with dad, so he could have tried, who knows. But still. A press release. He couldn't wait to fire me to my face.

I drive and drive until I find myself just a block away from the falls. The last place Anthony Donovan was possibly ever alive. Or maybe not. All we know so far is that his body was found on the rocks at the bottom of the falls.

It's then that I notice someone standing at the fence overlooking the falls. The silhouette is familiar. And suddenly, all the pieces of the puzzle start falling into place.

Oh. Fuck.

chapter 28

demons

Wes

I FUCKED UP.

I fucked up so bad I don't know if I can ever fix it. But I have to fucking try, or die fighting. Because this is everything. *She* is everything.

Twelve years ago, I was barely a man. I was infatuated with the idea of Claire finally becoming a woman. A woman that I could have, that I could touch. I was taken with her beauty, her hair the color of midnight and eyes so purple they belong to a witch. A beautiful witch who commanded my every thought. And with curves like hers, they were naughty thoughts. I thought of nothing but commanding her body, my mouth on her skin and my cock so deep in her pussy we lost where I ended and she began.

But I was unprepared for reality when I took her. I took her love and her body in ways I would dream about for years to come. I made love to Claire like I never have to any other woman because in my heart, I knew it was always her.

The hard truth was Claire was haunted by demons from her past and I was still tied to an enlistment in the United States Navy. I had planned to marry her as soon as I could and take her back to Coronado with me. However, I knew I couldn't take her away from her home and her family and move her all the way across the country only to leave her at a moment's notice when I was called up.

The life of a SEAL is never easy, but the lives of their wives is even harder. Your husband could leave in the middle of the day or the dead of night depending on the time of the call. Then you hope and you pray that your sailor comes home from that mission in the worst possible places all while knowing there is always a chance that they won't.

When I woke up the morning after spending the best night of my life with Claire, the girl of my dreams, I realized she was being held hostage in the tight in the clutches of a nightmare. When she screamed out, my heart broke because I realized there was no saving her. Claire had to find a way to save herself. I also knew that there was no way she was coming with me to California like this. And I knew without a doubt that my sweet, loving Claire would fight me if I told her the truth, so when she woke up, I broke her heart too. All while vowing that I would finish out my enlistment and come back home to New Jersey to start a career in law enforcement. Then, only then, would I claim my girl for once and for all.

And I did that. I did all of it, never realizing how badly I had hurt Claire. Never knowing that her heart was irrevocably broken and she would never trust me or any other man again. I had no idea how deep her pain ran. I also had no idea that she was still living within the nightmare she endured twenty-four years ago.

So, while I was forcing my way into her life and strong arming my way into her heart and her bed, never letting up, never giving her a moment to catch her breath, I didn't realize that she was suffering. I didn't realize that the nightmares gripped her so deeply. That is until last night when she woke up screaming in my arms again. But this time, I didn't force her back to her family for help. Help I now realize she never got because she hid her trauma so well, like a wounded big cat, never letting you see their weakness or vulnerability. No, this time, she ran. My girl was so afraid that I would break her all over again, that she ran. From me. And that stings.

I realize now that I should have hid the emotions rolling across my face when we woke up. But I was tired. Claire and I have been working the Donovan case for days with no breaks and her being poisoned scared the ever-loving shit out of me. Not to mention that instead of sleeping, I have been fucking Claire at every available moment. So, I was tired. Coupled with the fact that I want her as my partner in life and in my bed, *forever*, I did not think to mask my feelings. And that was when I fucked up.

I should have hidden my emotions because if I had known last night what I know now, I would see that showing her my sorrow for her suffering would only make her think I was disgusted with her, that I thought she was broken and unworthy of my love and affections. That couldn't be further from the truth. If anything, I don't deserve her. Sure, I'll give her shit and I will own her body, but in reality, we're equals, we're partners.

When she locked herself in the bathroom, I realized she was freaking out so I called Lee. Not only is he her brother, but he's my best friend. I needed his help. I knew he wanted her out of the field and behind a desk or at home in some man's kitchen, but I didn't realize how deep their feud over the matter ran. So by calling him, I fucked up again. Hindsight is always twenty-twenty and all that bullshit, but even I can see the pattern of my own stupidity where Claire Goodnite is concerned. Claire didn't see it as me reaching out to our family for help. Oh no, she saw it as me calling her brother to come riding in with the men with the big butterfly nets, elephant tranquilizers, and funny jackets to cart her off to the funny farm. Fuck!

Never in my wildest dreams would I have imagined the girl of my dreams, the woman I have been rapidly falling in a forever kind of love with, jumping out my guest bathroom window. That's the kind of moment that can traumatize a guy for life.

So, I chased her ass down the street. But Claire is one of the best fucking cops I have ever met. Even without her spare gun, boots, and underwear, she managed to escape me. For now.

Lee and I tracked her. From the moment I realized I had lost her, I back tracked to my house. I threw on jeans, a sweatshirt, my favorite running shoes. I also grabbed my jacket, badge, and gun on the way out before locking up my house.

Liam had shown up by then, a little irritated to have been forced out of some woman's bed but unlike usual, he wouldn't tell me who. I don't have time to question his SOP. I was so distracted that I missed the right hook that landed on my left eye when I opened my front door to him.

"Don't even ask what that was for," he shouted.

"I think I can draw my own conclusions."

"I told you not to hurt my sister," he growls.

"I didn't mean to, it was a misunderstanding, but now I have to find her," I pleaded like a big fucking baby. Thankfully, being my pathetic sad self seemed to pull Lee to my side.

"I'll help you, but let's not make a habit of this."

He then seemed to shake off his anger and was back to being my lifelong best friend. Here to help me get my girl.

I tracked Claire's whereabouts while Lee called in his dad who was none too pleased to hear I had taken up with his daughter before talking to him or Lee about it. Once he found out that Lee hit me when I opened the door, he roared with laughter and said he had an idea of where she might be. We just had to hang tight, but until then, I was going to trace all of the places I thought she might be.

By the time we hit the station I thought I had her, but once again, she slipped through my fingers. Lee chose to stay behind and keep me posted. His dad said he thought he had gotten through to her, but only time will tell. All I know is that I need to make things right with her, I need to stitch up the wounds that I didn't know I had cut into her so deep. Claire is mine, she's my everything and I need her to know that. I want to protect her, but I also want to stand by her side in all things. This case has shown me how great we work together both in and out of my bed.

So here I am, what feels like just a few steps behind her still, when I trace the different crime scenes of our case. I just left the suburb where the Donovan children lived with the Ascher's. Claire was right, we're missing something. I just can't figure out what.

I take the highway a few miles and exit at the falls. I make my way towards the falls, an iconic spot here in New Jersey, long before poor Anthony Donovan's remains were found on the rocks.

I'm maybe less than a block away when something tells me not to drive in so I pull into a lot and park. I lock up my vehicle and pocket my keys. I pull out my phone and send a quick text to Lee.

Me: I'm at the falls, something doesn't feel right. No sign of Claire.

Lee: I'll send a black and white by. Hang tight.

Me: Willco

My last message to Lee was willco, or I *will comply*, but it was a lie. I know in my gut that something is off. And my gut is never wrong. It saved both Lee and I on many an op so I know in the end he will understand that when it comes to his sister, I'm not waiting.

I take off on foot, careful to go unnoticed by those on the streets. At this point in the case, I'm not sure who I can and can't trust and that is not a good thing. It's damned dangerous. So far, the good guys are me, Lee, and Claire.

I turn the corner and I am across the street from the fenced in area overlooking the falls. I take one step across the street, and then another. I'm almost there when the world explodes around me. Or you could say, my world explodes as someone I do not recognize at first raises their arm towards Claire, with a gun in their hand, right before Claire goes over the edge of the falls.

I don't even think before I act, the movements ingrained in my brain and my body hardened by years as a SEAL and then with the FBI. I pull my own sidearm from my belt and fire before screaming.

"No!" Is torn from my lungs. And just like that, I have lost her again. My Claire, the only girl I will ever love.

chapter 29

in for a penny, in for a pound

Claire

"KASEY?" I ASK AS I step out from the shadows. Anger and malice flash across her face
before she drops down her mask of faux innocence.

All of a sudden the last tumbler rolls into place.
And it all makes sense. I'm not looking at a lost little
girl, I am looking at a cold-hearted killer.

"Is everything alright, Kasey?" I ask choosing not
to show my hand too early.

"Of course, Detective, why wouldn't it be?"

"We haven't found your brother's killer yet," I say
softly. "That has to bother you."

"You're not going to," she laughs a mean laugh. "I
heard your own brother booted you off the case.

"I admit that stings a little," I nod. "But it doesn't
mean I will stop before I find the responsible party."

"So, you're here alone?" She asks. "No one knows where you are," she surmises.

"Of course they do," I lie. "Captain Goodnite and Agent O'Connell know every move I make. In fact, I just got off the phone with them."

She chuckles again. This can't be good. And fuck if I'm not out here in the cold with no back up just like she said. Shit, shit, shit!

"You know what I think?" She asks.

"No, Kasey, what do you think?"

"I think no one knows you're here," she smiles a Cheshire Cat grin. "I think you figured it all out, didn't you?"

"Why did you do it, Kasey?" In for a penny, in for a pound.

She lets out a menacing laugh. "Why do you think?" she snarls. "They always left me to take care of him. I was tired of it."

"But Anthony was your brother, Kasey."

"Do you think I care about that?"

"Tell me what do you care about, Kasey?"

"I just wanted my own life, you know?"

"I do," I tell her. "My own family is very overbearing. Tell me about it?"

"I just wanted to go on a date with a boy," she whispers sounding all of the sixteen years old that she is.

"And what boy was that?" I ask softly.

"That's not important," she snaps.

"Okay," I hold my hands up, palms out, placating her. "Tell me what is important."

"They wouldn't let me go!"

"Who wouldn't let you go?" I ask all while knowing.

"My mom and Jonathan. He said he didn't want me dating boys but it was so he could keep playing his games with me while my mom was gone or asleep."

I knew it. That sick fuck was keeping his step daughter isolated so that he could keep molesting her for as long as possible. He kept her unsullied by teenage boys so that he could have her himself behind his wife's back. No wonder the kid snapped.

"I couldn't keep doing it, you know?" She asks, breaking the silence that surrounds us.

"I do, honey."

"But none of that matters now."

"Why is that?"

"Because I'm leaving Jersey,"

"How do you figure?" I ask. "You're sixteen years old. You need a car, a job, and parents."

"Parents?" She laughs again. "That's rich. Haven't you met my parents? My dad left me to my mom who doesn't give not one shit about me." I had to agree that her mom is kind of a huge bitch.

"And my mom left me to that monster who hurt

me, like all the time!" She screams. "And then when he wanted to parade my mom around I had to watch the baby! How unfair is that?"

"It's very unfair," I whisper. "Did you ever try to talk to your mom about the abuse?"

"Why bother?" She asks.

"Because she's your mother and could have stopped it." That little nugget of wisdom only makes her laugh harder.

"My mom married Jonathan so he could get to me," she looks at me with her cold, dead eyes. "He gave her and Anthony a lavish life in exchange for me. My own mother sold me." Oh fuck. I hadn't figured on that.

"So, you poisoned him in the jail."

"Of course," she looks at her fingernails with obvious teenage boredom. "He had to die."

"But what about me?" I ask. "Why poison me?"

"You ask too many questions," she sighs. "And Wesley is dreamy." Oh fuck. That's awkward.

"But why not your mom?"

"Oh, she's next. Just as soon as I get rid of you," she says. "Come over here . . . About how good of a swimmer would you say you are?"

Shit, shit, shit! I look around me for anyone who might have heard her. Someone who might have seen us talking at the falls. All I see is a drug deal going down about half a block away. A big, burly white biker guy and a couple of teenage thugs. What the hell?

I only have one real choice to make, so I take a deep breath and pull my gun from my hip. "I'm afraid I'm going to have to stop you right there," I tell her.

Unfortunately, during my survey of the land and various drug dealers, I did not hear the approach of a new comer. That is, until I heard the click of a gun being cocked behind my head. Well, damn.

Kasey's smile grows wide.

"I'd like you to meet my boyfriend, Detective. I think you know each other," she laughs again.

I turn around and come face to face with the last person I ever thought would pull a gun on me. "Bobby?"

"The one in the same," he smiles at me. "Drop the gun," he says as he points to my hand and I do because I'm out of options.

"You poisoned me?"

"Of course," he answers.

"And Jonathan Ascher?" I ask.

"I couldn't let him hurt her anymore," his eyes narrow and he gets visibly angry.

"But why Anthony?" I ask.

"He was in the way," Bobby shrugs. "And she asked me to."

"It's that simple?" I ask incredulously. "She asks and you carry out?"

"Yes," he says simply. "I would do anything for

her. No one is ever going to hurt my Kasey ever again."

"You won't get away with it," I say lamely. They both laugh.

"We already have," Kasey says. "Look around you. No one is coming to save you."

I do as she asks. It's just us here and the drug dealers in the twilight haze of early night. She's right. No one here is going to save me. Well hell, if I'm going to die, I might as well go down swinging.

Kasey is in between me and the fence to the falls behind us. Bobby is in front of me. He raises his arm holding the gun. I back up a few steps, getting some distance between us.

Bobby just laughs.

"Just shoot her already!" Kasey snaps.

"You have nowhere to run," Bobby laughs, obviously enjoying his cat and mouse game.

"Just watch me," I say as I turn around and run.

I hit Kasey in the middle of the chest with my arms, driving both her and I through the fence and over the edge of the falls. Her screams echo all around us but I still hear the two gunshots that rent the air.

We hit the ground with a thud, Kasey on the bottom of our pile after we hit every rock and sharp edge on the way down, her more than me. Not that I'm going to let myself feel sorry for her. I hit my head on one of the last rock outcroppings right before we land at the bottom.

I open my eyes and look straight into the blank, unseeing eyes of the dead. I try to push myself up off of her but my wrist snaps all the way through when I lean on it. My head swims and my stomach rolls. And then everything goes black.

epilogue

tell me a story

Claire

Four days later...

MY HEAD FEELS FUNNY *and my ears feel full of cotton like last summer when I got an infection from swimming too much. I open my mouth to tell him something is wrong, but my words don't work. They won't come out! I turn my head to look at him, a scream stuck in my broken mouth. He just smiles his big, creepy smile and everything goes black . . .*

When I wake up I'm on an old, yucky blanket on the floor of a dark, smelly house. It's not my house. I know that. I rub the side of my head, it hurts so much. When I look up, the strange man is leaning back in an old torn chair, his feet spread wide and there's a strange bump in the front of his pants that he keeps rubbing his hands on. He smiles when he notices that I'm awake and for the first time ever, I'm scared.

"Hello, Claire, I'm glad that you're awake," he says to me in a scary voice. I just sit there staring with my eyes big. "You may call me daddy."

A scream rents the air. My head is foggy, heavy even. My eyelids feel like they're full of lead but I have to open them. I have to get out of here. I have to help whoever is screaming. But then I realize . . . *it's me.*

"Claire!" I hear Liam shout. Someone shakes me. "Claire! It's me, Lee. Wake up. You're having a nightmare."

"It's no use, she won't wake up," I hear Wes say, he sounds broken. "I can't sit here, man. I can't sit by and watch her suffer like this. I have to do something."

"She's going to come out of it, Wes, you know it."

"At this point I don't know anything."

"You gotta have a little faith, brother," Liam says softly.

"Without her, Lee, I don't have any faith . . . I have nothing."

And then the darkness sucks me back in.

"It's time to come back to me, baby," I hear Wes's gruff voice say. I try to open my eyes but . . . *nothing.*

"She will, son," my dad says. "Now we just have to be strong."

"No, we thought we'd be weak," my mother snaps.

"Yeah, seems like a great day to pull her plug," my granny snaps. I can hear her roll her eyes out loud.

Pull my plug? What the fuck.

"You take all the time you need, my sweet girl," my dad whispers.

"That's right. We'll be here waiting, my lovely," Mom says. I feel someone's lips brush my hair and a strong hand squeeze mine.

And then the tide pulls me under. Again

"It's time to wake up, sis," Liam says.

He squeezes my hand.

"I need you to wake up, Claire. I thought we lost you once, I can't do it again. I barely survived it," he takes a deep breath. "Why do you think I try so hard to keep you out of the field? It's not because you're a girl. And it's definitely not because you can't do it. You're one of the best cops I know. But I can't live in a world without my baby sister."

I need to open my eyes. I need to reach out. I need to comfort my brother and tell him how much I love him. That I'm okay. That everything is going to be okay. I try and fight the waves that pull me under with everything I have. I feel a tingle zing down my arms and through my fingers. The warm current runs through my belly and down my legs and through my toes. Which I wiggle under my itchy blanket.

"If not for me, do it for Wes," he whispers.

"I would do anything for you," I rasp, my throat parched. I cough.

"Shit. Shit. Fuck! You're awake," my usually cool calm and collected brother flits around the room like a chicken with his head cut off. I never really understood that saying until right now, huh. I continue to cough. "Shit, let me get you some water. Fuck, let me get the nurse!"

"Water," I cough again.

Liam reaches for the cup on the bedside with the straw and puts it in my mouth and take several greedy sips and then cough again.

"Oh shit!" Liam barks again. "A nurse, we need the nurse!" He shouts as he bounces out of the room.

Does my brother, the Police Captain, calmly stand and walk out the door, or even pick up the call button and call the nurse on duty? No, he again runs all over and knocks a tray of medical tools over before shouting more curses and then running out the door. But only after he got tangled in curtain in front of the door to the room.

"Welcome back!" The nurse chirps as she walks swiftly in the room.

She checks my eyes, my throat and my blood pressure, all seem to check out, so she smiles sweetly at me.

"Your throat may be sore from being intubated. So liquid diet for the time being. I'll bring you some beef broth when you're up to it." I must have made a face because she throws her head back and laughs on the way out the door. I notice Liam watches her ass as she leaves.

I sigh.

"What?" he asks.

"You'll never change."

He laughs, "What? There is no handsome Fed waiting to sweep me off my feet. I just have to make due until then," he winks.

I sigh again.

"You need to talk to him," he says softly.

"I know."

"He's been beside himself. He helped pull you up from the falls. He chased you down when you went in with no backup and no phone or radio like a moron. You're suspended, by the way."

"I'm not fired?"

"No," he sighs.

"But on the radio . . ."

"Wes and I were hoping to flush the real killer out while taking the heat off of your back."

I nod, that makes sense. It was a great play, really.

"It was Kasey," I say softly.

"I know, honey."

"She killed her baby brother," I say.

"I know."

"She said it was because she was tired of baby-sitting, but Mrs. Ascher had said something about her missing pets. I missed so much."

"You can't beat yourself up over it. She was sick."

"Was?"

"You killed her with the weight of your fat ass."

"Not funny." Why do I have a brother again? Right now I'm not so sure. "And Bobby?" I ask.

"Wes shot him. It was a clean shoot. No suspension." After letting out a heavy breath he says, "I'm sorry, sis. I never wanted you to get hurt."

"It's not your fault, Liam," I say as I take his hand back in mine.

"I know. It's yours because you didn't let us help you."

"How long is it going to take for you to let that one go?"

"A long time. Longer than your suspension." I sigh. "Now about Wes . . ."

"I know."

"Just go easy on him, you put him through the ringer."

"Okay."

"He's out in the hall waiting."

"Send him in," I say. When Liam stands up and heads for the door. "I love you, fart breath," I say as I repeat the words of our childhood.

"And I you, dipshit."

I turn my head and look out the window. I don't know what to say to Wes. I don't know what he will have to say to me. I still have nightmares. I still don't know who took me, who hurt me all those years ago. I don't know if he can live with that. I only know that I have to for the time being.

A throat clears behind me. I turn to look at where the sound came from and there is Wes standing just inside the door leaning against the wall with his arms folded across his chest, his face blank but guarded. His hair is rumpled and he looks like hell. But still gorgeous. So much so, it's hard to stare at him knowing that he could hurt me so much. But Liam said to go easy on him.

"Hi," I say with an awkward little finger wave.

"Hi, beautiful," he rumbles from deep in his chest. But he doesn't move from his spot.

"Would you like to come in?"

"Yeah, baby."

"Okay."

Wes walks over and sits in the chair next to my bed

that Liam had just vacated. I keep my hands carefully open but still on top of the blanket on either side of my legs. Still, but open. Wes looks at me and then down at my hands, then back at my face again before sighing heavily and taking my hand in his. A golden glow fills my heart and warms my body. I want to smile but it's too soon. He could still dump me.

"I see you're going to make me do all the work this time," he sighs again.

"No," I whisper.

"It's okay," he says. "I fucked up, baby," he says the words coming out of his mouth shocking the shit right out of me.

"What?"

"I pushed you too hard. I backed you into a corner and I made you feel like you couldn't talk to me about your dreams. Your memories of when you were taken and that is not the case."

"But . . . but you said you couldn't do it. You said I was too much drama twelve years ago."

"I lied."

"What?" I shout but I can't really shout because my voice is still raw.

"I knew that I was tied to the Navy for the rest of my contract, honey," he continues to rock my world. "And so was Liam. When you woke up screaming, I knew that I couldn't move you across the country away from your family. So . . . I lied."

I sit there with my mouth hanging open for who knows how long until he touches my chin with his calloused fingertips and closes my mouth for me. I look into his eyes and for the first time feel . . . *hope*. It's all going to be okay.

". . . so I was thinking we could try dating . . ." I must have missed something important. How embarrassing that I was so lost in his eyes that I missed what Wes was saying to me. By the smirk on his face, that big bastard knows it too.

"What?"

"I was saying that I won't push you too hard this time. We can take as long as you need before we settle down."

"How magnanimous of you," I grumble.

"But then you looked at my mouth like that and I remembered how much I like to eat you . . ."

"Wes." I look at him with a wariness in my eyes.

"I know," he sighs. "Slow. But I'll be ready when you are."

"Okay," I say smiling easy for the first time in a long time.

"Okay?" He asks. "We can date?"

"Yes."

"But no one else."

"Wes—"

"What?"

I sigh.

"Okay fine. But now I'm going to kiss you."

"What happened to slow?"

"I didn't say I was going to fuck you."

"Wes!"

"What? You don't have to sound so put out about it," he laughs.

"Just shut up and kiss me already."

"Yes, ma'am," he smiles and then he does, kiss me, enough to make my toes curl and just how I like it.

"You guys are so gross!" Liam shouts from the other side of the door.

"Go home already, Lee!" Wes shouts.

I just laugh. Yes, everything is going to be alright. It's a leap of faith for sure, but with my family and Wes, I'm ready to take it. I'm going to take it all because my life is waiting for me to live it. So I will.

the end . . . for now

playlist

The Monster—Eminem ft. Rhianna

Bad Things—Machine Gun Kelly

Came Here to Forget—Blake Shelton

It Ain't Me—Kygo and Selena Gomez

If I told You—Darius Rucker

Black—Dierks Bentley

Better Man—Little Big Town

No Such Thing as a Broken Heart—Old Dominion

Best I Ever Had—Gary Allan

Fell on Black Days—Soundgarden

Tell Me a Story—Phillip Phillips

about jennifer rebecca

Jennifer is a thirty something lover of words, all words: the written, the spoken, the sung (even poorly), the sweet, the funny, and even the four letter variety. She is a native of San Diego, California where she grew up reading the Brownings and Rebecca with her mother and Clifford and the Dog who Glowed in the Dark with her dad, much to her mother's dismay.

Jennifer is a graduate of California State University San Marcos where she studied Criminology and Justice Studies. She is also a member of Alpha Xi Delta.

10 years ago, she was swept off her feet by her very own sailor. Today, they are happily married and the parents of a 9 year old and 7 year old twins. She lives in East Texas where she can often be found on the soccer fields, drawing with her children, or reading. Jennifer is convinced that if she puts her fitbit on one of the dogs, she might finally make her step goals. She loves a great romance, an alpha hero, and lots and lots of laughter.

stalk her

Website
JenniferRebeccaAuthor.com

Newsletter
JenniferRebeccaAuthor.com/Newsletter

Facebook
facebook.com/JenniferRebeccaAuthor

Twitter
@JenniRLreads

Instagram
@JenniRLreads

BookBub
bookbub.com/authors/jennifer-rebecca

Book+Main
bookandmainbites.com/users/22594

Dangerous Dames Facebook Group
facebook.com/groups/JRDangerousDames

also by jennifer rebecca

The Funerals and Obituaries Mysteries
Dead and Buried
Dead and Gone, Coming Summer 2018

The Murder on Ice Mysteries
Attack Zone
Layback, Coming 2019

The Southern Heartbeats Series
Stand (Vol. 1)
Joy (a Southern Heartbeat Holiday), previously featured in then Love, Snow, & Mistletoe Anthology for St. Jude
Whiskey Lullabye (Vol. 2)
Mercy (a Southern Heartbeats Short), free on Wattpad
Just a Dream (Vol. 3), Coming Soon

The Claire Goodnite Thrillers
Tell Me A Story
Tuck Me In Tight
Say A Sweet Prayer
Kiss Me Goodnight

The Wanted Kindle World
Church Bells

tuck me in tight

turn the page for a preview

prologue

this is how my heart breaks

WHAT. THE. FUCK.

I had sat down at my desk and opened the manila envelope that was left on top of my stack of mail. It had seemed harmless enough.

But it wasn't.

I blink my eyes over and over trying to make my brain process what it's seeing but I can't. I can't unsee the images in the stack of pictures in my hand. Giant glossy eight by tens from different angles so there is absolutely no doubt that my heart is breaking.

And it is broken. Shattered.

"It's not what it looks like," I hear from over my shoulder and I have to grit my teeth to keep from screaming.

I shuffle the pictures sliding the top one to the back of the stack so that I can see the next in the row. This one is zoomed in. His head is tipped back and his face is distorted in both lust and passion as she straddles his lap. Her hands hold his to her breasts and I can see the play of tendons flex through them as he grips them tight. It was only two nights ago that his hands were on my own breasts much the same way as I rode his cock on the sofa.

"Claire, did you hear me?" he asks but I shuffle the stack again. In this picture, he has his arms wrapped around her back and he's pulling her close, her breasts mashed up against his strong chest. Her hands with long, red painted talons press in on either side of his face and as they kiss hungrily, their mouths open as their tongues tangle. "Goddamnit, Claire! Did you hear me?" My spine turns to steal.

"I did. I'm just choosing to ignore you."

"Don't do this, baby," he growls.

"I'm not the one who did anything," I snap.

"I can explain." But I'm not interested in listening to him plead a case where he is more than guilty.

"I'm going to need you to leave, Wes."

"No."

"This changes everything.

"This changes nothing! Fuck that, Claire," he yells. "You want to run away. You have always wanted to run away. And here is your fucking reason served up to you on a goddamn silver platter."

"No," I shout back as I throw the stack of glossy

betrayal down on top of my desk as I push my rolly chair back and stand. It slams into the desk behind mine. "You do not get to come in here, where I work, and tell me that I am to blame for your bullshit."

"Okay," he says as he holds his hands up in surrender. "You're right. I'm sorry. I can see you need time."

"I need a lot of things. One of them is definitely distance."

"I don't know if I can give you that. I can't lose you, baby." His words burn hot behind my eyes and the last thing I want is for the other guys in the bullpen to see me cry.

"You should have thought about that before you fooled around with that stripper."

"Claire—" he starts but I don't let him finish.

"You need to go now," I say softly.

I stand with my feet apart, my hands on my hips, and my head bowed as if I'm waiting for a blow. He looks at me and opens his mouth as if he's going to try to explain again. Something in my stance must have told him it was a losing battle because he snaps his mouth closed before moving towards the exit.

Wes pauses just before opening the door to turn and look back at me, I see him in my peripheral, but I'm looking at his lies and deceit spread across my desk for all to see. He pulls open the door and then slams it on his way out. I'm Detective Claire Goodnite and this is how my heart breaks.

CPSIA information can be obtained
at www.ICGtesting.com
Printed in the USA
FFHW020322220519
52584765-58080FF